Prai...

LAWS OF ...
THE HUNT

"Fascinating . . . The characterizations are excellent, the plot strong, and the pace well implemented." —*SF Site*

"Calling this book a compulsive page-turner doesn't begin to do it justice . . . strong characterizations and crisply described, plausible action . . . the finale boasted more action than a Jackie Chan flick."
—*Crescent City Blues Review*

"A fabulous first book . . . her characters are crafted with a master's touch." —*Scribe's World*

"Pumps new life into a very old horror staple . . . Highly recommended." —*VOYA*

LAWS OF THE BLOOD

THE HUNT

SUSAN SIZEMORE

ACE BOOKS, NEW YORK

THE BERKLEY PUBLISHING GROUP
Published by the Penguin Group
Penguin Group (USA) Inc.
375 Hudson Street, New York, New York 10014, USA
Penguin Group (Canada), 90 Eglinton Avenue East, Suite 700, Toronto, Ontario M4P 2Y3, Canada
(a division of Pearson Penguin Canada Inc.)
Penguin Books Ltd., 80 Strand, London WC2R 0RL, England
Penguin Books Ireland, 25 St. Stephen's Green, Dublin 2, Ireland (a division of Penguin Books Ltd.)
Penguin Group (Australia), 250 Camberwell Road, Camberwell, Victoria 3124, Australia
(a division of Pearson Australia Group Pty. Ltd.)
Penguin Books India Pvt. Ltd., 11 Community Centre, Panchsheel Park, New Delhi—110 017, India
Penguin Group (NZ), 67 Apollo Drive, Mairangi Bay, Auckland 1311, New Zealand
(a division of Pearson New Zealand Ltd.)
Penguin Books (South Africa) (Pty.) Ltd., 24 Sturdee Avenue, Rosebank, Johannesburg 2196,
South Africa

Penguin Books Ltd., Registered Offices: 80 Strand, London WC2R 0RL, England

This is a work of fiction. Names, characters, places, and incidents either are the product of the author's imagination or are used fictitiously, and any resemblance to actual persons, living or dead, business establishments, events, or locales is entirely coincidental. The publisher does not have any control over and does not assume any responsibility for author or third-party websites or their content.

LAWS OF THE BLOOD: THE HUNT

An Ace Book / published by arrangement with the author

PRINTING HISTORY
Ace mass-market edition / October 1999

ISBN: 978-0-441-00660-1

ACE
Ace Books are published by The Berkley Publishing Group,
a division of Penguin Group (USA) Inc.,
375 Hudson Street, New York, New York 10014.
ACE and the "A" design are trademarks belonging to Penguin Group (USA) Inc.

PRINTED IN THE UNITED STATES OF AMERICA

16   15   14   13   12   11   10   9   8

This one's for me. So there.

Prologue

*When the blood fever rises, it is the Enforcer
who names the time, the place, and the prey.*

April

                    DAVY
*(Kneeling in the alley, surrounded by dead
bodies. Blood everywhere.) Stares at Sam:*
What happened?

                    SAM
Bares fangs:
Nothing you're going to remember.

"THAT SUCKS!"

Valentine snorted at the irony of what she'd said and
hit the delete key in disgust. She was very good at irony.
Her dialogue usually fairly dripped with it. Right now,
this script didn't drip with anything, not even the fresh
blood she was hoping to inject into her take on a vampire story. Everybody in town was looking to make
Scream-alikes; even she was in on it. Teen horror with
a cynical twist was staying hot. She could do cynical.

"What I don't do is horror," Valentine told her agent
when he first suggested the production package. "Es-

pecially not vampires.'' But it was a sweet, sweet deal. After she thought about it for awhile, Valentine decided, *Oh, what the hell.* There couldn't be any harm in it.

''And it's so . . . ironic,'' she muttered and went to get herself a cup of coffee.

The kitchen wasn't far away. Valentine was never far away from a cup of coffee. Her condo was expensive, but it wasn't big. Just a bedroom, kitchen, and a living room that doubled as an office.

There was a basketball game on the large-screen television in her living room. She glanced at it, saw the Lakers were down by eight points, and decided it was best to work and continue to keep the game on as background noise. Problem was, she didn't want to work. The night was flying by, and she hadn't yet put down a word that was worth keeping. ''Discipline,'' she told herself. ''You can do this.''

There was a terror inside her that told her she couldn't, that she was empty at last.

She noticed the blinking light on the answering machine as she returned to her desk. She had three phone lines, but only one person had the number to the phone hooked up to the machine. She didn't want to talk to him. She didn't even want to listen to his messages. There had been a time . . . She almost reached for the Play button. No. It would just be recorded pleas and demands. ''Reruns,'' she grumbled. ''And I'm talking to myself again.''

Came from being alone too much, she supposed. But everyone *knew* she was eccentric and reclusive. It added to the mystique to make people come to her. To make them want something that was hard to get. You had to use every trick you could to survive in this town.

''Get's boring, though, doesn't it?'' she complained and marched right past her desk and onto the balcony. She could feel the accusing glow of the empty computer screen at her back. ''I can't help it,'' she complained to it. ''The words just won't come.'' She'd always been a storyteller. But lately . . .

The balcony was full of flowering plants and was surrounded by a high, stucco wall. She leaned her elbows on the familiar rough surface and looked at the view beyond the walled garden that surrounded the building. The air smelled of jasmine and car exhaust, just as it always did. It was beautiful here, peaceful at this late hour. For all of its location near what passed for a heart in this splayed-out city, the building where Valentine lived conjured the charm and luxury of a different era. The Bunker Hill neighborhood was an old one; urban renewal had simply caught up with it and forced it to redecorate. She had preferred it before it became trendy but supposed the newfound popularity would pass, too. She'd still be here.

"I'm not bored," she told herself. "I'm not lonely. I'm not desperate."

She was all those things and knew it. It was time for a change. There was *something* going on, it was as pervasive as the smog around her. This restlessness was not her way. If there was one thing she hated, it was change.

She sipped coffee and listened to the song of a night bird for awhile, hoping for inspiration. Behind her, the game was getting noisy. The Lakers were making baskets. She had to get back to work. She had to put something resembling a story on disk soon, even if it was shit. She wandered to stand in front of the television, coffee cup clutched tightly in her hands. Shaq was on a rampage. Cool.

After a few seconds, Valentine sat down on the couch, attention riveted on the screen. She sat back. She relaxed. A camera panned across the crowd near the floor for reaction shots after a particularly beautiful pick and roll. Valentine sat up at the speed of light. The coffee cup dropped from her hands to crash into shards at her feet. Hot liquid splashed her legs.

"What? Show him again!"

But the camera had moved on to a close-up of a whooping Tom Cruise. Valentine snorted derisively.

She'd actually liked the boy in *Interview*, but it wasn't pretend vampires that interested her just now. She desperately wanted the camera to move left again, to give her another chance at viewing someone she hadn't seen in years.

"Had to be him," she muttered. "What's he doing in town? Can't be. And who was that pretty little redhaired thing with him? How long's he been in L.A.?" She pounded a fist on the arm of the couch. "And why don't I ever keep up with what's going on around here?"

Valentine smiled and rose slowly to her feet. She kicked aside broken china and ran to her desk. And what difference did any of her questions make when an idea was finally tapping on the back of her brain?

"I can do this," she muttered, then laughed wickedly as her fingers moved over the keyboard. "Can and will. Let's try this again, shall we, gentlemen? Davy and . . . what do I call him? How about . . . ?"

SULEIMAN:
What I just did was against the Law.

DAVY:
(Kneeling in the alley, surrounded by dead bodies, blood everywhere):
Kill a half dozen people? I'd say that's pretty illegal.

SULEIMAN:
That's not the Law I'm talking about.

DAVY:
Then what . . .
Stares at something in Suleiman's hand. . . . is that?
Suleiman holds up short dagger. It glitters in the glow from streetlamp.

SULEIMAN:

Silver? Yes.
(Smiles.)
Doesn't hold an edge worth a damn.
Moves forward, teeth bared to show fangs.
But I don't use the dagger on mortals. . . .

Valentine had to take her hands away from the keyboard because they were suddenly shaking too much to type. She barely stopped herself from looking over her shoulder. There were no accusing eyes in the night behind her, but she could feel them anyway.

"This is wrong. I can't do this."

Then again . . . She sat back in her chair and watched the words on the screen as if she waited for them to scramble, change, fly away, or catch on fire. The cursor just kept blinking, but the words didn't change. She didn't like the words particularly. They still weren't right, but that was because she was trying to tell the wrong story, wasn't it?

"But I don't have a story."

You know where to get one, an insidious voice in her head told her.

Valentine shook her head. "I haven't been there or done that for a long time." She hugged herself and wished for a cup of coffee. Somehow, even the short distance to the kitchen seemed like a dangerous journey. She wanted to hide here in her quiet corner, unseen and unnoticed, while she quietly contemplated treason, betrayal, death, and destruction.

"The box office could be enormous."

That is, if she found the right Dream to ride. She knew where to go to do her Dreaming, now, didn't she? There was a reason she'd seen him sitting in the audience of the basketball game. There was always a reason when their paths crossed. Right now, she needed a savior. Maybe it was his turn to get her butt out of trouble.

It was just a story. A movie. Her job. Her life. Of no importance to anyone but her.

Valentine noticed the clock on the bottom of the computer screen. It was hours until dawn. Too bad. For the first time in ages she was anxious to get a good day's sleep.

Chapter 1

ON NIGHTS LIKE this, Don Tomas showed that he was a traditionalist of the oldest school. To get his full attention, Selim had to show him the dagger. Without any sense of melodrama, he slipped it from the sheath strapped to his arm and put it silently down on the mahogany table, the point turned toward himself. Selim rarely thought about the dagger, though he wore it every night. He hadn't had any reason to use it for a long time. Los Angeles was a quiet town.

Kamaraju, Alice Fraser, and Michael Tancredi were at the table along with Don Tomas. The five of them watched each other in silence now that the dishes had been cleared away. The dining room's arched doorways were opened to the scents of a low-walled garden. The soft splash of a fountain made a soothing background noise in the quiet room. Beyond the garden wall a spectacular view of the city spread out from the estate's dizzying perch.

Considering that the people in the room rarely spent time together, dinner conversation had been surprisingly affable. Now they waited for Selim.

It was up to him to speak first, since the dagger was on the table. No one had commented on the absence of the Claremont vampire over dinner, so he rewarded their restraint by saying, "Miriam sends her regrets and apologies for not being able to attend. She has a situation that could risk our security and requested a private meeting with me later this evening."

"You will keep us informed of Miriam's actions."

Don Tomas was tall but slender in the wiry, muscular way many of them were, with a low, rough voice and deep, dark eyes. He sat back in the heavy carved chair at the head of the table, half-slouching, physically relaxed while radiating an air of tightly wound tension. His words concerning Miriam hadn't been a request, but they hadn't been a demand, either.

Selim nodded to him. "If her actions touch upon the Hunt in any way, I will inform you and adjust tonight's arrangements accordingly." As usual, Selim was very careful with his words. He was best known for being a diplomat, for finding solutions and compromises among the nests. But in the matter of the Hunt there would be no compromising. The strong-willed group before him had to know from the outset that he was the final authority here. From the hard looks in their eyes he knew imposing his will wasn't going to be easy. But, as Siri would say, he knew the job was dangerous when he took it.

Selim took a sip of after-dinner coffee at the thought and then went on. "What do you want?"

Everyone looked to Don Tomas to speak again. He sat very still and looked at Selim. His silence said that he accepted the role of host but refused to be a leader in any way.

Since no one rushed to speak or even think very loudly, Selim went on. "There's a ritual going on here," he reminded them. He gestured at the silver dagger. "Symbolism, remember? I ask the formal question. You tell me that you want a Hunt. I ask why. You explain. You name a body count. I name one. You don't like it.

Eventually we all go home." He looked around, coldly
eyeing them one by one, making sure every gaze was
on the dagger rather than on him before he went on. The
angry, outraged tension in the room was enough to raise
a heat haze and sear the skin right off him. Selim ate it
up, but he didn't smile. *He,* at least, still took the for-
malities seriously. Had to, actually.

"Shall we start over?"

When he looked back at Don Tomas, the *hidalgo* met
his gaze. There was humor and a hint of apology in those
burning, dark eyes. "We need to Hunt. We ask permission of the Strigoi Council. We ask the consent of the
Nighthawk, the Enforcer of the Law, Tytan, Bubo, De-
fender, Protector, The Hunter of the City of *Nuestra Se-
ñora la Reina de Los Angeles.*"

"That's you," Alice Fraser added. She turned her
fascinating smile on Selim. "Does that make you feel
better, darling?"

Kamaraju sighed. "This is all so last-century, Hunter."

"We know the drill," Michael Tancredi interjected.
He leaned forward, elbows on the table. "Let's get down
to business, shall we?" He sounded matter-of-fact, but
his gaze kept sliding back to Selim's silver dagger.

Finally, Alice said, "Please put that thing away. It's
so barbaric."

"It was made by barbarians," Selim pointed out.
"It's good to have the reminder."

"Is that what the Council thinks?" Kamaraju questioned harshly. "That we need constant reminders?" Of
all those present, Kamaraju was the least able to hide
his nerves, his needs, his contempt for Laws he hid behind when it suited him.

"There's no need to be so defensive, Kama," Alice
admonished. Her tone was firm but not judgmental. Alice made you *want* to do what she told you. Selim supposed that was why there was a waiting list to get
fostered in her nest.

Kamaraju proved to be as amenable to her charm as

anyone else. He gave Selim an apologetic nod, even if he didn't go so far as to say anything.

Selim slipped the dagger back into its arm sheath. He folded his long-fingered, elegant hands on the table before him, empty in sight of all of them. This gesture was even more of a threat than showing the dagger, but Kamaraju chose to ignore the meaning of it. He resented authority of any kind but was too much of a coward to challenge it openly. Though the dagger represented the authority of the Strigoi Council, his hands were Selim's real weapon; it was his right to use them as he chose.

Selim smiled brightly at the community elders. "Let's get this PTA meeting over, shall we? Yes," he answered Kamaraju, "the Council does think we need constant reminders of who and what we are. Fortunately, you have laid-back little me to deal with rather than some stuffy old by-the-Covenant Euro-trash type. We're all all-American vamps here." Looking at Don Tomas as he spoke, Selim asked, "How many?"

"Twenty," Michael answered. "At least twenty."

"We have a list," Kamaraju added.

"It's been twelve years," Alice pointed out. "That's a long time, Hunter. A lot of built-up frustration."

"Only twelve years?" Selim questioned. "It's been twenty years since a formal Hunt in New York. Longer than that in New Orleans. And Moscow—"

"Moscow—or anywhere else—doesn't have a tight-assed—albeit laid-back—control freak in charge of things, either," Alice interrupted, as sweet and calm as ever. "We do."

"We need twenty, Selim. Believe me," Mike went on earnestly. "Twenty is a minimum to cover everything on the agenda. We have the names. All you have to do is give your approval."

Selim admired the cold-blooded efficiency of the group, even admired that they'd worked together to come up with a list. He was almost tempted to sit back and let them do what they wanted. Almost, and even almost didn't last that long. As Alice pointed out, he was a tight-assed control freak. "Twenty is far too many," he told them.

"We have three births alone," Michael protested.

Selim had long ago perfected the art of canting a sarcastic eyebrow; he practiced it now. "Three fledglings? I don't think so."

"But—" Kamaraju began.

"No one's died recently," Selim went on. "Or moved away. I would have noticed. There isn't enough territory available to support the addition of three vampires to the community."

"You do know about the human population statistics?" Michael asked with equal sarcasm.

"I'm aware of them."

"How many millions more do you want in the game preserve before you'll let us at them?"

"I don't stop you from feeding."

"You regulate it."

"That's my job. I don't stop you from taking companions."

"You do a wonderful job of managing the city," Alice flattered him. "But, Selim, what about our population? Birth control is all very well and good, but . . ."

"But what? Birth rate isn't the question here. Not entirely. It's a matter of maturity."

"Whose maturity?" Kamaraju questioned. "Mine?"

"Yours," Selim agreed. "Remember Jager? He's a little problem *you* started that I'm going to have to finish soon."

Kamaraju didn't try to defend Jager. Didn't look like he was interested in saving the lad's life. Good. "Lisa's different," Kamaraju said. "And I promised her—"

"No way is that kid ready," Selim cut in.

Kamaraju pounded the table. "That is *not* your decision! I promised!"

"Oh, come on," Selim teased. "Won't you miss her when she's gone? If you're bored, take an extra lover," Selim went on. "But do not presume to tell me that a two-year-old companion is ready to change. It isn't going to happen."

"We still need twenty," Michael put in before Kamaraju could protest further.

"What about the other births?" Alice asked. "Perhaps Lisa isn't ready, but the other two . . . My own Angela?"

"Two," Selim told her. "Angela and Hallie. But at least one of them has to foster somewhere else." He looked coldly around the group as he continued. "Seattle lost quite a few when Istvan vacationed there last month. There are always half-empty nests looking for fledglings after he's passed through. Give Marthe in Seattle one, and you can have your two babies."

"You son of a bitch!"

Selim merely smiled at Michael Tancredi's angry snarl. Michael didn't want to know the nasty truths of their existence or remember the harshness of the Laws. Michael sold cars for a living. He believed in negotiations, in deals. He liked to think of himself as a member of some sort of vampire chamber of commerce. His appetites were small, his interests more on the other side of the glass wall than on the inside. He thought he could control the need by making a Hunt seem like some sort of civic activity, make it into a formalized initiation and show of ethnic solidarity. Vampire boosterism. Like a kind of St. Patrick's Day parade with human victims being herded through the streets on their way to being slaughtered.

"Maybe we could have a barbecue afterward," Selim murmured.

"What?" Alice asked.

Selim waved her question away. He concentrated, really *concentrated* the way only a Hunter could, on Michael Tancredi. Michael had no choice but to *listen*, his whole being completely attuned to Selim's unwavering attention. "You want me to let you kill twenty humans. It isn't possible. It isn't going to happen. You have a list. Business rivals the four of you would like to get rid of, perhaps? Personal enemies?'' Michael couldn't help but nod in answer to Selim's questions. Selim released his hold on the other's mind and looked around in disgust. ''Just how stupid are you?'' he demanded angrily. ''When did you get to be such amateurs?''

Of the four of them, Don Tomas was the only one who reacted, and that was to hide a smile behind his hand. Selim was gratified to know that at least Tom hadn't thought they could get away with it.

Kamaraju looked furious, Alice subdued, Michael frightened. Nobody argued.

''Six,'' Selim told them. ''You get six of my choosing, and you share with the strigs. On the day and time I set. Any questions?'' he asked politely.

The expected explosion didn't come from Kamaraju. It was dainty, delicate, hard-as-nails Alice Fraser who surged to her feet. ''Six! Two for the children and only four for the rest of us? Are you out of your mind?''

Michael turned a glare on Don Tomas. ''Leave him out of it. Then there'll be more for us.''

Alice shook her head. ''Don't be ridiculous, Michael. It's Selim who's—''

''If Selim says six, you know we won't talk him out of it,'' Michael went on angrily. ''He's a bloody selfish bastard.''

''Thank you.''

Michael ignored Selim as he went on. ''If there's only going to be six, we need to divide up the meat so we all get a fair share. Let the *hidalgo* go hungry this time. He deserves to.''

Selim knew this was bound to happen the moment he cut their rations. A group of hungry vampires was not a pretty sight; they were bound to turn on each other. Selim watched as Don Tomas rose out of his chair, eyes cold as stone. The Himalayas had probably looked like that, Selim thought, as the continents clashed and the mountains poured inexorably up out of the tumult, majestic and unstoppable. Only slower.

Michael Tancredi sprang out of his chair, pushing it

over in his haste. He was the size of a bull and looked like he'd just had a red cape waved in front of his face. The comparison stopped when he bared his fangs. No angry bull had ever looked that mean. It made Selim wonder where the reasonable car salesman of a few moments before had gotten to.

Alice backed out of the way. She stopped halfway between the table and the garden doorway, at a spot where she could fight, flee, or sit back down to the discussion. She flashed a glance at Selim that blamed him for starting this.

Kamaraju stayed where he was, though he looked like he was ready to duck under the table.

"You don't need to Hunt," Michael told Don Tomas. "You already had yours, didn't you?"

"It's been nearly five years," Alice reminded Michael. "Let it go, Mike."   Tancredi turned his snarl on her. Selim watched Alice back up another step. She looked like she was going to hold her hands up defensively before her but managed to turn the gesture into a shrug. "Fine. Don't."

"He should never have bled and bedded the bitch. Look at what happened."

"He didn't know she was Rom."

That was the problem with living in a melting pot culture. The seasoning was sometimes off. Cassandra hadn't been any more aware of her ancestry than Don Tomas had been. The result had surprised everybody. The result was nearly five years old. A healthy, happy, sharp-toothed little *dhamphir* menace that had every vampire that knew about him spooked. Selim was, so to speak, little Sebastian Avella's godfather. Cassandra was still living in the don's nest. Selim knew he needed to do something about it, but seeing Michael's open hostility reinforced his belief that Sebastian was safer being watched over by both parents.

"You are in my house," Don Tomas spoke to Michael, his voice a low rasp. "You will not speak of my companion."

"She's not your companion anymore," Michael shot back. "You killed for her, with her." He made a downward, slashing motion with his hands. "*You* cut the cord. She's one of us now."

"Then she needs to Hunt as well, doesn't she?" that hard, low voice questioned. "For the sake of the child."

"He's a sweet little *velociraptor*," Selim murmured.

Alice gave him an amused look when she overheard him. As the tension continued between the glaring men, she added her own low comment to Selim. "Don't you just love testosterone?"

"Not one of my favorite flavors."

"Not only tight-assed but straight."

"They go together."

"I suppose you're right," she agreed and backed farther from the continuing confrontation.

"You don't need the kill, Tomas," Kamaraju spoke up. "Michael's right. Cassie had hers."

"And the others in my house?"

"Let them pay a penalty for your Hunting out of season." Michael appealed to Selim. "That's fair. There should be more for the rest of us."

Selim sighed. He stood. Less than a heartbeat later, Michael Tancredi was sprawled out on his back, spread-eagled on the wide tabletop with his shirt ripped open. Selim's claws dug warningly into the spot over his heart.

Selim looked down into the surprised, frightened eyes beneath him and said gently, "Apologize to our host." He glanced momentarily at Kamaraju. "You, too."

"Testosterone," Alice said smugly from the doorway. "You just have to love it."

Michael was brave enough to meet Selim's gaze, smart enough to say, "You goaded me into this."

Selim nodded. "Thought the demonstration would do you some good." He sank claws ever so slightly into Michael's chest. Skin popped like bubble plastic and blood welled under Selim's nails. He could feel the other's slow heartbeat beneath his palm. "You'd be delicious," he said, smiling all the while. All of Michael's muscles went rigid. Nothing in his emotions suggested any hint of struggle. He was like a caught rabbit, hoping the owl would go away if he pretended he wasn't there. While Selim waited for Michael Tancredi to react in some way, he went on, "Should I invite little Sebastian in for a snack?"

"It's past his bedtime," Don Tomas said.

"Of course. Will you please apologize, Mike?" Selim asked in exasperation. "I've got spilled coffee dripping on my foot, and it's getting uncomfortable."

"My—my apologies," Michael blurted out.

Selim could tell from the look on Michael's face that the car salesman didn't remember what he was apologizing about. His emotions were just as confused; he wasn't thinking much at all. Good. Always good to keep them off balance. Selim backed away and helped Michael up. He refrained from licking the blood off his claws. He'd made his point, there was no use in being crude about it. He retracted his claws and put an arm around Alice's waist as she came up to him. She fitted nicely against him, all warm, willing curves and softness.

"To the victor go the spoils?" he whispered in her ear. He let his hand drift from her waist to her thigh. "Not that there's anything spoiled about you, of course."

Alice leaned her head back on his shoulder. "Take me shopping on Rodeo Drive and I'll show you differently. That wasn't a victory. Poor Mike," she added as Michael Tancredi moved to stand in the shadows away from the table. Within moments, only a pair of feral eyes glittered out at them as the embarrassed nest leader cloaked himself in darkness.

Alice put a hand over Selim's heart and turned on her most alluring smile. "I thought I'd try to seduce a few more people for the Hunt out of you. Will it work?"

Selim's breath quickened as heat flared where she touched. *Just how long had it been?* he wondered. The lure of the forbidden added spice to the moment. He kissed her forehead. "Alas, Alice, no."

She sighed and moved away. "Didn't think so. Can I get you another cup of coffee?"

The scent and feel of her lingered. Selim shook his head. "Thanks, no. I have to be going."

Kamaraju banged a fist on the table. "You can't walk out now! We have decisions to make."

"We?" Selim looked around. "We? Is this a democracy now?"

Alice chuckled. "You did say that we're all-American vampires."

"So I did. I lied." He looked at Kamaraju. "You already heard my decision. Six. That's it." He turned his attention to their host. "Thank you for dinner."

Don Tomas gave one of his tight, aristocratic nods. "Must you go so soon?"

"I do have to meet with Miriam this evening." Selim blessed them all with the one concession he was willing to make. "You can consider her nest out of the loop for this Hunt. That ought to make you happy."

It didn't. He could feel the anger from all of them. As he walked out of the room, it mixed sickeningly with the growing need. They hated the tight leash he kept them on, especially as the hunger grew. These were the civilized ones, the Law-biding ones. The strigs were going to give him even more trouble. It was only going to get worse, and he had to let it, walking the silver knife edge for them until the time was right.

Like Siri says, he thought once more. *You knew the job was dangerous when you took it.* He smiled at the thought of her and found Siri waiting for him in the car.

She didn't smile back. The petite woman turned a fierce glare on him as he slid into the passenger side. "Just what the hell was going on between you and Alice Fraser a minute ago?" she demanded.

Selim hunched down a little in the leather-upholstered seat. "Woman, I would hate to be as psychic as you are."

"Hmmph. Well?"

Selim winced. "Later. Drive," he instructed. "I'm a hen-pecked Hunter," he complained under his breath as his companion put the Mercedes in gear.

"And you love it," she added as she swung the car up the long, curved drive of Don Tomas's estate.

Selim put his hand over hers as she efficiently shifted gears. She was small, delicately made, and mortal. He didn't dispute her statement for a moment.

Chapter 2

SIRI TURNED INTO the parking lot at the entrance to Stone Canyon Park. They got out without a word and went to sit on the retaining wall that faced a the view of the city. The park closed at dusk, and a cop or private security car would pull up soon and they'd be told to move on. In the meantime, Siri snuggled up in the crook of his arm and they gazed on the lights spread out for miles and miles below them. The touch of her warmth in the cool of the evening was sweet. He put his arm around her shoulder and pulled her closer.

Siri sighed. "Isn't it beautiful? Don't you just love this town at night?"

"I've never seen it any other way."

"You know what I mean."

He remembered the way this view had looked before the sprawl of light was quite so wide, before the freeways formed bright flowing rivers, before the city noise reached all the way up here. That was what he disliked the most about change, he decided, the noise.

"I grew up in a quiet spot in a noisy city, but I never heard it," he told her. "Maybe the only quiet spot in the whole . . . in a garden surrounded by squalor." He felt her curiosity but said no more.

She tilted her head, concentrating. "You grew up in a cage?"

Psychic. Far too psychic for her own good. Far too psychic for his good. "Never mind."

"I don't understand."

It was always tempting to explain and far too dangerous to give in to the temptation. It wasn't that he didn't trust her, it was that he didn't trust anyone else. What Siri knew could be forced from her.

"Right," she said. "What I don't know can't hurt either of us. You're a pain, Selim."

He squeezed her shoulder. "I haven't caused you any pain in ages."

She squeezed back. "You wanna?"

Her enthusiasm rattled him. He wanted. He wanted very much. But . . . "No. Let's just talk. I don't have much time."

"You have to go to Claremont. But you don't want me to drive you. Why?"

"I need the exercise." A stinging insect landed on his cheek, then flew away without trying to bite—professional courtesy and all that.

"Right."

Her disapproval amused him, her jealousy didn't. She knew he wasn't interested in Miriam. Siri, in fact, knew everything that went on. That was why they needed to talk before he got back to work. He'd been at home for nearly a month before tonight's meeting, meditating, thinking, dreaming, leaving the outside world and grocery delivery in Siri's capable hands while he prepared for the Hunt.

She put a hand on his knee, then ran it up his thigh. "Skinny but cherse," she judged.

"Stringy," he answered.

Her lips found his throat, her kiss a soft, teasing plea. The night went red and warm around him. He smiled and licked his lips. Then he forced his mind back to business while he let himself enjoy her touch. They hadn't talked much on the ride over. He'd been concentrating too hard on the upcoming meeting to pay much attention to her, even though her resentment had filled the car, acrid as smog. They were comfortable together for the moment, and he reveled in just being with her. He wanted to tell her how much he loved her, but he didn't want to go where that would lead.

He waited until she stopped kissing his throat and snarled a few forceful swear words into the night before he spoke again. "I trust you didn't get bored while waiting." He carefully refrained from mentioning that Cassandra had invited Siri in. She carefully refrained from reminding him. They both carefully refrained from mentioning Cassandra, keeping the subject at bay by avoiding it.

He did admit, "I made the mistake of mentioning Istvan."

"What'd you do a thing like that for? That could only get them thinking about Sebastian."

"As if being in the same house with a *dhamphir* wasn't on all their minds already. I ended up using the reference to stir them up. We Enforcers like to remind the ones we oversee that things could always be worse."

"And somebody ended up accusing Don Tomas of unspeakable acts because of it."

Selim scratched his ear. "That's pretty much what happened."

"Oh, honey. Why'd you have to go start a fight?"

"I let Mike start it. The resentment of Don Tomas was bound to come out. Better now than later."

"I suppose."

"Were you bored while I was having fun tossing Mike Tancredi around the dining room?"

Siri laughed at the idea that she could ever be bored. "I had my cell phone and palmtop with me." She tapped her forehead. "Not to mention my own personal radar. How could I ever be bored?"

"Palmtop?" He frowned. "'You were on-line, weren't you?"

"Of course not."

He accepted the lie. Another case of what he didn't know wouldn't get anybody killed. Many members of the Strigoi Council hadn't yet adjusted to the idea of telephones. So far, the Internet was strictly forbidden to vampires. He wasn't going to tell anyone on the Council about his web site—or anyone else's, as long as they used to the web to advertise their legitimate businesses. People had to make a living, which was something else the Council didn't understand. Own a few slaves and make them support you was still the dominant opinion of those in charge. It was pleasant, Selim agreed, but not always practical.

"You know what I told you about E-mail," he warned.

"Don't get caught?" Her tone was sweet as baklava. He could feel the breeze from her innocently fluttered eyelashes. Some night—not tonight—she was going to get herself into deep trouble. *Pushing the envelope* was the term he believed best defined his companion.

Selim chuckled. "Something like that. What's the news, owl bait?"

"Well, I talked to Rene. He's with Alice," Siri said after a moment's puzzled silence from Selim. "He saw the news reports and wanted to reassure us that they aren't involved."

"News reports?"

"The Griffith Park problem?" She swiped a hand in front of his face. "Hello?"

After a few more seconds, Selim finally made the connection. "Someone is killing people and horses in Burbank and North Hollywood. Alice lives in Burbank."

Siri nodded. "Rene's upset."

"Tell him not to be. Anything else?"

"Well, there's Jager."

"Consider him taken care of."

"Kamaraju won't like that."

"He'll cope."

"Okay. Got another strig situation, though."

"Why me?" He sighed. Los Angeles attracted more loners than anywhere else. Problem was, there really was no such thing as a lone vampire. "What now?"

"You need to have a talk with Geoff Sterling. That boy's got himself into a situation."

The name wasn't familiar. "A new strig?"

She nodded. "Moved here after that mess in Seattle. Wasn't looking for a new nest. Then . . . he met a girl."

"How does that constitute a situation?"

"Been stalking her." Siri sounded outraged. Probably thought he should be. He waited until she went on. "The girl's an actress. Has a role on a television series."

Ah. That was decidedly different, one of the hazards of living in this town. "I'll have a talk with him."

He could tell that there was more she wanted to discuss, but a patrol car slowed and turned into the parking area before they could continue. He waved as the beam from the headlights swept over them. They stood and headed for the car before they could be told to leave. Selim opened the driver's side door for Siri. "See you later." He kissed her cheek. The gesture left her stiff with disapproval.

He ignored it, closed the car door for her, took a deep breath, and began to run. As he picked up speed, what she'd told him about this Geoff Sterling got him to thinking about how they'd met.

Murad fingers the gold coins. One slips from his fingers and falls to the floor. A woman seated at the next table picks it up.

SARA

(Looks at coin):
An owl.

MURAD

(Holds out his hand):
Yes.

SARA:
Night hunter. Silent. Deadly. Beautiful.
(Their gazes meet. Lock.)

MURAD:
Thank you.

SARA
(Tosses coin; catches it):
Dumb as posts, though.

MURAD:
What?

SARA:
Owls. Gorgeous creatures. Efficient. But nothing
like their PR reps. Of course, how much brains
do you need to catch mice?

MURAD:
I don't know. Why don't you tell me, owl bait?

Valentine finished rereading the pages she'd faxed to
her agent. She was almost pleased with them. She wasn't
pleased by the tone that had been in her agent's voice
when she picked up the phone and heard, "We have to
talk about this latest draft."

When she was done reading, she spoke into the
phone. "Just what is it you don't like about this?"

"I like the woman," her agent told her. "Adding the
romantic element is nice. I'm not sure about the direction you're taking the romantic element, though."

"Sex sells."

"Yeah, but a romance with the vampire? Shouldn't
the hero be the romantic interest for Sara?"

"The vampire *is* the hero."

"That's right, you got rid of Davy in the last draft. I
don't know, Val, a vampire as a love interest is kind of
sick."

"Depends on the vampire. Murad's a nice boy."

"Vampires aren't nice. And what's with the name change?"

"You didn't like Suleiman."

"But why Murad? Who's going to see a movie about an Arab vampire who's not only the hero but the love interest?"

Valentine began to experience outrage for the first time in years. She gripped the cordless phone so tightly that the black plastic began to crack. The only light in her apartment came from the glow of the computer screen on her desk and the blinking answering machine she hadn't checked in days. She scrolled through a few pages of the script file, reading as she answered, "I don't see anything wrong with that."

The voice on the other end of the phone was reasonable, coaxing. "We both know there's no money in that, Val."

Valentine's attention was only half on the conversation as she reread the words she'd written the night before. The woman's character needed more fleshing out. She wanted to know more about the girl. That would be tricky, but she thought she had a way. She answered her concerned agent. "Don't call me Val. What about truth? What about originality? What about my production deal? This is the movie I want to make."

"What about a reality check, Valentine?" There was a pause, then her agent went on. "Assuming you can get the movie you want made, nobody will come to see it. Not with the story as it currently stands. What you're writing isn't what I asked for, what I promised you'd deliver."

"I haven't finished the rewrites."

"That's good. Because I think you need to trash what you've got and go back to the original premise. Monster movie, remember? Lots of blood, smart-ass dialogue, screaming teenage girls."

"There's nothing real in that idea."

"There's nothing real about vampires, Val."

"But there could be. What's wrong with a story about how vampires really live?" She knew how that sounded and she didn't care. She was on fire with her vision. "I can make a movie that will have humans believing in vampires," she promised.

"I'm beginning to think you believe in vampires."

"Of course I do. I've been working in Hollywood too long not to know a few personally."

Her agent laughed shakily. "Me, too."

No. Valentine forced herself to calm down, to keep from blurting out the truth to someone who wouldn't believe her anyway. "So," she said. "What do I have to do to get this movie made the way I want it?"

Another laugh, cynical, not shaky. "You tell me, Val."

She considered her answer carefully. What were her options? The independent film route was fraught with more complications than she was prepared to cope with. It wasn't the financing that bothered her or even all the other endless details. She planned on producing anyway. But there was no way she was prepared to stump the film festival circuit in hopes of romancing studio interest in a distribution deal once she put the movie in the can. She'd done Sundance once. The desperation at the parties had left a very bad taste. Being near all those film school *auteurs* pretentiously pretending they weren't hungry to sell their souls for big Hollywood deals had actually given her a skin rash.

She could get the movie made, then try for a cable or a straight to video deal. She shook her head. She didn't like those options, either. She was used to being part of the system, to being on the inside. She wasn't prepared to start over now.

Fortunately, there was one other thing she could do. Her stomach curdled at the very thought of it, but she couldn't keep from smiling. "I can do this."

"Do what?"

She deleted several pages of dialogue. She'd been

talking to herself, but she answered her agent. "I want you to arrange some meetings for me."

"You?"

Her agent's surprise registered against her senses even at a distance. Valentine's smiled sharpened. "Me. Don't remind me that I never take meetings. I have to do this in person." She named names, said, "Bring them here."

Instead of waiting for arguments, she hung up the phone. Then she stared at the screen some more. "Definitely have to flesh out the woman." She had some ideas, some knowledge, but not as much as she needed. All right, not as much as she wanted. She was curious about the girl.

Valentine's Dreaming had brought her bits and pieces of information in the last few weeks. Enough for her to start weaving a story, but she still hadn't pinned down exactly what it was she both wanted and needed to tell. That the notion of telling the truth had turned into a hunger was something she didn't deny. She knew hunger so rarely lately that she found the growing sensation very pleasant. Pleasure was something else she'd almost forgotten about. She'd lived her life in limbo and liked it, then desperation drove her to take the first step into someone else's private world. Maybe she should be ashamed of herself, but voyeurism was proving to be fun.

The girl was very prominent in the dreamworld Valentine had chosen, but there were many things about her that Valentine hadn't been able to sense. She wanted a complete picture. She wanted more information than she could pick up on her own. Valentine sighed and glanced over at her personal phone line. The answering machine light blinked accusingly at her, bright red. She bit her lip and tapped a finger thoughtfully on the wrist rest of her keyboard while the light kept on blinking. She was going to need help, she decided. Not just with the girl but with the whole project. She simply could not do it on her own. She was going to have to call him, get him involved, make him do what she wanted.

He would complain. Accuse. Rage.

She could live with that.

But not right now. She turned her attention to the computer screen and thought about the script. How many drafts had she gone through? How many more? She was getting close, but not quite there yet. There would have to be a Hunt, of course. She'd finally admitted that a Hunt was the only kind of dramatic element a studio would go for: All the visceral drama and excitement and gore potential of the chase scenes would be a director's wet dream. She could envision the shots done with a handheld camera.

"You're not a director," she reminded herself. She shrugged and settled for telling a truth she did know, and decided to change the characters' names one last time. This time the words on the screen said,

SIRI

(Looks at body):
That was . . .

SELIM

(Draws Siri to her feet):
Alive a moment ago. Let's not talk about what he was.

SIRI

I've seen him before. Around.

SELIM

Of course you have. He's been stalking you for months.

SIRI

He has? How do you know?

SELIM

Because I've been stalking you, too.
(Takes Siri in his arms.)
I won.

Chapter 3

IT WAS A modest one-story house, set well back on a sleeping street in the quiet college town. Surrounded by a large, elaborate garden of night-blooming flowers, it wasn't so far from the houses on either side as to be conspicuous, but it wasn't all that close to the neighboring buildings, either. A porch light was on, attracting moths, but curtains were drawn, blocking any other light from escaping the house. Streetlights shed small pools of light above the cross streets at both ends of the block, but the house was well away from the lampposts. The only car parked on the wide street was a Jeep Cherokee on the opposite curb a few houses up.

Selim checked his watch, then looked at the gold coin carefully before he knocked on the door. He wanted to make sure he had the right one. The coin was twenty-four-carat gold, about the size of a nickel. It bore the image of an owl on one side and an inscription in a dead language on the other. Selim carried five such coins. Each one was slightly different.

When he knocked, a slave named Gary answered the door. "Hi, Selim," he said casually. His eyes narrowed as he looked around, but his attention wasn't focused on the Hunter on the front porch.

Selim frowned and held up the coin. "This is the point where you bow and grovel."

Gary stepped aside and let him in. "Yeah, right. This is L.A., man."

Gary was a postdoctoral candidate in human geography. "It's Claremont," Selim informed him. "And I'm not a man."

"That's not what Siri says. Come on in."

"And Siri would know," Selim agreed. "Your Lady around?"

"In the bedroom. Come on."

Gary led Selim through the house's small living room and into the heart of Miriam's home. The bedroom was actually a library with a bed in one corner. Even the headboard contained a bookcase, and there was a pile of paperbacks on top of a crocheted comforter with a sleeping cat curled around them. Miriam sat on the floor, with her knees drawn up, leaning back against one of the bookcases. Her companion was seated next to her, head in a book, though he looked up as Selim crossed the room. Miriam was deep in a conversation with her fosterling, who was perched on the top of a desk in the middle of the room.

Miriam jumped to her feet when she saw him. "Selim. Hi." She waved a hand toward the vampire on the desk. "Andy and I were just discussing Hume."

"Hello Miriam. Andrew. Who's Hume?"

"You don't want to know. She's gotten into all things Scottish lately," Andrew said as he rose to his feet. He shook Selim's hand. He was tall and lanky, with big hands and feet, like a puppy. He wore his brown hair unfashionably long, having never quite recovered from being a guitarist in a rock band for awhile, back when he was human. "She's thinking about moving us to Edinburgh," he went on. "Please make her stop, Hunter."

"The nights are cold there," her companion said. He rose to stand protectively behind Miriam with one hand on the short woman's shoulder. His attention focused warily on Selim.

Miriam tilted her head back. "But long, Joe. You'd like that."

Joseph looked between her and Andrew. *"You'd* like it. I'm a day person."

Andrew snickered. "Give it a few years." He returned his attention to Selim. "Thanks for coming."

"You look winded, Hunter. You didn't come here on foot did you? Would you like coffee?" Miriam asked. Selim nodded, and Gary headed for the kitchen.

"Sorry we couldn't do this with just a phone call," Selim said after the slave left the room. He wanted to ask her to have her companion leave as well.

"We're all involved in this," Joseph said belligerently before Selim could speak. "Gary as much as the rest of us."

Andrew nodded. "We're a family, Hunter. No secrets."

"That's true, Selim." Miriam's tone was much milder; hers the only voice that mattered to Selim.

He shrugged. He wanted to say that how someone ran their nest was none of his business, though it wasn't true, and they all knew it. He did let it go, a concession, something to remind Miriam of if she balked at being left out of the official Hunt.

They all trooped into the kitchen and took seats around the table so that Gary could be part of the conversation while he busied himself with domestic tasks. "I made spice cake," Gary said after the coffee was on and a pot of tea was brewing. He began cutting large slices and putting them on plates. "Siri says you love spice cake, Hunter."

Siri talked too much. But, what the hell? "I do," he said, and accepted a piece graciously. "Thanks for going to all the trouble, Gary."

"We don't get many visitors. And *she* only likes chocolate," Gary complained jokingly.

His mistress laughed and patted the place on her left. Joseph was seated on her right. Andrew was perched on the counter that separated the cooking from the dining areas in the small kitchen. His long legs rested on the back of one of the ladder-back chairs. Gary finished passing out dessert, then sat next to Miriam. The blended aromas of hazelnut-flavored coffee and Earl Grey tea filled the air.

"So," Andrew asked after Selim took a few polite bites of the cake, "do we get to kill the fucker?"

"This is quite good," Selim complimented Gary. He noticed Miriam's slight grimace of disapproval at the fledgling's language. "Siri only passed on the sketchy details you gave her about someone needing to be dealt with."

"I couldn't go into specifics over the phone," Joseph pointed out.

"I appreciate that. But I trust you, Miriam. I still thought it best to speak with you in person first."

She smiled graciously. "Thank you. I didn't think it would be safe for me to try to make it to the meeting tonight, knowing he might be watching me."

"I appreciate your concern for security."

"Did you see the Jeep outside?" Joseph asked Selim. "He's taken to hanging around outside the house. He claims that he first saw her coming out of a theater at the Ontario Mall and fell instantly in love. That he had to have her. It started with letters and progressed to phone calls. He's sent photos of her along with some of those love letters."

"And your response?" Selim asked Miriam.

Joseph answered. "First Andy tried putting the eye on him, but the dude doesn't hypnotize."

"He's gifted?" Selim asked.

Andrew shook his head. "A little. Not enough to do anything productive with. Enough to form this obsession for Miriam, though. Enough not to respond for more than a few hours to the deepest command I can manage. His *need* has too deep a hold on him for anything to break it. I did beat the shit out of him," he added. "There weren't any phone calls for three weeks after that."

"I don't want to go near him," Miriam apologized. She dragged her fork across her dessert plate, gathering crumbs and frosting without showing any real interest in eating.

"She shouldn't have to," Joseph spoke up. "Touching a mind like that freak's, one that's full of filth aimed at her, could overwhelm her. It'd be like he mind-raped her before she could do anything about it. She'd be trying to tell him to leave her alone, and he'd be showing her all the things he plans to do to her. It would be giving him what he wants." Joseph and Miriam held hands while his fierce, protective anger boiled around the room. They all absorbed the righteous feel of it, and after he calmed, he went on. "I thought about getting a restraining order, but Miriam vetoed that."

"I should think so," Selim responded. "You should have called me sooner, Miriam."

"I didn't want to bother you."

She didn't want an Enforcer bothering her happy little nest, she meant. He didn't blame her. Her quiet household was happy with their intellectual pursuits and each other. Joseph taught at UCLA, Selim believed, Gary studied at one of the small colleges in town, Andrew owned a coffeehouse that catered to the student crowd, and he played folk music there on weekends to pick up girls. Miriam wrote history books and biographies. They all went to a lot of movies. Siri had talked him into joining them at a multiplex for a screening of *Fargo*, then he'd had to listen to Joseph going on for hours about some people named Coen, and he had neither cared nor understood about any of what he'd heard. Siri had enjoyed herself, though. Selim used the old excuse about vampires not socializing with each other the next time Siri tried to get them all together.

Selim wondered if this nest's contented isolation from the rest of the Southern California vampires insulated them from the growing tension in the larger population.

"No," Andrew answered his thought. "I'm getting hungry."

"Do you think that anyone with the slightest psychic ability isn't aware that *something* is going on?" Miriam asked. "I don't think all the daydreams I'm having lately have to do with being watched by some annoying mortal stalker."

"Even I'm antsy," Gary spoke up. "Can't keep myself from ordering rare steak anytime I go out . . . and I'm a vegetarian."

"So, if there's going to be a Hunt anyway—" Andrew began.

The telephone rang before he could go on. Gary got up and picked a cordless receiver off a wall cradle over the counter. He listened for a moment, then passed the phone to Andrew. Andrew listened, gave a bark of laughter, then brought the phone to Selim. "It's for you, man." He was grinning in that bright, sharp-toothed way the young cultivated.

Selim was not surprised when a deep, angry voice asked him, "What are you? A cop? Another one of her lovers? She knows how I feel about her having more men in her house. You better leave, or she's going to be very, very sorry."

"Well, someone's going to be," Selim replied. He switched off the phone and looked at the waiting nest members. "Does this . . . fucker . . . have a name? I need pertinent details before I can set it up for you."

"We get to kill him?" Andrew jumped happily to his feet. "Cool."

Like called to like often enough that Siri wasn't in the least surprised when the big blond man walked into Jamba Juice, gave her a long look, then took a seat on the other side of the busy smoothie shop. She took note of him, then paid him no more mind. Her thoughts were on Selim, as was right, proper, and usual, so nothing else held her interest for long. Not in the mood she was in, anyway.

Three hundred and eighty-four days, she thought sourly as she glanced through the shop's wide side win-

dow toward the tall old building down the street from
where she sat. It was six stories high, took up most of
the block, was topped by domes and fake minarets, surrounded a garden full of palm trees and roses and a high
wrought-iron fence. It was an altogether hideous piece
of architecture left over from the last century, a local
landmark. Fortunately, its overdone facade was mostly
in shadow now that the sun had gone down. She always
sat at this side table because of the view. It was the
closest he let her get to him in the daylight these days.
The time was currently just past sunset. It was precisely
fourteen minutes before she was allowed to approach
him. He said he needed time alone when he woke up.
"You know what I'm like until I've had coffee." He
used to let her make the coffee after *they* woke up.

They needed to talk about the last year. More than a
year. Three hundred and eighty-four days, to be precise.
And counting.

Not that I'm counting, of course. "What is the matter
with that man?"

She was going to confront him for sure this time, she
decided. Point out that he wasn't the only one with
needs, wants, desires. It was just that he was so busy
lately and—

Oh, stop thinking like a honeymooning companion!
She chided herself, just as the cell phone on the table
beside her rang. Siri knew who it was before she answered. It was a gift with her. "Cassie, what am I going
to do with him?" she demanded as she flipped the phone
open.

"Slip a little Viagra in his dinner bowl?" her friend
answered promptly. Cassandra and she had had this conversation before. Cassandra yawned. "What am I going
to do about Sebastian?" her friend questioned Siri back.

That wasn't a question Siri felt qualified to answer.
After all, how many parents had to deal with a son who
could have gone through the terrible twos as a serial
killer? Not that Sebastian had, of course. Cassie and
Tom were doing a pretty good job raising their baby. It

was just that no one knew what to expect from the first *dhamphir* born in the last six hundred years.

"What's the problem?" Siri asked, as sympathetic as a woman who had no children could be to a friend with a rowdy four-year-old.

"His birthday's coming up," Cassandra answered.

"He wants to have a party?" Siri guessed. "Invite all his little friends over?"

"Can you imagine Tomas letting him do that? It took me a year to talk Tomas into letting Sebastian play with anyone but the . . . help. He still throws one of his glaring fits every time I schedule a trip to the park for Sebastian."

"He's just being a concerned parent," Siri soothed.

"I know. Do you know what else Sebastian wants? He wants to go to school like everybody else. Where does he get these ideas?"

Siri shrugged. "I don't know. *Sesame Street*?"

"Probably." Cassandra sighed. "I know there's nothing you can do to help me, girlfriend, but you're the only one I can vent with." Cassandra wasn't even supposed to do that with another vampire's companion, but neither of them mentioned that. Besides, everybody talked to Siri. It was well known that she was the reason the Hunter was so well-informed. That sort of made it okay to bend the rules. "I better go," Cassandra said. "Gotta see to the needs of the lord and master."

"Tom or Sebastian?"

"Both. Bye."

When Siri put the phone down, the blond man was sitting on the other side of the table from her. He'd been there for several seconds, but she'd been ignoring him. Oh, he'd moved swiftly, silently, and cloaked in a cloud of telepathic you-don't-see-me projected thoughts, but Siri was good. The best in L.A. This guy was good, too, but he was still just some vamp's companion, while she was the City Enforcer's girl.

"You're wearing sunglasses at night," she said. "Very Hollywood, but not the way we do things around here.'' She didn't recognize him, and she knew everybody. ''You're new in town.'' She held out her hand. He kissed it. Very old-world. ''I'm Siri.''

''I know.''

The accent was old-world, too. ''And you are?''

''Yevgeny.''

''Nice to meet you.'' She glanced at her watch. She was very new-world. ''I've got five minutes. What can I do for you? Make it fast.''

Chapter 4

"YOU COULD HAVE told me you weren't going to be at home."

"I forgot how far it was to Claremont. It's not as easy as it used to be to take shortcuts; jumping over all that razor wire on fences takes time. Then we ended up working late. Miriam has a spare bedroom. She let me stay through the day."

"Gary could have driven you home."

"In the trunk of his car? I don't think so."

"So you took a commuter train home? You couldn't call and tell me where you were?"

"I called."

"To have me pick you up at Union Station. I was waiting for you in Pasadena."

"You didn't have to be."

"I always do. You know that."

Selim stared out the windshield as they waited for the streetlight to change. He watched a bus lumber by. The headlights of the Mercedes raked across the ad for an upcoming blockbuster movie painted on the bus's side. Something mind-numbing, with lots of explosions, he supposed, from all the flames boiling up in the background of the advertisement. The sight of the flames lingered in his mind after the bus was gone. Or maybe it was Siri's seething fury that ignited images of fire. The girl could project when she wanted to. The girl could do anything she wanted to, he thought proudly. She was the most amazing woman he'd ever known, even if he hadn't told her so recently.

Maybe that was what this was all about. From his point of view, he'd simply behaved in a logical manner. He had a busy evening ahead; a run home as soon as he woke after sunset would have been tiring. His actions made perfect sense, but women were strange. Maybe he shouldn't even have had her drive him now, but she knew where to find this Geoff Sterling, which saved him the trouble of hunting the strig down on his own. All he had to do was show up and act omnipotent. That was another wonderful thing about Siri; she always made him look good.

"I was inconsiderate," he admitted. "I'm sorry." Damn it! He wasn't supposed to do that. He was the vampire. She was the companion.

"I'm supposed to await with breathless eagerness on your beck and call."

"I was just going to think that."

"Never complain or ask questions or make demands."

"That, too."

Her small hands were white-knuckled on the steering wheel. "I do."

"Yeah. Right."

"I would if you'd let me."

"You have better things to do with your life than await on my beck and call. With or without breath."

She snarled and swung around in the seat to face him. "I hate you."

He ignored her blistering look and ruffled a hand through her short red hair. "Sure you do." Behind them, people were honking their car horns. "Light changed, Siri. Drive."

"Yes, master," she mimicked an Igor accent. Her foot came down hard on the accelerator. "Driving, master."

He drove her crazy! He knew he drove her crazy, and he didn't care. He thought it was funny. Thought she was funny. *Life,* she thought, *after three hundred and forty-eight days, is not funny. Okay, sometimes it was.* She wasn't one who could stay despondent, or even angry, for long, especially not when she was around Selim. But he was driving her crazy. *"I was inconsiderate. I'm sorry."* Yes, he was; and no, he wasn't. She growled, deep in her throat. Sometimes she just wanted to rip his throat out!

"Going to have to get you to a vet, girl, if you keep that up."

Any other time she would have laughed. Now she just kept her attention on the road, resentment glowing like a hot coal deep inside her. She'd get over it, she knew she would. In a few minutes. There was work to be done. In the meantime, she nursed her hurt and kept the things she'd been going to tell him about Yevgeny to herself.

"Get in the car."

Siri heard Selim through the closed window of the Mercedes and couldn't stop the smile. His voice was low, menacing, dangerous, utterly butch. And a complete turn-on. That wasn't the reaction Selim received from the young strig outside.

"I don't think so."

She heard the deep anger in Geoff Sterling's voice. The hate. She also read that the strig was scared half out of his wits. Which was actually a very good reaction as long as he didn't do anything stupid. Selim had her chase Sterling into an alley off Melrose after spotting him cruising the busy street. Sterling looked conspicuously Goth, all done up in leather and torn black lace. "It's a wonder the fashion police haven't gotten to him first," had been Selim's comment as the strig began to *feel* his presence and took off. She'd backed Sterling into a chain-link fence at the end of the alley with the bumper of the car. Selim got out to talk to him before Sterling could make the leap to the other side of the fence.

"Do you know who I am?" Selim asked.

Siri frowned as a glob of spit landed on the windshield. The strig either had bad aim or a certain amount of sense; Selim was standing right in front of him.

"Pervert," Sterling said to Selim. "*Dhamphir.*"

Selim didn't bother to correct the youngster's misapprehension, but Siri took immediate offense. Just because all *dhamphirs* were Enforcers didn't mean that all Enforcers were *dhamphirs*. It was just that the one *dhamphir* that was an Enforcer, and totally insane but efficient, gave all the others a very bad reputation. She knew that Cassie didn't want Sebastian to grow up to become one of the Enforcers of the Law, but did the little boy have a choice?

Siri took a great deal of exception to Sterling calling her Selim a pervert because he had the ability to do what others couldn't. Vampires could not kill each other, despite the hideous battles they sometimes got into; they couldn't even commit suicide. The only kind of vampire that could bring death to another vampire was an Enforcer. It was a skilled profession, not a perversion, or so the Enforcers and Strigoi Council chose to believe. It was an honorable profession, no matter how hated and feared they were by the others of their kind.

Not that Selim had told her any of this. Vampire stuff was all supposed to be a big secret until companions came of age and all that bullshit. She had her sources; she had a brain to figure things out. She could read Selim's mind a good deal of the time. Siri loved being married to a cop and did what she could to help. Lord knew, he needed it.

"Hey! Watch the finish!" she complained as Geoff Sterling landed forcefully on the hood of the car. She winced as she heard his shirt buttons scrape against the glossy enamel.

"Sorry, hon!" Selim called and pulled Sterling off the hood by the back of his leather coat. A moment later, the rear passenger door opened, and Selim pushed the strig into the car ahead of him. "We'll be going now," he said to Siri.

She saw Selim flash her a quick grin in the rearview mirror as she backed out of the alley, but she did the proper, subservient companion thing and drove in inconspicuous silence. *Damn but Selim was hot,* she thought as he settled into the seat beside the sulking strig. Sterling was a pretty boy, slender and androgynous, with dark hair and bright green eyes. Her vampire was skinny, but in a wiry, muscular way that looked great naked. Selim's face was angles and shadows, with big, liquid brown eyes, a high forehead, and a sharply pointed chin.

"When are you going to kill me?" Geoff Sterling asked as the Mercedes pulled out on the freeway.

The question broke a long, tense silence. Siri was glad; all the emotion the young vampire projected into such a small space had given her a headache. Selim, she could tell from the Cheshire Cat grin she glimpsed when she glanced in the mirror, was eating all the fear and loathing up with a spoon.

"Why would I want to kill you?" Selim answered the question with a question.

After another silence, a sullen one this time, Geoff said, "Seattle."

"You weren't involved."

"How do you know?"

"You're not dead. Besides, I'm sure you're very sorry and will never be bad again, especially now that you're on my patch."

"I don't acknowledge your authority," the young one replied.

"Will that stop me from ripping out your heart? Should it become necessary, that is."

A spike of fear registered on Siri's senses. She just barely managed not to swerve the car across lanes in reaction. *Stop that!* she thought loudly at Selim, but gave no outward sign of being involved in any of this.

"It's about the girl," Selim said with no further games.

"The girl?" Sterling sounded outraged. And jealous. "What about Moira? What's she to you?"

A complication, Siri thought. *Don't worry, hon, he doesn't want your girl. He better not.*

She hoped.

Never mind that vampires often had more than one companion. She had no business being jealous of this Moira, no more business than Geoff Sterling had being jealous of Selim. But both she and Geoff Sterling were jealous at one mention of a name. Everybody was *so* touchy lately. She hated that she was being drawn into this nonsense. She'd be so glad when they got it out of their systems.

"Back off, boy," Selim said. "My interest in you and Moira Chasen is strictly professional. Do you know who she is?"

"Of course I know."

"Until yesterday, I was blissfully unaware of her existence. I'm told she's a black-haired beauty who plays an angel on some highly successful television show."

Sterling chuckled. "That's what first drew me to her. Seducing an angel. Sounds like fun, doesn't it?"

"A make-believe angel? If that's fun for you, who am I to stop you?"

"A *dhamphir,*" was Sterling's bitter answer.

"Hunter will do. Juveniles are so ignorant. But then, you were orphaned so young. You're what? Two, three at most?"

"I was a companion for—"

"Doesn't matter. It's not the same. If you weren't young and inexperienced, you wouldn't even remember how many years you were a companion. You certainly wouldn't think those years counted for anything."

Thank you very much, Siri thought. What was Selim talking about? What was his point? Why didn't he just tell Sterling to leave the girl alone and kick him out of the car? Instead, he wanted her to drive them to a mall. What for? Was Selim planning on doing something to improve this kid's wardrobe?

"Do you think you're ready to take a companion of your own? Or is there something else you have in mind?"

"I don't know," was Sterling's answer to both questions.

"You haven't thought about it? I see. The girl caught your attention, and you started stalking? You're just playing owl and mouse without thinking about where it has to lead?"

"I want her," Sterling answered sulkily.

"Does she have the gift?"

Sterling nodded. "I've never wanted anyone like I want her. Wanting's enough."

"Dead or alive? Either way is complicated," Selim went on without giving the other vampire time to answer. "She's famous. Her face is known. It's time you made a choice. Ah, here we are."

Siri pulled into the parking lot of the large mall, found a parking spot near the neon-lit main entrance, and shut off the car engine. She didn't like where this conversation was going. Mostly because she didn't understand where it was going. It had seemed simple and straightforward to her when she found out about Sterling's unhealthy interest in the actress. She'd told Selim, assuming he'd nip the problem in the bud. Suddenly, she didn't have a clue as to what he was doing. This was abnormal, and she didn't like it one little bit.

She didn't like it when he said, "Wait here," and dragged Sterling out of the backseat. She heard Selim say, "Come on, I have something to show you," to the younger vampire as they headed toward the mall's main entrance.

"Stay here, my ass," she muttered. She checked her watch, then got out of the car. "Wait for lord and master to return? Not a chance. Not when Macy's is open for another hour."

Chapter 5

"I KNOW WHAT it's like," Selim told the boy as they walked across the parking lot. "To want someone so badly that you *ache* all the time. You follow them at night, you dream about them during the day. Do you ride her in your dreams? Do you have it that bad?"

He asked the questions as they reached the row of glass doors at the main entrance. Moths buzzed around the overhead lights. A group of teenagers loitered just beyond the glow of the lights, smoking by the side of the building. The confusion that emanated from Sterling, as acrid as the cigarette smoke, told Selim all he needed to know. The look on Sterling's face was priceless. Selim pushed open a door. Artificially cooled air with no scent of its own surrounded him as he started walking down the wide, shop-lined corridor. Geoff Sterling hurried to catch up with him.

"I've never quite made up my mind about air-conditioning," Selim said as the strig put a hand on his arm. "On the one hand, it's convenient. On the other . . ." He shrugged Sterling off. "It's just so much dead air. What do you think?"

"I think you better tell me what you're talking about."

Selim gave Sterling one of those slight little smiles he was told had quite a chilling effect of their own. "Think about it. How do you spend your days? Dead to the world? Or do you dream? Do you dream about her? What she's doing? Where she is? Do you call out to her in your sleep? Go to her?"

Sterling looked at him strangely, thoughtfully. He sat down on one of a row of benches that lined the middle of the wide corridor. He ran his hands through his thick, slicked-back hair. Selim stood with his arms crossed and looked around. There weren't very many people in the mall. It was a Wednesday night, and quieter than usual, even for the middle of the week. Miriam and Andrew were seeing to that. While he waited for Sterling to adjust his thinking, he added his *go home, get out of here* thoughts to the mix. Wouldn't work on everybody, of course. There were plenty of people who could resist vampires' telepathic commands, but it didn't hurt to exercise one's will on those who couldn't resist every now and then. Safer for everybody in the vicinity on a night like this.

After a few moments of staring at his shoes, the young vampire looked up at Selim. "I can do that? Project my thoughts while I'm out of it?"

"Have you tried?"

"To control my dreams?"

Selim nodded.

Sterling looked momentarily outraged. "Why didn't anyone ever tell me about this?"

"Because your foster parent screwed up and got caught before teaching you half the things you need to know. Then *you* got all pouty about it and decided to go strig before anyone could beat any sense into you."

Sterling came angrily to his feet. "So now you're going to teach me, *dhamphir*?"

Selim was hardly impressed by this show of temper. He *wasn't* all strung out and in need of a Hunt like every other vampire in town. It helped to have his aggression under control when everybody else was on the verge of losing their heads. "I am." He waved away the inevitable protest. "This is my town." He took the young vampire by the arm and pulled him toward the courtyard at the center of the shopping mall. "Come on. There's something I want you to watch. When it's over, we'll discuss your Moira's future."

There were four entrances, with a fountain and palm trees in the middle of the court. A glass dome arched overhead, letting a small circle of darkness into the heart of the suburban shopping center. Shiny, molded plastic tables in black and white were lined up like chess pieces in the tiled circle between the fountain and the fast-food stalls. Bright red trash containers circled the fountain. A smell of hot grease assailed the senses, masking the warm scent of human that was already dulled by the cold air. Gary waited for them, seated near the west entrance. He was one of about ten people scattered at the tables, none near where Gary sat. The slave was sipping on a soft drink when they came up. There was a pile of french fries spread out on a tray in front of him, and a great many empty packets of ketchup were scattered around the fries. He nodded amiably as Selim took the seat across from him.

Selim dipped a fry into a pool of ketchup in the middle of Gary's tray. "Don't bother to get up."

"I won't." Gary hiked one shoulder higher than the other and assumed a stupid accent. "Unless you want me to fetch you a hamburger, master."

"Nah. The meat's always overcooked at these places." Selim popped the fried potato in his mouth, then let ketchup linger dramatically on his lips for a moment before licking it off.

Gary snorted and dropped the Igor pose. He glanced briefly at Sterling, who remained standing uncertainly by the table. "Your friend's being obvious."

"He's not my friend," Sterling answered.

"He's talking to me," Gary complained to Selim.

"Don't get formal on me now," Selim said to the slave. To the vampire he said, "Sit." Sterling sneered but did as he was told. "If you're looking for a foster mother, you can talk to Miriam after the hunt. Until then, strig," Selim informed Sterling, "you will leave those in her nest alone."

"Oh. Sorry." Sterling looked at Selim as he spoke, but the word was aimed at Gary.

Finding a well-mannered vampire in need of a good home beneath the posing and silly getup gave Selim hope for the boy. The strig pulled up a chair and took a seat without noticing how obedient he was. Selim turned his attention from Sterling to concentrate on the more important part of the evening. "Is he here?" he asked Gary.

The slave nodded. "Following Miriam. I saw his car follow hers away from the house. I wish you hadn't told her to lure that creep into the mall alone."

Miriam was small, a good-humored intellectual who lived in a world of ideas and clever conversation. She was shy, as many of their kind were. Selim could see how the members of her family could be concerned at the idea of her being out alone with a sicko stalker on her tail. He didn't bother reassuring Gary that she'd be fine. He ate another french fry and waited.

Gary took the hint. "Joe's at the east entrance of the court now. Andrew's in the north. Miriam said she'd come in through the south. What do we do once he gets here?"

"Miriam and Andrew will know."

Selim knew exactly where each member of Miriam's nest waited. Andrew was hungry and surprised at the intensity of it. Joseph had never been more excited in his life, but he had no idea why. He thought it had something to do with righteousness, with justice, with protecting his lady. Curiosity was almost as strong in Gary as his urge to protect his mistress. Miriam was the most in control of the group. A fine sense of irony edged her hunger, and the hunger was overlaid with the need to protect her people. She wanted to get this over with and get back to her normal life. Her stalker was happy, gleefully obsessed with having the woman he wanted so vulnerably within reach. He was too focused on Miriam to notice anything else. The few humans still in the food court were alert to danger, on some primitive, subconscious level. Selim was reminded of nature programs he'd seen on television, the sort that showed wary herd beasts scattered across the Serengeti as hyenas stalked prey around them. Beside him, Geoff Sterling's sulky anger was giving way to restlessness and growing arousal.

Selim picked up some more ketchup-dipped potatoes. "Want some of these?" He asked the strig.

Sterling looked around at the scattering of humans. One of them met his gaze for a moment, then hurriedly departed the food court, leaving an untouched meal and an overturned chair behind. Sterling covered his mouth with his hand when he looked back at Selim. "Yes," he growled around a mouthful of fangs.

Selim stared him down. "More than you want Moira?"

Sterling shook his head. He closed his eyes, his hands knotted into fists to keep them from shaking as much as to hide the claws.

"We'll see." Selim stood as Miriam entered the courtyard. He put his hands on Sterling's shoulders to keep him in his chair. "Watch and learn," he said. "Then we'll talk." He didn't ask the boy to calm down. From this point on, it wasn't going to be possible for any of them to be calm. He even found himself running his thumbs slowly up the sides of Sterling's throat, all too aware of the warm pulse of blood just below the skin.

Gary jumped to his feet. Joseph and Andrew moved into position at their entrances to the food court. Several nervous humans looked frantically around, adding spicy flashes of fear and uncertainty to the mix—a condiment, like ketchup on the french fries. Miriam's glance swept quickly around the area, coming to rest on Selim. The stalker trailed in behind Miriam at a leisurely pace.

Everything was now in place. Selim gave Miriam the briefest of nods.

The Hunt began.

Of course Siri knew where Selim was; she always knew where he was. That wasn't what drew her away from the linens department at Macy's and sent her running toward the food court. It was hunger, overwhelming hunger, and not her own. Hunger and a vision. She was used to having visions, she just hated having them in public. One moment she was discussing Ralph Lauren sheets with a bored salesclerk. The next—*Miriam moved.*

The man was behind her, then she was behind him. Miriam put her clawed hand on the man's shoulder. When he turned, she laughed. The man went pale; primitive fear shot through him. Miriam let him go, but not before briefly burying her claws in his shoulder. "You belong to me now," she said. The scent of blood was in the air. A small red stain welled up to mark the man's white shirt. He backed a step as she touched her tongue to each of her claws, fastidiously tasting the man's life. "Run," she suggested as he stumbled backward, knocking over a chair.

He fell over the chair. Black plastic shattered beneath him, throwing up knife-sharp shards. He sprawled onto his back, and Andrew was beside him. The young vampire helped the man to his feet. Andrew slashed the man's arm as he pulled him up. More red on white. He looked from one vampire to the other and his mouth opened to scream. Selim was inside his mind by now. No sound was allowed to escape. Not here. Not yet.

The man looked around for help, and though people watched the scene, no one rose from their tables to help or to run. Those who had the strength to get out already had. Those that were left were slaved to Selim now, held tight, as witnesses to the carnage. Sometimes vampires just had to put on a show.

Andrew tossed the man a long wedge-shaped piece

of broken plastic. It looked like an ancient obsidian blade. No reason for the prey to be helpless. What was the fun in that? The man tossed the plastic aside and pulled a small gun from an ankle holster. Andrew and Miriam exchanged a happy glance.

"Of course he has a gun," said Miriam.

"Don't you just love L.A.?" Andrew responded. "Such a well-armed city."

"Good boy," Miriam told her prey. He pointed the gun toward her face. His hand shook as she took a step closer to him. Her voice was full of sultry suggestion as she added, "Show me you know how to use that thing."

Miriam was no more than two feet in front of the prey when he squeezed the trigger. Of course she was behind him by the time gun was fired. The bullet smashed a gouge in the cement fountain. None of the humans in the court reacted to the gunfire.

The victim didn't try to turn the gun on Andrew. He dropped the weapon and ran toward the east exit of the food court. Joseph headed after him, human matched against human. Miriam and Andrew lingered, poised like a pair of eager hounds, their attention on Selim. After a few heartbeats, Selim decided that their prey had a good enough head start. He nodded, and the vampires gave chase. A few moments later, frowning at Miriam's insistence on ignoring custom, Selim allowed Gary to follow the rest of her nest toward the killing ground.

The vision was gone as she reached the entrance. Siri saw Selim haul Geoff Sterling to his feet as she entered the food court. The nest of vampires was gone, but the energy lingered. Danger, fear, power, and anticipation all mixed into a heady, erotic perfume. Siri had never been more aroused in her life. She trembled, not with fear but need, as she approached Selim. Siri was drawn to him by a frenzied hunger that went deeper than the connection they already shared. It was all some part of the Hunt, though she couldn't put any coherent defini- tion on what was going on. Other than the fact that she wanted to strip naked and fuck Selim blind and wasn't sure she'd be able to stop herself from doing just that, no matter how public they were. She couldn't take her eyes off him, not that she ever wanted to anyway. Right now, though, he was the most potent, beautiful creature she had ever encountered. And after she fucked him? Damn, but she was hungry. And thirsty. She hadn't tasted him for a long time, and right now, she wanted to drink him dry. She wanted to sink her teeth into those long, stringy muscles of his and—

Her fangs ached at the sight of him.

"Wait a minute. I don't have fangs."

A shiver went through Siri. Realization brought her to a shocked halt a few feet away from Selim and Sterling. Maybe she was still caught in the vision. Or maybe the world just was a weirder place than she already knew it was. She glared at Selim, still wanting him, but that was normal. "Just what the hell," she asked her lord and master, "is going on here?"

Selim was very aware of Siri's presence but fought to ignore her. Not because he wanted to. In fact, he wanted exactly what she did. To push her clothes aside and bury himself in her. To take her as hard and fast and furiously as she could stand while he drank her damn near dry. But he denied himself, and he denied her. He wouldn't do that to her. Not tonight. It was her question—beloved, caustic, as inquisitive as ever Siri demanding answers—that saved him from temptation one more time. He didn't answer her, but the evidence that she had some measure of control helped him keep his. Besides, his work for the evening wasn't done yet.

Selim focused his attention on Sterling. The strig's control was flimsy at best. An erection pushed against the tight crotch of his leather pants; his claws and fangs were at full stretch, too. His eyes were changed, effectively blinding him in the artificial light of the courtyard. Selim pushed the boy closer to the darker area by the fountain. Siri followed. He held Sterling easily, despite the strig's efforts to follow the Hunt.

Not your prey, he warned the strig's inner vampire.

"Don't even think about it," he said aloud. He shook Sterling a little. "Calm down."

Sterling's wide gaze focused on Selim's face. "How?" The word was a howl of frustrated pain.

Selim patted him on the shoulder. "See. You're feeling better already."

"Where?" Sterling pushed ineffectively against Selim's chest. The younger vampire was taller than Selim, his heavier build disguised by his androgynous getup, but he was—younger. Selim was immovable. "I need—"

"One like that," Selim finished for him. "Yes, I know. You and the other strigs. As to where Miriam's nest is right now . . ." He closed his eyes for a moment to get a better view. "They have their human cornered in the storage room of Victoria's Secret. I wonder if Miriam planned it that way as a romantic interlude for her and her young men? Never mind. What happens now isn't any of our business." It would only be his business if Miriam's household didn't clean up afterward, but Selim was sure he could trust her nest to leave everything neat and tidy behind them once they were done. He pushed Sterling down to sit on the edge of the fountain. "I need two things from you," he told Sterling. "Two, and then I'll let you play, too."

Selim watched approvingly as Sterling worked hard to get himself under control. It took a few minutes, but eventually curiosity got the upper hand over need. "Two things?" Sterling asked, voice rough. He wiped sweat off his forehead, then through his slicked-back hair. His eyes looked closer to normal as he glared at Selim. "What?"

Siri came up and took Selim's hand in hers while Sterling calmed down. Selim didn't really want Siri to hear this conversation, but he didn't have enough stamina to deal with her, Sterling, and the Hunt. He sacrificed secrecy for controlling as much as he could. It felt good to have her close by. Besides, Siri found out everything eventually, anyway.

"One," he told Sterling, "I want a liaison for the

Hunt with the other strigs. You're it,'' he said, not bothering to give the boy any choice in the matter. If Sterling was smart, he'd realize that the only way he would be allowed a taste of the kill was by cooperating. For the second thing, Sterling did have a choice. ''About Moira. You want this actress?''

Sterling didn't hesitate. ''I want her.''

Selim nodded. ''Fine. Now all you have to do is decide whether she's going to be your companion or your prey.''

Chapter 6

"IT'S VERY HIGH concept," Valentine explained. "Think *Get Shorty* . . . with vampires."

"Okay, I see that," the man sitting on the couch across from her answered. He leafed through the script pages she'd given him to read. He sounded less than enthusiastic. She knew he'd only come to her home because of the chance to say he'd actually met the writer who was so reclusive she didn't even allow her name to appear on the title credits of the hits she'd scripted. His name was Art Rasmussen. He like to boast that his name was Art, but he wasn't interested in art. That was fine with Valentine. She was trying to get a movie made.

"You have some good stuff here," he told her. "Story's not quite there yet, is it?"

His instincts were good, whether he believed in art or not. She glanced at the script. "I'm still working on it."

There was a CD playing quietly on the stereo, David Bowie's *Diamond Dogs* as background music on continuous replay. She'd had this need to listen to *"We Are the Dead"* just as the doorbell rang. She'd let the music keep playing as they talked. She'd been in movies too long not to think that one of the problems with real life was the lack of a soundtrack. This was her fourth such meeting with production executives, the second one this evening. Even though she was playing each meeting as though it were part of a structured act in a script, she was still getting nervous from being around so many people. She thought she was doing a pretty good job of keeping her nervousness under control, of staying focused on her objective.

You really ought to get out more, Valentine, she told herself. She noticed that her hand shook as she reached to pick up the blue ceramic mug she'd set next to the pile of script pages on the coffee table. *No, I shouldn't.* She took a sip of coffee, then focused her attention on Art Rasmussen. She caught his gaze. "Talk to me," she said as *"Future Legend"* began to play again.

Rasmussen thoughtfully rubbed his jaw, obviously uncomfortable at the intensity of her gaze. "Sex is good. Sex sells. But does the vampire have to be the heroine's boyfriend? I'm mean, the guy's dead. The dead can't get it up."

"He isn't dead; he's different."

"Of course he's dead. He's a vampire. And he's Arab."

Not that again! "Turkish and Egyptian," she explained, not for the first time. First her agent, and now every executive she'd talked to was concerned with audience identification with the hero. "I'm emphasizing his being Egyptian for a reason." *Because he is,* she added to herself.

"I don't like it."

"I don't care."

He pretended not to hear. "Black, I can see. Snipes opened *Blade*. Denzel, Will Smith, they could make it work."

She went on. "You see, Selim is a prince. Every other vampire knows he's a prince, but they think he's an Egyptian prince. Ancient Egyptian. They're thinking pyramids and pharaohs, and he's letting them believe he's thousands of years old.''

Art Rasmussen did not see the obvious humor. ''And this is important how?''

''Because he's an Enforcer of the Law, but he's only about two hundred years old. Here he is, in charge of the city, bossing all these ancient strigoi around, when, in fact, he's just this wet-behind-the-fangs kid. They all think he can take out any one of them any time he wants, so they always back down; but the truth is, almost any nest leader could take him on. They couldn't kill him, but—''

''Nests,'' Rasmussen interrupted. ''You've got it structured like a kind of vampire Mafia. That's good. I like that. Different families running different parts of the city, fighting each other. With this Selim keeping everything in checks and balances.''

''Think of him as the marshal of Los Angeles,'' Valentine went on. ''He makes sure everyone keeps to their own territories, sets up what kills are allowed between Hunts, makes sure no humans find out about the vampire community, enforces the Laws.''

''Laws? Vampires have laws?''

''They used to when I—All societies have laws,'' Valentine hastily corrected herself. ''That's what makes Selim the hero. He's upholding the Laws.''

Rasmussen looked disgusted. ''He's a vampire. Vampires are evil. I'm not making a movie about a vampire hero. No studio will support this; I don't care how it's bankrolled, I don't care who's pitching it.''

''Think of it as very hip, cynical, and postmodern.''

''There are no good guys.''

''Rather like in real life,'' she suggested with a smile. ''Tarantino never has good guys. Moral ambiguity sells these days. I'll put explosions in it,'' she offered. ''Car chases. More sex. Vampires love sex. How about a human villain for the vampire hero to fight? No. I don't like that. I want it to be about real vampires' problems. It's a story that needs to be told.''

He stood up. "I think it's been nice meeting you." He didn't say, *You're crazy, lady,* but he didn't have to. He was shouting it inside his head loud enough for Valentine to wince from the volume.

"I am not," she answered his thought. She pointed at the couch. *Sit.*

He eyes widened, his shoulders strained under his dark silk designer jacket, but he promptly obeyed.

Don't move, my dear. And stop thinking so loud. "Nod if you can hear me," she said.

Rasmussen nodded. Slowly. He stared at her, his gaze having gone soft and worshipful, quite without any choice in the matter. There was surprise and outrage buried deep inside him, but the surface of his mind was detached from it. The surface was hers, and all she'd done was barely suggest that his brain pay attention. The telepathic connection had come almost too easily. She guessed she still had it. What a shame.

Valentine sighed. "I hadn't planned on doing this the easy way," she told him. "I really hate this sort of thing. But a girl's gotta do what she's gotta do, I suppose. Too bad."

She rose to her feet and approached the human. It required touch to go deeper inside. She was small, delicate-looking. He was tall and beefy, not at all bad-looking, though she didn't find the collagen he'd had injected in his lips attractive. It didn't make him look younger or sexier, just vain. It would have to go. No, no, she reminded herself. He wasn't going to be that kind of slave. She'd outgrown her interest in playthings. Her movement was tentative at first, as she rested a fingertip on his artificially puffed lips. They were soft, and really felt quite—nice.

"Mmm," she murmured and cupped his face with her hands. Her skin absorbed the warmth of his. Heat spread through her, a simple pleasure, unfamiliar and unwelcome, but marvelous all the same. Maybe she could play with him . . . a little. They were more like cats than owls in some ways, despite the emblem they'd

adopted for themselves thousands of years ago. He
moaned at the dual touch of her mind and hands on him.
Moaned with pleasure and alarm. She tried not to enjoy
his dual reaction. This was a business deal.

"You see, sweetheart," she explained as she probed
deeper into Rasmussen's thoughts, "I've always liked to
think of myself as the only vampire in this town—bar-
ring producers and studio heads, and agents, and—well,
you know what I mean. I've spent far more time with
you human vampires than with my own kind. But
they're out there, on the move, and I can use that. Have
to."

Valentine stroked his face and throat, let the need
build in both of them. He was addicted to power. He
was beginning to learn what it was to be addicted to
subservience. "Vampires invented d/s games, did you
know that, darling?" She let him nod. "Well, not
games. I'm the real dom, and you're the real sub." She
let him put his hands on her and lick his lips. He was
beginning to sweat. She went on, digging mental hooks
deeper into his consciousness as she spoke. "I prefer
living a quiet life and playing by your rules when I have
to play at all. But I've been having this really big problem with writer's block. Until I came up with the best
idea I've ever had. The idea is to tell the truth. Nobody
tells the truth in this town. But I'm going to, and you're
going to help."

She stepped back, abandoning sensation for clear,
precise thought once more. Rasmussen was horny, hum-
ble, and ready for the next step. She wasn't. "I hate this
crap," she complained as she went into her bedroom.
She came back with a very specialized blade. She approached the couch, held the dagger up in one hand, and
sliced open a fingertip on her other hand with it. "Ouch.
Damn. Here." She stuck her bleeding finger in Rasmussen's mouth. He didn't need any instructions to begin suckling. As she whispered powerful words, blood
and magic flowed out of her, a few drops at a time, and
into Art Rasmussen.

Valentine threw back her head and laughed. "You don't need the gift to be a natural-born bloodsucker, I guess."

He did have the gift, of course, just a little. Enough for her purposes. She'd had to go through three meetings to find someone with just the degree of mental talent she needed. She'd been intending to do this since having her agent arrange the meetings. Why else take a face-to-face when there were faxes, phones, and E-mail in this day and age? She just liked pretending to herself that she was above her kind's usual parasitical behavior. *And which kind would that be?* she wondered. The strigoi or the moviemakers?

She ruffled Art's perfectly arranged hair. "Hey, it's real."

It was soft and thick and smelled wonderful, a sensual delight to touch. She'd tried to forget how good this felt. Valentine wanted to resent Rasmussen for forcing pleasure on her, but it felt too good just now for her to be grumpy. She let the blade fall from her hand. It landed on top of the pile of script pages, leaving a small splatter pattern of her, damp red on the white paper. Valentine closed her eyes, listened to David Bowie's seductive voice, and let the throb of exhilaration within take over for a few moments. But only for a few.

Art Rasmussen let out a piteous, hungry groan when she pulled her hand away from his mouth. He looked up at her with begging, puppy-dog eyes. She wanted to let it go on, too. "No," she told him firmly and wiped her wet finger on her slacks. "I want to work with your studio, not make you my baby." She pointed at the door. The cut on her finger was beginning to heal. Time for him to get out before she put a few puncture wounds in his skin. "Go home now," she told him. "Call me this time tomorrow night. No, make that Wednesday." She wanted to do another treatment, nail the outline for sure. She had some research to do before she could really get into the final draft. "After the playoff game," she added as Rasmussen headed obediently for the door.

He glanced at her over his shoulder and ran a hand through his mussed hair. He smiled, his eyes full of love. "Fine. I'll call you then." He blinked, and puzzlement was added to his adoration. "Something seems to be missing. What do I do now, call you Mistress, and grovel?"

"Nah," she said, waving toward the door. "Just go on home. And don't expect me to be wearing some kind of dominatrix rig when you see me again." Valentine felt a stab of guilt over the need she had just forced on Rasmussen, and she relented a little. There was someone she'd heard about. Valentine had her own suspicions about the girl, since she'd heard about her off and on for at least sixty years. She gave Rasmussen her name.

He'd obviously heard of her. "I don't use hookers."

Valentine shrugged. "Just a suggestion, sweetheart. In case you get the itch I have no intention of scratching."

He took it well, but then, of course, he was in no condition to argue with her over anything. "Okay." He grinned. "Can I see your fangs?"

"No. Go home. Men," she grumbled as the door shut behind Rasmussen. "They always want to see a girl's fangs."

"I'm a tit man myself," Yevgeny said as he came out of the bedroom. When she turned toward him, he was leaning against the door frame, arms folded. "Of course, I didn't used to be. You've got the best pair on the planet."

"Tits?"

"Those, too."

He was tall and blond and broad, arrogant as ever. Valentine's bare toes curled in the thick carpet as he looked her over. She hadn't let him come to her in a long time, but her reaction to him was just as strong as ever. That was why she hadn't let him come. He was here now, and she wanted him. She told herself it was because of what she'd been doing with Rasmussen. The truth was, she always wanted Yevgeny.

Besides, she owed him. He wasn't likely to let her forget it. There was only one way for her to pay. Besides, she wanted to.

He held his hand out toward her. Fire caught between them.

"Oh, what the hell," she murmured, and went into the bedroom with him.

Chapter 7

"DID I SAY you could come in?"

"Do you think you can keep me out?"

He'd taken the elevator. Siri had taken the stairs and was waiting for him at his door. Siri hadn't spoken a word to him since they left the shopping center. Hadn't even reacted when he'd kissed her cheek before getting out of the car. He'd assumed she was too shocked and angry for communication. He'd told himself that was all for the best, that she'd get over it if they left it alone, but he knew it for a lie. Now here she was, at the place where he wanted her, which was also the place where she shouldn't be. He'd miscalculated again. He didn't know if it was Siri or celibacy that was driving him crazy. Both. Oh, and there was this Hunt thing he was attempting to deal with.

"It's late," Selim told his companion. "Nearly dawn."

She looked at her watch. "You've got time."

"Go home."

"No." She tapped her foot, making sharp rapping sounds on the hardwood floor.

Selim unlocked the door and let her walk in ahead of

him. It was just as well to capitulate on this. A shouting match out in the hallway might call attention from his neighbors. The walls of his home were thickly insulated. No screams would ever disturb the neighbors from the inside. He knew that from experience. He'd been living in the same apartment for over sixty years, and nobody had heard anything yet.

She followed him down the long entry hall like an angry little shadow. Her gaze stabbed him in the back, irritating as a wasp sting. What her emotions did to him was even worse. He'd had a rough night. He was drained. Tired.

"You do know I've already got a headache?" he questioned as they reached the living room.

"Am I making it worse?"

"Yes."

"Good."

Redheads. And their tempers. Why were vampires always so attracted to redheads?

Selim turned on Siri. He wanted to grab her shoulders and shake her, but if he did that, it was likely he'd kiss her. That would just be giving in to what she wanted, what they both wanted. Then he saw her face, blazing with fury and disgust. Maybe that wasn't what she wanted. Maybe that wasn't what this was about. It hurt him to think that her show of temper wasn't about the way he was hurting her lately. What was the use of—

It was too close to dawn. He didn't have time for this.

"What?" he demanded.

A start of fear went through Siri when Selim turned on her. His pupils were wide, a hint of fang bulged beneath his lips. A glance at his hands showed her that the nails were sharpening. Her heart slammed hard in her chest, but she lifted her chin defiantly. "What are you going to do? Eat me alive?"

"It's too late for that, we're already married."

Her fear didn't lessen any, and laughter died in the tightness of her throat. She saw what he wanted to talk about, what Selim was finally ready to talk about. She let it go. It hurt like hell to throw away the opportunity, but she wouldn't let him distract her now. She glanced out the arched balcony doorway. Faint gray light showed beyond the fanned-out tops of the pair of palm trees just outside. Selim was right. He didn't have much time. Better to get to the point then and not waste it.

"What did you mean by telling Sterling that he could kill Moira Chasen?"

Selim's features had settled into a more human cast by the time he spoke, which somehow made his words more chilling. "I meant he can kill Moira Chasen."

Siri suddenly found it very hard to stand. It wasn't as if she hadn't expected the answer. And it wasn't that she didn't want—need—to hear it. It was just that she didn't know what to do about it.

"You can sit down," Selim said. "You look terrible. Do you want a drink?"

Solicitous as ever, he helped her to the old camelback sofa, then went into the kitchen and came back with a glass of ice water for her. Siri had fought down her revulsion and regained her temper by the time he returned. She thanked him for giving her the time for that. Taking the tall, frosted glass from him as he bent over her, she asked, "What am I supposed to do with this? Throw it in your face?"

He slid to sit cross-legged on the floor in front of her. "I'd prefer that to your throwing breakable objects this time. Cold water might help keep me awake."

"That won't work."

He shrugged. "They say people need less sleep as they get older."

Siri balled her hands into fists to keep from reaching out and ruffling his thick, dark hair. "Don't."

"What?"

"Don't be cute."

Siri looked around the room rather than at Selim. He was radiating persuasive charm at the moment, and she didn't want to be affected by it. Having him close to her never helped when she wanted to be clear-headed. She often advised him to move out of this old building, to get rid of all his accumulated stuff, but for the moment she was glad of all the *tsatkes,* photos, and *things* he kept around. Every horizontal space was covered with the mementos of a longer-than-mortal lifespan. Things she could look at. Things she could throw if the need arose.

The carpet was old, Persian, the pattern deep red and gold and cream. Soft and thick, comfortable to sit on. Comfortable to make love on, as she well knew. Except for the computer and a thirty-two-inch television set she'd given him two years ago, the furnishings in the big penthouse were mostly from the 1920s and '30s. They reminded Siri of the set of some sophisticated, witty old black-and-white movie. Only she was feeling far more *film noir* than screwball comedy right now.

She finally looked back at Selim. She wasn't any calmer, nor was his look of patient concern in the least bit endearing. Having lived through one Hunt when the prey deserved to die had been bad enough. She didn't see how she could survive one when it was murder rather than execution. Her soul wouldn't survive that. Neither would Selim's, and she *knew* he had a soul. "Why would you let Sterling kill that girl?"

"Not just Sterling," he answered. "It would be a Hunt for all the strigs in town. I have to give them someone," he went on. "Might as well be the girl."

Her blood curdled at this matter-of-fact reply. Did he have a soul? A conscience? She swallowed bile. "Why her?"

"It's not my choice. It's up to Sterling."

"But she hasn't *done* anything!"

"There are several good reasons to let the strigs have her. A celebrity's disappearance could focus attention away from other, less famous peoples' going missing. The media would concentrate on a beautiful television actress rather than some homeless junkie. So would the police. I can use that to cover the nest Hunts."

"You'd let her die as camouflage?"

"Sure. You have a problem with that?"

"Of course I have a problem!"

He looked offended. "I think it's a pretty good idea. That is, if Sterling wants to take out a celebrity."

"If he wants to take out a celebrity, I'm sure O. J.'d be available!"

Selim shook his head. "Too famous."

"But Moira Chasen hasn't done anything!"

She seemed to think that if she kept repeating this point he would finally *get* it. He had several other reasons for letting the strigs hunt the girl if Sterling was stupid enough to want a kill instead of a companion. Selim decided not to try to explain them to Siri just now. His companion seemed fixated on this innocence issue.

"If she isn't one of us," he told Siri with brutal frankness neither of them appreciated, "Moira Chasen is just meat."

Siri's skin had gone beyond pale to sickly, nauseated green. Her revulsion was nearly enough to make her faint. It radiated back at him, turning his stomach as well. She went on doggedly, "Moira is an intelligent young woman who never asked to have a vampire come into her life."

"Neither did you."

"We aren't talking about us."

"Aren't we? You're pretending we're something we're not. Very bad move, darling."

Siri kept doggedly to her point. "Moira doesn't deserve to die. I thought you would help her."

"Deserve has nothing to do with it. Why would I help prey?"

"She needs to be saved from Geoff Sterling!"

"No. Geoff Sterling needs to make up his mind what to do about her."

"What about Moira!"

"Not my species. Not my problem."

He meant it. The callous bastard meant it! "I don't believe what I'm hearing."

"Yes, you do." *You knew the job was dangerous when you took it.*

She flinched from his thoughts; something she'd never done before. "Don't."

Selim rose to his feet in one of those faster-than-the-human-eye-could-see moves that had stopped impressing her—but did this time. Siri gulped back tears. She fought fear.

"Don't what?" he asked. There was nothing human in his cold voice. "Don't get inside you any damn time I want because I *own* you? Don't let them kill people? Don't let them Hunt? I can't stop it. I don't want to stop it. Contain it. Control it. That's what I do. Vampires live to hunt. That's what they do. There is no version of PETA in the world *you* and *I* live in. Vampires for the Ethical Treatment of Humans does not exist."

Siri jumped to her feet. "Then maybe we should start it!" She threw the ice water at him, glass and all. "And you don't *own* me!"

"No?"

The word was an arrogant shout, both inside and outside her mind, vocal and telepathic denial ripped into and through her. The intensity of his possessive protest surprised them both. Her knees went weak as the vampire's angry roar reverberated around the room. Siri stumbled forward. Selim grabbed her and pulled her close. His grasp was rough. The look on his face was savagely angry. He was going to kiss her. And she wanted him to.

Except that the sun came up and he passed out before he got the chance.

Siri was left to look down at the lean body crumpled on the carpet before her with nothing to show for the evening but the worst case of emotional trauma she'd ever experienced. A mindless shudder of reaction overtook her, and she had to run to the bathroom to throw up before she could do anything else. Once she finished retching and washed her face, she was able to think again, only she didn't want to. She just wanted to get out, get away from Selim. *Escape* was the correct word.

All right. She wanted to escape from Selim. From the life. Loving him made her an accomplice, an accessory, a participant. She couldn't deal with that anymore. At least she couldn't deal with it right now.

She went back to where he slept on the floor, insensible until the sun set once more. It took a great deal to fight the impulse to drag him up onto the couch or at least get a pillow and blanket for him out of the bedroom. He was a soulless creature of the night. If he woke up with a crick in his neck and an aching back from sleeping twisted up on a cold floor, he deserved it. He deserved a whole hell of a lot more. A hell of a lot worse.

A stake through the heart was what he deserved, but all she could manage was to nudge him in the ribs with her foot. "I've had it," she told the sleeping monster. "I'm gone. Out of here. History. I never want to see you again."

It was something she should have told him years ago. Or at least 385 days before.

He couldn't hear her, of course. He didn't even hear her slam the door on the way out, though she, at least, got some satisfaction from doing it when she gathered up some things and left—after she got him that blanket.

Chapter 8

"You're not asleep, are you?"

No. She didn't sleep much anymore. Valentine wasn't quite sure what it was she did in the daylight. At least not before she took up dream riding as a recent hobby. She wasn't awake, certainly. Not in the sense that she could get up and walk around and go to the bathroom if she wanted to. Which she did at the moment. Way too much coffee last night was proving inconvenient. Maybe it was the caffeine that kept her up, though she doubted an artificial chemical stimulant had anything to do with her state of awareness. And a very odd state of awareness it was.

Maybe it was having Yevgeny beside her. She'd been sleeping alone for a long time. How many years?

"How many years?"

He echoed her thought, but with bitterness rather than the bittersweet contentment she felt. Too many, she guessed from the tone of his voice, from the tension in the hard body stretched out next to hers. He moved, and she could hear the subtle sounds the bed made as the big man shifted his weight. She could feel his hands on her. Not just the normal things—his body heat and the

texture of his skin. She wasn't just aware of his hands
moving over her inert flesh. It was more than awareness,
but not quite reaction. Memories of the night, perhaps?

Valentine didn't want to feel. Not now. She was busy.
Come with me, she thought to Yevgeny instead. *Come
into my dreams.*

No. He laughed. She felt his finger tap the center of
her forehead. "You're not alone in there, are you?"

Never mind the vampire telepathy nonsense, she was
a storyteller. Of course she was never completely alone
inside her head, but that wasn't what he meant. She
wasn't doing what he thought, not yet. She wouldn't, if
he decided to keep her company instead.

"You want to drain what I've learned from me. Take
it without having to pay." Yevgeny ran his fingers along
her jaw and down her throat. There was tenderness there,
and an implied threat.

She smiled in the only way she could, letting him
feel her amusement. *You want to have your fun.*

"Yes."

Sadist.

"It goes with the territory."

You haven't told me anything yet.

He cupped her breasts in his hands. "I've been
busy."

So had she. *Tell me something now.*

"She's a pretty little thing. I asked her for a date."

Good. Anything else?

"Aren't you jealous?"

No.

"You're so smug," he said. "So superior. So beautiful."

Goes with the territory.

He kissed a spot between her breasts. Valentine's reaction was no sensory memory from the night before.
"Distracting, isn't it?"

He continued kissing her for awhile, in various
places. Valentine decided he was just trying to be dif-
ficult, stubborn, jealous, angry, and taking it out on her

the only way he could. She didn't tell him to stop. She didn't tell him anything at all. She did stay half-tied to her bed, half-awake, half-alive in a way she'd never known before. That didn't stop her from hunting in her own way, from seeking the mind she'd been riding for weeks, from hunting the story that mind didn't know it was waiting to tell her. Selim was hiding something, protecting some important secret from her. She hadn't been able to dance it out of him yet, not even in his wildest dreams. That made her chase of him even more exciting. She was going to have to resort to inducing his worst nightmares soon. She didn't look forward to that, but too much depended on having the Enforcer's story for her to give up now.

She sought, and after a while she found. He lay in a twisted heap, passed out on the floor of a room that desperately needed redecorating. He was more dead to the world than usual, sleeping as much from sheer emotional and physical exhaustion as from what their kind so evocatively referred to as the Curse of the Night. Did they still call it that? She wondered. Did they count the curses—the Hunt, the blood, the loneliness and the night?

The Goddess had certainly done a number on them in her righteously angry fit of revenge all those thousands of years ago. The Great Loneliness was the worst curse of all. Now, how did that little old Law go? *"Your lovers will become your children, and your children you may not touch."*

Yevgeny was right. She was distracted. Or maybe it was just some kind of residual guilt popping to the surface at what she'd been doing with Selim. She didn't have time for guilt. And what was that boy doing on his living room floor? What had he been doing that tired him out like that? She concentrated on finding out, on settling onto him, softer and more encompassing than the blanket he was wrapped in. Never mind that Yevgeny's body now covered hers. She settled into Selim.

Dream it all out, my child, Valentine whispered. *Tell Mama why you're so sad.*

"Okay, I admit to being a hypocrite," Siri said. She paced back and forth across the living room with the phone held to her ear while her friend waited patiently for her to continue.

Siri lived and worked in a stately old house in Pasadena. She was a matchmaker; an old-fashioned job, perhaps, but she made a good living at it. While she used all the latest in electronic gadgets to impress her clientele, she relied on a natural-born talent for putting people together. Even when her own world began to fall apart, her hit ratio among human couples hadn't suffered. She hadn't been open for business today, hadn't returned any client calls or E-mail. What did it matter if she helped people find true love when Selim thought it was perfectly all right to feast on any mortal that happened to be in the neighborhood when he was feeling peckish?

"It's not as if I didn't know that they kill people," she went on. "I know they get off on stalking people."

"It's part of the hunting instinct."

"But I saw what they do to any human who dares to stalk them. And what he plans for this young actress is completely unacceptable. And it's my fault. I took her problem to Selim. If she dies, it's going to be my fault. I can't warn her. I mean, who believes in vampires, for God's sake?"

"Siri, maybe you should come over."

This was not a conversation she should be having on the phone. At the very least, she should be using euphemisms. Security was always an issue. Secretiveness imperative for survival. Face-to-face was always the preferred communication method among them, or mind-to-mind. "You know that's *forbidden*," she reminded Cassie.

"Not for you."

"Not for the Enforcer's companion, you mean. I'm not. We broke up."

Cassie's laughed sharply. "Yeah, right."

She was wearing a hole in the carpet with her pacing. She hadn't been able to sleep today. She'd called Cassie the instant the sun set. "Really," she told Cassandra. "Selim doesn't care. You know what he's been like lately."

"Inattentive?"

"He's a heartless bastard. Besides, I've met someone else."

Cassie laughed again. "Sure you have."

"I have." She made herself think about the arrogant blond. It wasn't easy. She told herself she was just too used to thinking about a skinny Egyptian jerk. "He's a companion. Gorgeous—in an Aryan master race kind of way. He *was* a companion, actually. Knows exactly what I've been going through."

"How?"

"Some strig dumped him."

"What strig?"

"I don't know. Yevgeny won't tell me."

"You can't just dump a companion." Cassie was outraged. "It's—"

"Against the rules. I know."

"It's against nature."

"So's being what you are."

"Thank you very much."

"It's not your fault. Yevgeny wants to see me," Siri hurried on before she and her best friend got into an argument. "He's interested. Says he hangs at the Viper Room, and I should meet him there. I've never been to the Viper Room. What should I wear? Something black?"

"Black is good . . . since you'll be going to this guy's funeral when Selim finds out about it."

That sounded so sweet. It just didn't ring true right now. "I don't know if I'm going," she told Cassie. "I don't know what I'm going to do." About anything. The phone signaled, and Siri sighed. "Got another call."

"It might be Selim."

If it was, she'd hang up. Surely she had enough independence left to do that. Time to forget about Selim. Move on. "It might be work," she told Cassie. "I'm going to concentrate on my work for now."

"And hope the Hunt passes you by?"

Siri didn't answer the question. She hung up on the vampire. There was a vampire on the other line, but it wasn't Selim. She hung up on him anyway.

"You're having trouble with your love life." It wasn't a question.

Selim put his feet up on the couch and shifted the phone to his other ear. He'd woken up from a day filled with really bad dreams to the sound of a ringing telephone. He hadn't expected the voice he heard when he answered, but he adapted quickly. "It happens," he responded. "Everybody has problems." *Bloodsucking fiends are people, too,* he added to himself. He didn't mention this thought to the caller. Don Tomas wasn't exactly famous for his sense of humor.

"This is no time for it to happen."

Selim did not appreciate the reminder. "I need her eyes and ears and other gifts," he agreed.

"You need to be clearheaded when the rest of us can't be."

"Thank you very much for that reminder, Don Tomas," Selim answered acidly. "I've got an idea. Why don't you take over my job in this town?"

Selim expected outrage in response, arrogant denial that Tomas Avella was *that* kind of man. Or at least haughty silence. Instead Don Tomas answered, "Cassandra would like that."

Selim's feet hit the floor with a painful thud as he sat up quickly. "Do you know what you're saying?"

"That there would be no vampires in this town if I could hunt them."

"Tomas—" Selim warned. "Careful." That the old vampire felt no compunction about using such blunt language over the phone shook Selim.

Tomas took no heed. "I would do anything to protect my son. To protect my family. They'll kill him if they get the chance. You know that."

Selim shuddered. Had Tomas been walking inside his dreams today? Or were they sharing a dream? Or was there a vision they were sharing? He was too polite to ask, but he did promise, "I won't let that happen."

"I prefer the safety of my loved ones to be in my own hands, Selim. I've already sired a monster. I could change into one for his sake."

"No, you couldn't, Tomas. Do you really want to?"

"No. Got your attention, though, didn't I, Hunter?"

Selim relaxed. He laughed. The sound was unconvincing to his ears, but acknowledging Don Tomas's words as a joke was better than pursuing them as treason. Don Tomas would never have been so direct, so out of line, if the bloodburn wasn't starting in him. People said stupid things when the hunger got them. Got reckless. They all thought they could rule the world, have everything their hearts desired, run in the daylight just because they wanted to.

"You've reminded me to look out for Sebastian," he told Don Tomas. "Believe me, I will."

"With your thoughts distracted by your own problems? Can I trust you to keep the Laws when your own house is in chaos?"

"We're not in chaos. We're just . . . What are you suggesting? That we go to a marriage counselor? Are you offering your services as one?" There was vast amusement in the silence on the other end of the phone. Selim smiled. He got up and walked to the balcony with the cordless phone tucked under one ear. He already knew that she wasn't waiting at the Jamba Juice bar up the street. He stepped outside and looked that way anyway. "I miss her."

"It drives you crazy," Don Tomas said in his ear. "But you have to do it."

It wasn't advice, it was just the truth. Selim went

back into the living room. "It won't get in the way of my job."

"Good. What about Jager?"

Selim knew that this question was the real reason Don Tomas had called. "Just a friendly reminder?"

"Exactly. You'll be taking care of the problem soon?"

Selim was restless and wanted to pace. He sat back on the couch. "Tonight."

"Good."

Selim could feel Don Tomas preparing to hang up. He asked a question quickly. "You've met Istvan, right?"

"You haven't?"

"Never had the pleasure."

"We met once."

"What does he look like? Tall, slender, but with broad shoulders and long arms, big eyes under heavy brows?"

Selim wanted to ask if the *dhamphir* in any way resembled Nicolas Cage. That was who Istvan looked like in the dream. It had felt like someone had cast the actor for the part of the world's most dangerous vampire. Like he'd been watching a movie. Weird. But that was only a dream. Some dreams were real. Most weren't. Besides, Siri was a big Nicolas Cage fan, and most of Selim's dreams were about Siri. He was very confused.

"He looks like that. Why?"

It had just been a bad dream. Either that, or Istvan was coming.

There could only be one reason. Selim wasn't about to discuss it with Sebastian's father. "Nothing," he told Tomas. "Just wondering, that's all."

Selim hung up the phone and checked his watch. It was time he got going. He needed a shower and some breakfast before he went out and killed a vampire.

Chapter 9

In the end, Siri simply couldn't make herself do it.

She couldn't wear black. Not even to the Viper Room. The whole Goth vampire thing just wasn't her. Neither was looking cool and hip and with it and just like everybody else. She'd done her short, sexy, little black dress thing back in the eighties, at the Rainbow, the Whisky, the Roxy, and the other rock clubs on the Strip. She missed the eighties, but she couldn't make herself dress like that anymore. She was a grown-up now, for God's sake!

She did go to the Viper Room, though.

She remembered when the club at the address was called Filthy McNasty's. That had been a lifetime ago, but Sunset hasn't changed much, Siri decided as she waited by the velvet ropes outside the club. There wasn't any more traffic or any fewer tourists. The giant billboards that lined the street were gaudier and more numerous than she remembered. There were fewer hookers, or they weren't as obvious as they used to be. The tattoo places, strip clubs, and psychic reading rooms hadn't gone away, though there was a darker, more degenerate feel to them than she remembered.

People just don't know how to have fun anymore she thought. Getting tired of waiting to get inside, Siri made her way to the front of the crowd and caught the doorman's attention. She smiled and thought about how much he wanted to open the door for the nice redhead in the slinky emerald green dress and he eventually smiled back and did as her thoughts told him. "Good boy. Have a biscuit," she added as she forked over a generous tip on her way in.

It was very noisy inside, the music from the stage overwhelmingly so. Siri didn't expect to be impressed in any way with this hangout for the trendy but changed her mind the moment she let herself listen. The place had the best sound system she'd ever heard. All right, she decided as she made her way into the main room, she wouldn't pretend to be bored and blasé about hanging out at Celebrity Central here. The music was great. She wasn't sure whether to wander toward the stage or look for Yevgeny. She'd been listening to the Melissa Etheridge CD with "No Souvenirs" over and over in the car on the way over. She felt the need now for a song that was a bit less desperate. One that would help keep her mind off Selim.

Yevgeny solved the problem of what she should do by stepping up behind her before she got very far into the crowd. "Let's talk," he said, and took her arm. His grip was hard enough to keep her from arguing. His whole attitude was more domineering than she wanted or liked. She went with him, willing to keep him company for now.

"Macho, aren't we?"

"Yes." He flashed her a grin. "Chicks dig it."

"What century were you born in?"

"Nineteenth. Want a drink?"

A few moments later, they were seated side by side at a small table. The couple who'd been occupying the table had felt a sudden, overwhelming urge to dance. Siri and Yevgeny smiled at each other as the couple, both bleached blonds, wandered off.

"Was that someone famous?" Siri asked as she watched the pair disappear into the crowd.

"Probably. Who cares?" Yevgeny looked at her with the sort of intense concentration she hadn't felt from a man in over a year. It was the sort of look that made the temperature of the already hot room rise significantly. "Let's talk about us."

O-kaay. Siri licked her lips. She chose to take his words in a general way. "How long have you been a companion?" she asked him. "Who were you with?" She'd asked Yevgeny these questions when they'd met. She asked them for Selim then. Now she asked because *she* wanted to know.

As before, he avoided answering her. "Too long. And does it matter?" Yevgeny took her hand. He gazed into her eyes.

She felt his thoughts probing her. She gave him a hard mental swat. He blinked. Anger blazed in his face for a moment. His grip on her fingers grew crushing. He relaxed before Siri could begin to struggle. He let her go and smiled.

"You are very good."

"You know that already," she told him. His eyes were an incredible shade of blue, the lines around them when he smiled were intriguing. Attractive. So were his broad, Slavic cheekbones. He certainly wasn't hard to look at. Very different than Selim. For some reason that annoyed her. Which was stupid, since, if she was going to go looking, she should be looking for someone different from Selim.

"You don't want to look," Yevgeny said, reading her surface thoughts whether she liked it or not. "That's the way it is with us. Once we're hooked, we're hooked. That's the strongest weapon they have. They make us drink in loyalty."

She did not want to think about that. She didn't want to talk about it. A waiter came with drinks ordered by the dancing couple. She and Yevgeny accepted the diversion and the glasses. "Were you really born in the nineteenth century?'' she asked when the waiter was gone. She supposed it was possible. Not likely, of course. But Yevgeny *felt* old.

He looked around.

''Were you?'' Siri insisted. She trusted the sound system and crowd noise to cover any confidences they shared.

He shook his head. ''It's a good line. How old are you? And where are you from, little girl? Where did you meet *him?*''

''Right here on Sunset,'' she answered and wished she hadn't. Just driving up the street had done enough to flash her back to memories of that night she'd been drawn to a man playing with a handful of gold coins as he sat alone in the Rainbow Bar and Grill. A few minutes later, she watched him rip the heart out of a vampire. She'd woken up in his apartment the next morning. ''Ten years ago.''

''You sound surprised.''

She took a long sip of very good scotch. She felt breathless, but not from the whiskey. Not from the cigarette and cigar smoke in the air, either. Not from the electronic music pounding in her ears. Not from the glint in Yevgeny's eyes, nor the intense interest he radiated at her.

''Time flies,'' Yevgeny went on. ''Among our kind.''

She made herself put down the glass when it was still half full. She stared at the amber liquid as she spoke. ''It just doesn't seem like I've known him for ten years. That we've been together for so long.''

''It seems like you just met him yesterday, doesn't it?''

''Day before,'' she answered. The day before yesterday she'd been a happy, if restless, companion. Now, here she was talking to this ... stranger. Companions didn't do things like that. Didn't even think about it.

''Why not? Because you're happily married?'' His large hand covered hers, though she didn't see him move to do it. Yevgeny stroked her cheek with his other hand, the touch gentle and intimate. ''You think he has his reasons for the way he's treating you now, don't you? That he'll get over it?''

Shock seared down inside her, all the way down to the fear that nothing would ever be right between her and Selim again. Yevgeny's touch felt wrong. Different. Good. "I don't want to talk about him."

He stopped touching her. He sat back in his chair. "You can't think about anyone else."

"Shut up." She finished off the scotch. Considered ordering another. When she looked up to get a waiter's attention, a pale face in the crowd caught hers. "Shit. What's he doing here?"

Yevgeny turned in his chair to follow her gaze. "You know Larry Jager?"

She flashed him an angry look. "Do you?"

His answering smile was of the annoying, enigmatic kind. "We've had a few encounters."

"Is he the one who dumped you?" That would explain Yevgeny's antivampire bias. Did one actually need a reason for antivampire bias? Would a real human think you needed a reason to hate vampires? Was she a real human? And did being a real boy—girl—matter to anyone not named Pinocchio?

"I don't hate them," Yevgeny told her. "Not at all." He pointed toward Jager. "But you certainly know how to hate that one. Don't think so hard at him, he'll come over here. He's not very good company."

"Not very good—? Do you know what he's done? What he's like?" Just thinking about Lawrence Jager left such a bad taste in her mind that she wanted to spit.

"He likes them young." Yevgeny shrugged. "Younger than you or me, certainly."

"You condone what he's done?"

"It's not my place to judge them. Being one's a bad habit to begin with."

"Bad habit." She sat up straight and jabbed a finger, hard, in the center of Yevgeny's broad chest. "Did you know that he had a fifteen-year-old companion?"

"I know."

"Do you?" The man feigned indifference very well, but she could feel *something*, something strong and dark and unhappy beneath everything he said and did and thought. His knowing good old Larry Jager only served to make Siri more suspicious of Yevgeny than she already was. "Did he dump you for her? Do you know what happened to her?"

"Selim let him have her."

"He didn't want to," she found herself automatically defending her Enforcer. "But she was a tough street kid. A runaway. It was decided that she was old enough, at least mentally, to be a companion for a strig . . . like being runaways together. Then Jager let her get hooked on heroin. He let her die of an overdose. They don't let their companions die."

"More's the pity, sometimes," he said quietly.

"That's not even the worst part," she went on. She wanted to stop. To shut up, but being so close to the loathsome strig triggered an indignation she couldn't tone down. She could feel Yevgeny probing around her shields, too, urging her on, urging the words out. She didn't know why he wanted to hear them, but she couldn't stop them. "Now he's sniffing around an eight-year-old. A child."

"You have great fondness for children, don't you?" Before she could snarl an answer that her feelings were irrelevant, he went on, with deep sympathy and sadness, "It's a pity our kind are barren."

A jolt of disagreement shot through her. She felt him catch it, question it, but she didn't give voice to her knowledge. Cassie's child wasn't this strig's reject's business. "Jager intends to molest a human child. Kamaraju bit and abandoned Jager. Now he thinks he can do anything he wants."

"He's a loner. The risks are his to accept."

"Not in this town."

Yevgeny threw back his head and laughed. The sound infuriated her. "You really expect Selim to ride to the rescue, don't you? To protect the world."

"No. Just that child." She did. She really did, but that wasn't realistic, was it? He'd disclaimed any responsibility for humanity last night, hadn't he?

"Haven't you learned that they only care about themselves? That they've forgotten how to be guilty?"

"Guilty of what?" When he waved the question away, Siri went on, "There are limits. Child molesting is one of them."

"But it's all right to eat them when they're young and tender."

The words turned her stomach, but Siri persisted angrily, "Physical and mental rape of children is not allowed. You do know what happened when someone in Seattle tried it, don't you?"

He leaned close to her, intensely curious. "No. What?"

The world blurred around her before she could answer. When her vision cleared, Yevgeny was gone. She was standing. And Jager was standing beside her. His hands were on her shoulders, with just the faintest touch of claw pressing into her skin. The thin silk of her dress offered no protection.

"Well, if it isn't Martha Siriaco. I haven't seen you in a long time." Jager smiled with all his teeth showing and drew Siri close.

Selim couldn't get a stupid song he'd never heard about some ex-lover leaving no souvenirs out of his head all the way from Pasadena to the Strip.

He put on speed, but the music matched itself to the rhythm of his steps. He counted blocks and streetlights. He made a game of jumping fences and dodging speeding semitrailers on the freeway. Some of the drivers saw a blur as he passed, most didn't notice a thing, and none heard his laughter as he ran by. Selim loved to run. Speed was the one gift he'd worked harder than any other to develop. He was probably the only vampire in history who would have taken up marathon running if it was a nighttime sport.

Maybe it's something I could organize, he thought wryly as he ate up the miles to his destination. *Get a group of dedicated runners together and sponsor a charity event. Blood bank donations, maybe?* He laughed and wanted to share the thought with Siri. Only she probably wouldn't be amused by the idea at the moment. The girl was taking humanity far too seriously lately.

The smoggy air began to burn in his lungs. He even began to sweat a little, as much as his kind could. The song kept going round and round in his head.

He hated being haunted by songs, though it was a common enough occurrence. Being haunted by a song that was probably something Siri listened to was not so common. It made him think of her more than he wanted. Everything made him think of her. He didn't have time for that sort of nonsense right now. He should never have let her get angry; she projected far too much when she was angry. It could be dangerous. Not just for his peace of mind. The city was full of hunger-crazed vampires. It wouldn't take much to set thé less stable ones off. A whiff of Siri's energy could be enough. It occurred to Selim that he shouldn't have allowed so many years to pass between Hunts, but it seemed like a good idea at the time.

He knew it wasn't a good idea when he heard her scream.

The sound drowned out the song. It drowned out everything.

He heard her. Saw her. Knew where she was.

It brought him to a dead stop in the middle of Santa Monica Boulevard.

"Oh, my goddess!"

Car horns blared and brakes screeched. People swore. Somebody shot at him. Selim ignored it all. These people had no idea what road rage really meant. As fear and fury built in him, it was a wonder the pavement didn't melt beneath his feet.

"The bastard was dead already. Now I'm really going to *kill* him!"

Siri was still miles away. All Selim could do was run faster.

Chapter 10

"WHAT ARE YOU doing?"

Geoff Sterling stepped out of the crowd as he spoke. His hand landed on Jager's shoulder. Jager snarled at him. Geoff backed away, but the younger strig's puzzled presence was enough to divert Jager's attention momentarily from her. Siri grasped the diversion. Cloth tore as she twisted away. She ignored the pain, though pulling away from his claws left a faint scent of blood in the air.

"Running," she answered Geoff's question, and took off.

Siri caught a glimpse of Moira Chasen's beautiful, curious, faintly freckled face somewhere in the background as she turned. She couldn't tell whether Geoff was here with the actress or had followed Moira to the Viper Room. At the moment, she didn't care about this particular vampire soap opera. All she wanted was to put distance between herself and Jager's fangs and claws.

She was used to fangs and claws, it was the mad hunger in his eyes that set her heart racing. That triggered the very human instinct to escape.

As she fled, she heard Jager say casually to Geoff, "Wanna hunt the Enforcer's bitch with me?"

Screaming black panic took hold of her. The screams were all inside her head, along with the prayers, and the calls for help. People moved out of her way. That was all she cared about, just getting to the door. She could hear Jager's laughter, knew he was giving her a head start. Playing with her.

Jesus. They were like big cats in the way they loved to play with the prey.

Her heart hurt, a hard, burning knot in her chest, hammering like it was trying to get out, abandon her to flee on its own. The world around her was all pulsing light, black and red on the edges.

Calm down.

The voice in her mind wasn't Selim's. She didn't pay attention to it. She found the door and rushed outside. It was just as crowded on the sidewalk outside the club as it was inside. Too many people. A damned, mindless, milling herd.

It's your fear he wants.

He's got it!

Calm, little sister. Calm.

The voice in her mind belonged to Geoff Sterling, and it was none too steady. He was close to losing it. Doing what he could to help, but he had the scent of her emotions as well. He managed to project that if she didn't get herself under control, he would be Hunting, himself, in a moment.

Knowing that there was about to be another vampire on her trail had an oddly calming effect on Siri. No way was she going to give either of them what they needed. She wasn't cattle. She wasn't prey. She wasn't prepared to die tonight.

The problem was, how was she going to stop it?

She looked up and down the street. She knew Sunset. Maybe it had been a decade since she used to hang out at the clubs and bars, but the terrain hadn't really changed. It was brighter than she remembered, with more streetlights and car lights and gaudy, illuminated billboards. Light had to be her friend, didn't it? Against a creature of the night? Yeah, right. No light but sunlight would do any good. It was a long time until dawn.

Would being in a crowd protect her? From a crazy, Hunt-crazed strig? Chances were, the only thing being in a crowd would do would be to get other people killed. Public. Messy. Out in the open. This was L.A. Who would notice any longer than it took to hose the blood off the street? Where the hell was Selim when she needed him? The Lakers game wasn't tonight, was it?

Irrelevant. It was all irrelevant. She could *feel* Jager stalking toward her. No time. No time. She cast her head from side to side. *Which way? Left.*

She went left, away from the crowd waiting to get into the club. They were hardly alone on the busy street, but it was his laughter she heard, Jager's footsteps that sounded close behind her. He wanted her to run. Her own voice inside her head told her to run. She didn't run. Siri moved quickly. When she reached the end of the block, she dashed across the street against the light. Better to face traffic than what was coming up behind her. He could outrun her, of course. She knew he didn't want that yet. The crazy strig was enjoying stalking her. She knew he was there, even though she couldn't see him when she glanced quickly behind her. He knew she knew. He was getting high on the knowledge they shared.

His thoughts buffeted at her shielding, a cat's paw swiping at her mind. Siri stumbled, barely able to keep her feet as she made it to the other side of the street. Where she walked straight into a plate glass window of a sushi shop. Raw fish. Raw meat. *Yum. Oh, God!* Her outer senses were blinded while she struggled to keep the hungry strig out of her head. She'd be damned if he was going to mindfuck her as well as murder her!

They say we can't kill our own, Jager's thought whispered to her. *Let's prove 'em wrong, bitch. Bitch. Selim'sfuckeddeadbitch.*

Yum, yum, yum.

A vivid image formed in her mind. A sending? A vision? She didn't know. Siri knew she'd kill herself before she let those things happen to her. Somehow. Suicide was against the Laws. Then she'd kill Jager. It was against the Laws for a companion to injure a vampire.

She bounced off the glass, stumbled blindly on. She heard sobbing, was furious to find out the sound came from her. She bit her tongue to keep the fearful whimpering inside. Footsteps. Laughter. The brush of claws caressed the back of her neck.

"Fuck the Laws."

"You tell them, sweetheart."

She couldn't tell if the voice was inside or outside her head. She felt a hot, stinking breeze from an alley entrance against her skin. Her arm was grabbed roughly. She was pulled into the alley.

"Stay here," Selim said. "No. Wait at the car."

He kissed her. Brief, hard, reassuring. He was breathing harder than she was, radiating hard-held fury. She tasted her own blood when his mouth left hers. His tongue swiped across her lips, taking the blood for himself. His eyes had turned to pure night. His hand brushed across her cheek, touch gentle, though mostly claw at the moment.

It had been his hand that had touched her neck. He had called her to this spot. He'd been waiting for her!

"No, you weren't bait," he said, before she could even think it. "What the hell are you doing here? Never mind."

The alley was dark. Her thoughts were still scrambled. She suddenly couldn't see a thing. Siri reached out to grab him. Her hands closed on air. Selim was gone. The Enforcer of the Law was hunting.

Where are you, owl bait?
   Owl bait?
   Here, little girl.

Nobody called his companion things like that and got away with it.

Selim snarled, but he kept to the shadows, spreading them wide and thick around him. He was between Siri and the creature after her. Jager was lost in the dark, but so into blood fever, he didn't quite realize it. Selim felt her moving from the alley, racing back up Sunset Boulevard. She was on the other side of the busy street from Jager now, moving in the opposite direction. Jager sought, with eyes and ears and mind. He didn't see her. Didn't feel her. Selim kept the shadows a hard and solid wall of smoke between the vampire and the one he hunted while she got away.

Where are you, bitch? Jager made a wet, lip-smacking noise. It reverberated through Selim's head. It was meant to chill the prey's soul. *You're old, but you'll be tasty.*

Old? How dare he?

"Yo, Hannibal Lechter," Selim whispered. "You talking about my girl?"

Selim smiled at the thoughts he intercepted, thoughts that didn't get a chance to touch Siri's mind. *"Not a pretty smile,"* Siri would have said. *"Too many teeth."* He laughed. *Oh, yes. Far too many teeth. Even for a vampire.* That was one of the differences between Enforcers and their prey. You needed a lot of teeth to bite a vampire. And really long, sharp, nasty, hard-as-titanium claws. Vampire hide was tough stuff. Especially old vampire hide.

"Come here, young and tender one," Selim murmured.

Jager's frustration cut through the night. He was about to lose his concentration on taking a specific prey. About to turn on someone, anyone, on the street. Couldn't have that. Way too public. Damn sloppy strigs. Selim shed the shadows and moved to intercept the other vampire.

Jager was standing in the center of the sidewalk, just out of the light of a streetlamp, a snarling, fanged creature, hardly hidden from view. People saw him, all right, and hurried to move out of his way. No one was running in screaming panic. Not yet. He wasn't trying to eat their emotions. Once he picked one out of the herd and concentrated on the victim, the fear would spread to every mind in the vicinity. Panic and riot would ensue. Vampires from all over town would be showing up to join in the fun.

For now, though, people just walked on by. Jager ignored them, and they paid him very little attention. Selim thanked several gods that this was a town full of weirdos and makeup artists. Then he laughed, remembering that Jager had once had a day job working in the special effects department of a movie studio. Back when he was Kamaraju's companion.

Selim moved, too fast to be seen. People only felt the brush of air as he passed. Jager felt his scream of challenge and rage. The strig whirled, answered the challenge with a bellow. Selim ran a circle around Jager. Jager clawed the air, great, long-armed swipes, trying to connect with fast-moving muscle and bone.

It was Selim's turn to whisper inside the vampire's mind. *Run, little one,* he suggested. He didn't have too much time to play, but it added a little necessary spice to the night. Added a little revenge for the bastard's hunting Siri.

Weren't you expecting me? Selim stopped a few feet away from the strig. "You happy to see me?" he asked around a mouthful of fangs. He caught Jager's gaze with his and held it. He reached out with his thoughts and sucked in the strig's anger, lust, and madness. He sent back all the terror Siri had experienced, tripled and concentrated.

Jager froze, still as a statue of a dead thing, his arms up, claws catching only air.

Selim clouded the minds of most passersby as he walked up to the frozen form. Frozen like a rabbit. The pounding of Jager's wild heartbeat was loud in Selim's ears. His fear scent was an overripe, strong perfume.

Selim sniffed and put his hands behind his back. He tilted his head to one side, as though studying a piece of bad sculpture. "You waiting for pigeons to land on you?"

Run!

The strig turned and ran. Panting, pushing humans aside. Any thought of hunting them was gone from Jager's mind. Death was after him. Selim was happy to have distracted Jager from the people on the street. Now he had to get the strig somewhere private. Selim felt someone running behind him, another vampire trying to catch up. He'd deal with the intruder later. First things first.

It was Jager himself who provided Selim with what he needed when he veered off the sidewalk at the base of one of the tall billboards that reared over Sunset. Selim followed as Jager dodged through a forest of metal legs and struts. The shadows under here couldn't hide him. The metal obstacle course didn't slow Selim down. When Jager jumped for an access ladder high overhead, Selim leaped onto the ladder a second after him. Selim scrambled up onto the narrow catwalk at the top of the ladder to find that Jager had led him to the base of a gigantic, brightly lit movie advertisement. He raced after the strig, vaguely aware that he was passing the wide expanse of some actress's lovingly rendered, mostly exposed breasts. There were painted explosions somewhere in the background of the movie ad as well. The whole scene was lurid and eye-catching. Hopefully, the young actress's twenty-foot breasts were of far more interest to anyone glancing up than the swiftly moving shadow images that raced briefly in front of them. For a few moments, Selim felt exposed and naked himself, as though he were caught on a movie screen. Then Jager ducked to the back of the billboard, and Selim followed him into darkness.

Jager would have leapt from the top of the billboard onto the roof of a truck on the street below, but Selim grabbed him by the back of the neck before he was able to jump. Selim dragged him back to the darkest part of the narrow catwalk. Jager turned to fight, now that the chase was over. He slammed into Selim. Desperation turned him into a snarling, furious animal. He was strong, with years of martial arts training as well as his natural weapons.

Selim dodged and ducked and blocked, dancing back and forth across the billboard with Jager. A few of the strig's blows landed. Jager didn't draw blood, but a kick cracked Selim's ribs, a closed fist grazed his jaw. Jager descended into frenzy while Selim fought to keep his head through the growing blood hunger. The hardest fight Selim had on the catwalk was with himself. Instinct told him to just jump for Jager's throat, to go for the jugular kill as he would with human prey.

That was no way to kill a vampire.

Selim waited until the moment was right. Then he drew the silver dagger. He smiled and got Jager to look him in the eye one last time. There was nothing rational left about the strig. It was a pure animal that met Selim's gaze.

That was how you killed a vampire.

You waited until there was nothing to them but the hunger, until they descended into frenzy, with no more brain than a shark. Anyone could kill a shark. You just had to be careful about it. Smarter and better equipped, too. It wasn't the dagger that killed Jager; burying it in his bared throat was just a symbolic gesture.

The dagger that killed Jager came from Selim's mind. A thought, sharp, penetrating, aimed straight into the strig's brain sent Jager staggering. Another mental blow knocked him onto his back, legs and arms splayed out as much as the narrow space allowed. His breath wheezed as thick blood welled around the silver hilt sticking out of his throat.

Selim crouched by the body. He pulled the dagger from Jager's throat and cleaned the bright blade on Jager's shirt. "Doesn't hold an edge worth a damn," he said and slipped it back into its arm sheath.

The Hunter ripped the beating heart out of Jager's body with his bare hands. He swallowed it whole. The strig wasn't going to be causing any more trouble for Siri, for the child he'd planned to repeatedly rape, or for anyone else. Dead vampires did not get resurrected; they got digested.

Chapter 11

SELIM'S ACHING RIBS were healed by the time he'd sucked and licked all the blood away from the open chest wound. There was still plenty of blood left in the body, still plenty of fresh meat. Selim just didn't have the time or privacy to take advantage of the feast right now.

When the vampire that had been following the hunt jumped on the top of the catwalk, Selim's reaction was instant and violent. He slammed Geoff Sterling against the back of the billboard, held him there with an arm against the young vampire's throat. He held the claws of his other hand a fraction of an inch from the strig's darkened eyes. "What are you doing here?"

Sterling didn't resist. He kept his lips over his fangs, his hands rigidly at his side. He didn't try to shield his fear from Selim. Or the worry. "Your companion?" he asked after a false, squeaking start. "I—I wanted to help her. She's safe?"

Selim was almost moved by the young strig's concern. "Of course." He believed the boy enough to let him go.

Sterling slumped against the billboard for a moment,

letting out his breath in a rushing sigh. He brushed a fall of hair out of his eyes. Eyes that were just beginning to show normal pupils once more. "I did what I could to help. The blond just ran."

I bet you did. Selim kept the thought to himself with effort. Jealousy ripped through him. "What blond?"

Sterling shrugged. "The one she was with. Don't know him." He shrugged again. "I don't know the community."

Selim made his claws withdraw into their sheaths. He forced himself not to see the young vampire as either a threat or a scavenger come to fight for a share of fresh meat. He forced the jealousy down. Siri would tell him about the blond. She didn't keep things from him. Jager must have interrupted a meeting at one of the clubs strigs went to. Maybe Sterling had tried to help Siri. At least he hadn't joined Jager in the Hunt. That was a point in his favor. The other strigs were probably all nearby as well.

Selim stood still and let his awareness spread from the perch high over Sunset. His perceptions roamed over the neighborhood, drawn to moving hot spots of lust and hunger. Yes, they were out there, all of Los Angeles's population of loners, drawn to the double aphrodisiac of fear and blood. Selim considered the simple expedient of spending the evening killing all of them. He had promised them a Hunt, but he hadn't said who would be the prey. Primitive peoples thought that eating the heart of an enemy made a warrior stronger. It was true.

He looked speculatively at Sterling. A little torture would be in order to distract and excite the strigs. The boy's silent screams would make an excellent lure to draw them in. Then again, he thought he could get to like the kid. Selim decided he'd rather find Geoff Sterling a good home than rip his heart from his body. Besides, he wanted to get to Siri. He needed to see that she was safe, and killing the other strigs would take too much time.

"It was just a thought."

"What was?"

Selim shrugged. "Never mind."

He nudged Jager with his foot. It was Kamaraju who should be lying there dead, instead of the companion he'd let hunt long before he was ready. But Kamaraju hadn't broken any Laws. Skirted them, gained the contempt of many, but he hadn't done anything that wasn't allowed by the code set down by the Strigoi Council.

"Jager never had a chance on his own," he pointed out to the young vampire. Better to offer instruction than violence. "I told you that how long you'd been a companion was irrelevant. That's not true. When you have a lover," he warned, remembering Sterling's interest in the actress, "keep her as long as you can." *If you don't kill her, that is,* he added to himself, remembering the decision Sterling had to make.

Geoff Sterling nodded. "Jager and I used to talk." He didn't go so far as to claim that he and Jager were friends. Strigs liked to pretend that they never had anything to do with each other. "He went crazy," Sterling said. "Kept trying to get Kamaraju's attention."

And Kamaraju loved it, Selim knew. He and the nest leader were going to have to have a talk about that. But he had other things to occupy the rest of his evening right now.

There was a saying Siri had quoted to him once. Something about how friends help you move, good friends help you move bodies. Sterling wasn't a friend. He was wearing a long, draping leather coat, impractical for even the coolest desert nights, but stylish. It would do. Selim held out his hand. "Give me your coat."

Sterling looked disgustedly at the bloody body on the catwalk. "Shit." He didn't argue, though, just stripped off the coat and handed it over.

"Thanks."

Selim bagged Jager's remains in the coat. The makeshift shroud would be enough to keep any blood from trailing on the ground. He then hefted the body over his shoulder. He glanced at the ground below the billboard and jumped. It was a faster and easier way than taking his burden down the spindly access ladder. Hell on his knees and arches when he landed, though. At least he was wearing a decent pair of Nikes to help take the impact. It was little comfort to know that the fall would have killed a human. He wasn't human; he was a hungry Enforcer with a curious young strig on his tail. He snarled at Sterling when the boy landed lightly beside him. Sterling grinned at him. It was a gesture of cheerful enthusiasm rather than a threat display. Which was good, since Selim was in no mood to play alpha games.

"I have to get to Siri."

"You need help with—"

"Go home, boy."

Sterling took the hint. He went. So did Selim, trotting under shadows to where he felt Siri waiting, blocks away.

There was valet parking in this lot, but the young men who worked in the place didn't notice Selim as he went past the booth at the entrance. Maybe they caught a faint scent of blood on the air, but they didn't see anything. Selim walked directly to the back row. There were many Mercedes among the neatly parked rows of cars, but only one of them had its trunk open. Only one had Siri standing apprehensively next to it. After he dumped Jager inside, Selim slammed the lid and turned to the woman cowering by the side of the car. All right, maybe she wasn't cowering, but her shoulders were hunched and her arms were crossed defensively over her stomach. Her face was pale, but for a bruise forming on one cheek. Her dress was torn. Anger flared in him at the sight of her exposed flesh.

"You did that," she said, in a small, tired voice. "When you grabbed me from behind."

"Oh." That didn't make it all right. She'd been threatened, in danger. It didn't matter who had caused it. He held out his arms, and Siri rushed into them. Hunger gnawed at him, so he didn't dare let himself kiss her. It would lead to his dragging her into the backseat and having her, letting her taste him. All his pulse points throbbed at the thought of Siri's teeth sinking into his flesh; of her mouth sucking, drinking deeply.

He held her for a few moments, taking and giving comfort, fighting the rush of need. A faint stain of Jager's blood was on her dress when he stepped away. He turned toward the car. "Give me the keys. I'll drive you home."

She looked at him strangely. "You can't drive."

"I can drive. I just don't like to." He took her arm. She was shivering, still unsteady. He gently guided her into the passenger's seat of her precious dark red Mercedes. She sank into the seat and put her head back as he started the engine.

"Anything you want to tell me?" The question came out of him in a far too casual tone. He winced at the suspicious sound. He might as well have asked, so, who's the blond?

Siri didn't move. Didn't open her eyes. "No," she answered, even though she had to feel the prick of his jealousy.

"Fine." He put the car in gear. "You can sleep while I drive."

They didn't talk on the trip out of Los Angeles. Siri put her hand tentatively on his a few times as he shifted gears. He wasn't sure if she was looking for reassurance or worried about his driving. He didn't ask. She didn't say anything until he pulled up in front of her house and got out to open the passenger-side door for her.

"You could come in."

"With a body in the trunk?" He glanced at the rear of the Mercedes. "I don't think so."

She followed his gaze and sighed. "You have to dispose of it, don't you? Will you be safe? Do you know where to—?"

"I've had practice," he reminded her. He wished he could keep her out of this. He always had before. It was a shame that real life wasn't like the movies. It would be very convenient if vampire remains simply turned to ash. Of course, if they did that, what would Enforcers have for dinner?

He escorted Siri to her door, made sure it was locked behind her, then drove the Mercedes somewhere safe and secure. He made a call to Mike Tancredi on the way. Siri would have a brand new Mercedes delivered to her the next morning by one of Mike's slaves.

"She's deep in denial."

"She's holding onto her humanity," Valentine said. "That's good."

"Why?"

Yevgeny's sneer of disgust did not amuse her, but she let it go. She reached around where he sat, perched on the edge of her kitchen counter, and poured herself another cup of coffee. "It's none of our business," she told him. He held his mug out, and she tipped steaming espresso into it. He took a long sniff of the coffee's aroma, then drank from the mug in silence, without even thinking that she was being a hypocrite.

She asked, "What else?"

Yevgeny put the mug down, then slid off the counter to stand next to her. He was a very big man, and she was a very small woman. His size hadn't been what attracted her to him. She didn't normally have any interest in big, hard-bodied palomino stallions. It wasn't his looks that kept him fascinating. Companions came in all shapes and sizes and sexes. There had been a eunuch once . . . long ago. She hadn't been able to get his manly bits to grow back, but she'd loved him anyway. His company had been rather restful, come to think of it. She didn't want to think about long ago, but how did one help it?

She concentrated on Yevgeny, loving him, feeling his love for her, strong still, despite all the anger and necessary frustration. What she loved in this beautiful man was the strength of his gift.

"We used to call it the Curse," she told him, answering questions that had been in his mind so long he'd stop thinking them consciously.

"What? You mean the gift?"

"Psychic ability, psi, telepathy, empathy, precognition, premonition, the sight," Valentine said. "Whatever the sense is that most humans don't have. Call it what you like. We saw it as a brand, a mark of sin. We believed that every human born with psychic ability was a child of the Goddess, just like us." She touched his cheek. "You were born with our version of original sin. We believed that you deserved to suffer the same punishment as us. But that was a long time ago," she added. "I don't believe in that religion anymore."

He didn't care. He didn't want her excuses. He wanted what he wanted. His indifference hurt her. "It is your fault." His tone wasn't even accusing. It had become too rote for that.

He was right. It was. *So what? Get over it, Yevgeny.* It was better not to humor him. She took her coffee and went to her desk.

Yevgeny sulked in the kitchen for a while, but eventually he followed her. He perched on the edge of the desk. Yevgeny wasn't much for chairs. Valentine kept typing while silence drew out between them. There was no comfort in their silences anymore. Mostly, the silence was a long-distance one these days. She should never have called on him for help. It had just been another excuse when she told herself she couldn't do this without him.

"How's it coming?" he asked at last. "Your script?"

"Good," she answered, though she wasn't certain that was true. She kept changing the story. "I think I'm finally on to something. You've been a big help." She looked at him instead of the computer monitor. "No, you haven't." She put her hands flat on the wrist rest in front of the keyboard. "Tell me more."

Instead of complying, he got up and came to stand behind her. While waiting for him to say something, Valentine went back to work. After a while, she grew anxious. Not at his stubbornness, but because all writers are insecure, neurotic creatures.

"What do you think?" she asked as Yevgeny read over her shoulder. She dreaded his answer, since he was the most honest critic she'd ever known. She both loved and hated that about him. He put his hands on her shoulders and leaned down a little. She scrolled the screen up a few times as he read, and she waited.

"Istvan?" he finally said. "That's going a little too far, isn't it?"

"He's a good boy."

Yevgeny snorted. "He's everyone's worst nightmare."

"I've never approved of what was done to him." She didn't reward Yevgeny's curiosity with an explanation. She did add, "He never liked me, of course. He never liked anyone."

"He still doesn't. I can't believe you're using Istvan."

"I'll probably change his name," she said and shook her head in disgust. "I've already had enough trouble with the hero's character not being a blue-eyed white guy. Of course, my dream casting's Nic Cage for the villain."

"I think you're missing the point, Valentine."

"And you're stalling." She tilted her head back and smiled at him. "Did you miss me that much?"

He bent to kiss her forehead. "Of course."

A wave of affection flooded her, but she didn't let it overwhelm her. "Nobody's biting anybody tonight." She'd felt a chase earlier, the first one in years. She was interested, excited, but she didn't let it show. She didn't suppose Yevgeny knew the details of what had happened. It didn't matter. She'd draw it out of Selim's mind in the morning.

"Bitch."

How true. "Tell me something I want to know. You said you'd help me."

He withdrew from her, sat back on the corner of the desk. "You ordered me to help you."

"I asked nicely. You didn't have to."

He laughed. "I had to. I had to see you," he added grudgingly.

"I didn't answer your calls," she mimicked. She swiveled the chair face him. "I didn't let you come to me. It's better, and you know it."

"I want to be with you."

She laughed softly and stroked his thigh. He tensed beneath her touch. "I know what you think you want."

"Need." He gritted out the word. The pain he felt was in his mind and very real.

"You're just infected with all the psychic energy being put off by the others. It'll pass," she reassured him. "It did last time."

He gave a hollow laugh. "The last time, you took me on vacation. Somewhere boring in Utah."

"You said you liked the skiing."

"You said you enjoyed the film festival."

She shrugged. "We both lied. You should get away this time. No," she agreed before he could say it. "It's too late. You've caught the scent."

"So have you."

She looked at her computer. "I have my own coping mechanism."

"I need to Hunt."

Valentine shook her head. "It's not going to happen. Do you hear me?" Her voice was hard as iron. She remembered an age of iron. And one of bronze before that. She put the authority of all her years in her words. "I forbid it."

Yevgeny shot to his feet. She rose from her chair. They stood toe to toe; a very large man loomed over a very small woman. A portrait had been painted of her once, on a palace wall. Someone in this century had found that portrait and dubbed it "La Parisienne." She had lived in Paris, too, once. But she'd seen sunlight last on the Isle of Crete. Hers were a little people, lithe and supple and strong. She was not afraid of bulls. She had danced with them in her youth.

She stared down her great, angry bull of a man now. She put her hand on his chest and pushed, just a little. Yevgeny sat with a hard thud.

"I forbid it," she repeated. "I love you."

His head came up sharply. The bright blue eyes beneath the golden arch of brows met hers. His mouth worked. "But—"

"It's not good being a vampire," Valentine said. "Trust me on this." She stepped back, put her hands on her hips. "Now, tell me something I can use."

"There's a child."

She needed to sit down. She did. On the floor. Dizzy at the notion, shaken, she felt the truth of his words deep in her bones, in the marrow where blood was born. She looked up a long way to where Yevgeny smiled viciously down on her. The world faded in and out and in. Valentine blinked. "A child?" The question was no more than a faint, frightened rasp.

"Siri knows about him," Yevgeny told her. "She hides it well, but I got through her shields. A little. Her and Selim's real worry was that Jager would somehow attack the child. She's good," he added. "But then, you know that. You wouldn't have called on me if you could have gotten to her yourself. Why can't you ride her, the way you do the other one?"

Yevgeny's jealousy was a strong, hot stink in her mind. She ignored it. Valentine stretched her legs out in front of her. "A child?" she repeated. "I'll be damned."

"That's the traditional view, yes."

She ignored his sarcasm as well. "Who? How? So that's the secret he's been keeping." She'd been rummaging around in poor Selim's head for weeks, hunting for material she could use, and here he'd been dodging her, faking her out all the time. How'd the ungrateful little bastard manage to keep something so momentous from her? When did he get to be so good?

It had been a couple hundred years since they'd seen each other. Time flew. People changed. "Damn."

"I detect more admiration than complaint in your tone," Yevgeny said. "About what?"

Her mind was racing. She ignored his question. She almost forgot his presence as she got up and began to pace. She moved with growing restlessness from the office corner through the living room to the kitchen, from the kitchen out to the balcony, then back through the living room. Yevgeny stayed perched on the desk, arms crossed over his wide chest. He watched her as she circled the apartment, but her muttered words weren't directed at him. "A child. There has to be something going on with the child."

"What's so important about the child?" he asked her. "How did a vampire have a baby in the first place?"

"Is it a boy or girl?" she asked. "Who's the father? Was it on purpose or an accident? What happened to the mother? Where's the kid being hidden? What's Selim planning to do to the little darling?" She rubbed her chin. She paused in her wanderings and discovered she was back by her computer. "Boy," Valentine said. "A little boy. A cute, adorable, big-eyed little boy."

"How do you know?"

She sat down and flexed her fingers over the ergonomically designed keyboard. She closed her eyes. Ideas popped and flowed. She knew suddenly what she had to do, where all her searching and agonizing and false starts had to lead. Her restlessness was gone. She was sharp and alive once more. Possibilities were suddenly endless. She hadn't felt this good in years.

She laughed. She closed the file on the screen. She began a new file. The blank white screen was a beautiful landscape before her. She didn't need Selim's dreams anymore. She could take it from here.

"This is going to be so good," she murmured and began to work. She barely noticed when the door slammed behind Yevgeny, and she was having too much fun to care that it did.

Chapter 12

"YES, THANK YOU," Selim said, though there was no one there. "I slept very well." In fact, the recent pattern of dreams that featured reruns of his life alternating with possible futures had continued. The lights were programmed to come on at sunset, so the room wasn't dark. It was big and messy, his clothes from the night before left scattered where he'd dropped them, a fresh layer over the clothes from the night before that. He stared upward, with his head resting on a pile of four pillows. Two of them were hers. She'd tell him he was a pillow hog if she were there. The ceiling, he thought, could use painting.

He kicked off the covers. "Everything could use fixing up." There was no one in the bed with him, but he stretched a hand out across the queen-size expanse just the same, searching for . . . what? He was talking to . . . who?

Stupid question. His first thoughts were always of her. His first words always to her. Even when she wasn't there.

Where was she? What was she doing?

"Who's the blond?"

He kept his thoughts to himself, and reached toward the bedside table to take the cordless phone from its cradle. A moment later, Selim put down the phone. There had been no irritating beeping signal telling him there was voice mail waiting when he picked it up. That was odd. It was irritating. It was damned irritating.

"This is what you wanted," he told himself. "No."

That he was feeling sorry for himself after his first meal in years and his first good day's sleep in weeks irritated him. Last night had been a very good night. Of course, the evening would have been perfect if he'd gotten laid.

"How crude," he chided himself as he got up and set about preparing for the night's work. Was that any way for the son of a sultan to think? Just because he'd had a harem once . . .

Why not now?

Perhaps he had become too American, too modern, he thought as he began to shave. Perhaps that was his problem with Siri. That he had allowed one partner to become too important to him. If he wanted to get laid, all he needed to do was take a second companion or a slave or even spend an evening with one of Alice Fraser's possessions, one of the girls who gave blood.

No. Definitely not. What would Siri think? He would not hurt her like that. What would everyone else in town think? And they were bound to find out about it. She had her pride. Her place. He would not do that to Siri.

"And who is the blond?" he asked the angry man who looked back at him out of the bathroom mirror. *Put it out of your mind,* he ordered himself. He had work to do.

He didn't need Siri's help with this. He'd do it the old-fashioned way. He turned on the television and channel surfed. Within a few minutes, a local news program caught and held his attention. He sat impatiently through a long, lurid report of another murder in Griffith Park. It was the sort of story the media loved to sink its teeth into and gnaw on, one with sound bites from experts on serial killers and cult rituals. There was much indignation and calls for the authorities to move quickly to bring peace and safety back to blah blah blah.

It was the story about the convenience store robbery that interested him. The one where the police who arrived on the scene shot the store owner. People in the neighborhood were angry, bitter. This wasn't the first time the cops had hassled and harassed them. Now someone was dead. Tensions were running high. People were ready to take to the streets.

"I can work with this."

Selim clicked off the television and went to have a look at the scene in person.

"The new car's dark blue. I miss the burgundy red one."

She'd found the new Mercedes in her garage that morning. Flowers, with a note from Selim, had arrived in the afternoon. The note said he hoped she liked the color. No apologies, certainly no explanations. No invitation or mention of seeing her soon, either. But he had kissed her last night, and the fire between them had been just as strong and deep as ever. She touched her bruised lips; the only marks on her from last night came from Selim. *Son of a bitch.*

She wasn't going to let herself go to his place. He made no effort to see her. Impasse. *He saved your life last night,* she reminded herself.

He's still a son of a bitch.

You like him that way.

What's to like? He's a killer.

Two nights ago, that didn't bother her. The truth was, she didn't object to people being killed. There was nothing wrong with people being killed. Certainly nothing wrong with vampires being killed. There had been a dead body in the trunk of her car last night. She hadn't objected to that at all. She would have been happy to help kill that particular vampire. *Yeah, but Larry Jager deserved it.*

"It's a beautiful new luxury car. Blue. Red. What's the difference at night?" Cassie's voice called Siri's attention back to the conversation.

"I can see them in the daylight. Besides," Siri complained to Cassie, "you see just fine at night. I thought your eyes picked up a different spectrum or something."

"Or something," Cassie answered. "It's hard to explain."

"And you're not going to."

"Can we talk about something else?"

Even though the conversation wasn't being conducted on cellular phones, circumspection was always—mostly—the order of the day. Siri and Cassie still got together for the occasional private chats, but vampires weren't supposed to socialize with other vampires' companions. They were being real sticklers for their stupid rules right now. Companions weren't even supposed to talk to other companions. Everyone was supposed to stick to their own nest and wait for the night of the Hunt. It was the Law.

The rules were complicated and stupid, and they were never fully explained. She doubted if they'd even been codified or written down. Were there vampire lawyers? Loopholes? You were just supposed to obey without question. Until she'd come on board as Selim's girlfriend, no one in Southern California had ever talked to anybody else. There wasn't any Law against it, she'd discovered, it was tradition. Even Selim rarely had contact with the others, though he kept tabs on them in a quiet, secretive way.

Siri simply couldn't stand the lack of communication. Besides, she was endlessly curious, a professional busybody, and had this tendency to see things about people she knew before the events happened. The fact that there was anything resembling a vampire community these days was her doing, but she was a mere mortal, to be ignored when it suited them. They were up to important vampire stuff right now. Life-and-death decisions. Mostly death. She had no place in their—Selim's—

councils while he picked and chose which humans died.

"Bullshit," she muttered.

"What?"

"Nothing. What do you want to talk about?"

"About . . . last night. You're sure he's—"

"You don't have anything to worry about. I promise." Her friend's obvious concern helped get Siri's mind off her own complaints. Never mind that she felt used and unloved. There was a child's life at stake, and that was more important. Selim considered Jager a threat to Sebastian. She'd found out the hard way that the strig was totally out of control. "It's taken care of," she promised Cassie. "You and Tom can relax."

Cassie sighed. "I wish. Sebastian's so vulnerable," Cassie went on. "There are some old stories about children like him."

"What stories?"

"I don't know."

Of course not. "Don't you people ever talk to each other?"

"You don't have to sound so annoyed. We're a secretive people."

"You mean Gypsies?"

Cassie laughed with no great enthusiasm. "I mean that Tom says I don't want to know."

"So you don't want to know. Honestly, Cassie, what's wrong with a little knowledge?"

"It can get you killed."

Siri had the distinct impression that the "you" in this case wasn't just the object of a sentence or an offhand comment. She refused to take it personally, as either threat or warning. Not from Cassie. She did take time to count to one hundred rather than go into a lecture about the unreasonableness of it all. Cassie had her own problems with all those Laws, much worse problems than Siri's.

Siri curled her feet under her on the couch and switched the receiver to her other ear. The television was on, but the sound was off. Who needed sound to watch a Timberwolves-Bucks game on ESPN?

Maybe it was Selim's constant secretiveness that was getting to her, even more than that other thing. No, it wasn't.

"I'm thinking about getting a cat," she told Cassie. "It's getting lonely around here."

Cassie laughed. "A cat. To go with the crystal ball?" They'd met at a New Age bookstore, back before either of them met the—persons—they were currently involved with. "You sound like an old-maid witch."

"I don't need the crystal ball. I'm not old. Or a maid . . . though I'm beginning to forget what sex feels like. And didn't you used to read Tarot cards?" Siri reminded Cassandra. And it wasn't like one of them had set up a date for the other one with their new boyfriend's best friend. Neither had known that the other was involved with a vampire; they'd actually gone their separate ways, lost track of each other. Neither was surprised, though, to meet again the way they had. They'd warned each other for a long time that the cards and the visions held strange, dark fates for them both.

"Still read the cards," Cassie said. "Maybe it's a Romany thing."

Until five years ago, Cassandra Widdoes didn't have the faintest idea she had any Rom ancestry. It wasn't until after Cassie became pregnant that Siri's research proved that Cassie's grandmother, who'd been born and orphaned in a refugee camp just after World War II, wasn't Jewish, as the family had always assumed, but a Russian Gypsy. Further research showed that Tom Avella had some Spanish Gitano ancestry, as well. Aristocratic old Don Tomas hadn't like hearing that. At least the proof of Romany blood had convinced Tom that Cassie wasn't cheating on him and that the baby was his. Things had been a little tense in the Avella household for a while, if you wanted to be so low key as to call a vampire in a murderous, jealous rage tense.

The amniocentesis and other medical tests had

helped, too. Not just to convince Tom of his companion's faithfulness but to convince Selim that the impossible was indeed happening. She and Selim had been involved in that bizarre, long night at the hospital. Strange how all the medical personnel involved in giving those tests had no, or a very confused, memory of doing them, and how all the results had disappeared. Science was all right, but psychic talent was often much more efficient.

Siri said, "I miss having adventures." Before Cassie could answer or she could remind herself about last night, the phone signaled a call on the other line. "Hold on." The basketball game wasn't holding her attention. She clicked the remote to a random channel. A local news program came on the screen as she switched to the incoming call. "Hello."

"Hi, Siri, it's Joseph." Miriam's companion sounded cheerful and relaxed now that his household's little problem was taken care of. "Saw an item in the trades this morning that you might be interested in."

Joe taught at the UCLA film school. He'd once joked that he'd personally turned down Steven Spielberg's student application, but she knew he wasn't that old. He kept his finger on the pulse of pop culture and the business, though. Joe's tidbits were always interesting. Siri perked up. It would be more fun to hear Hollywood gossip than vampire gossip. "Oh?"

"I know how you love vampire movies."

"Oh, lord," she groaned. "Not another one!" One news story ended, another one began with a shot of a reporter standing before an angry crowd in front of a Hispanic supermarket. There was something disturbing about the scene. She knew without having to check that Cassie had hung up on the other line, that Tom wanted her for something. Siri didn't try to discern what the Hollywood Hills vampires were up to. She clicked the sound up to whisper level on the television set. A shiver went through her, but she kept most of her attention on the other companion.

"Yep," Joe confirmed. "There was a press release from Arc Light Productions this morning." He laughed. "Says that production is starting on a film about 'real' vampires."

The shiver hit her again. Siri sat up straight. A line of ice crawled up her back. "Real?"

"I'm looking forward to this one," Joe went on. "We're going to have to do another companions film festival at your house before going to see this one. Think we'll like it better than *Near Dark*? Though, as I recall, you voted for *From Dusk 'til Dawn* as best vamp movie the last time."

"Real," she said again. She gripped the phone tightly in her sweating palm. The world was burning up. The walls of the room were made of glass. Beyond the glass were . . . stars. Burning, falling stars. No, flames tearing up through the night sky, reaching to burn the stars. The city was on fire.

The voice on the television shouted at her, "Can't you see the city's on fire?"

Of course she saw it. "What do you want me to do about it?"

"It's just a movie, Siri," Joe said, a million miles away. "You don't have to sound so scared."

Why was this fool talking about movies when real people were dying in the burning streets? She stood up and threw the cordless phone toward the melting glass wall. It bounced off and hit the television screen. Siri sat back down. She blinked, and her living room returned to normal.

"Damned visions."

What had Joe been talking about? Why had she turned away from the basketball game? What had the vision of flames and destruction been about?

"No, wait," she said, rubbing her temples and thinking hard. "I know that one."

Selim was up to something. Something actually quite clever. No, no. It was diabolical. Evil.

Siri looked up and spoke to the large photograph of

Selim that smiled down from a silver frame hung on the blue wall. "Did you have anything to do with the Rodney King riots, you bastard?" She thought the words louder and angrier than she said them. She hoped they gave him a headache. "If you think I'm going to let you get away with it," she added, "you are sadly mistaken."

Siri tapped her fingers on the arm of the couch and imagined that she heard the click of claws instead of the tap of human nails. She glanced at her hand. Still human. But for how long? Some secrets they kept very well, despite her information network, despite the visions. Selim had never told her *exactly* how vampires were made, though she knew it involved more than just sharing blood with companions. Cassie refused to talk about her own change. Siri admitted that she had never let herself think about it. Or maybe Selim hadn't *let* her think about it. She knew he made her forget things sometimes, only because they eventually came back to her, and they had fights about his messing with her mind. She guessed the birth process involved something to do with the Hunt. There was so much she couldn't see, so much she didn't know despite phones and faxes and E-mail and face-to-face conversations. Oh, and the visions, of course.

The Hunt was inevitable as night. She accepted that humans were going to die. But did the strigs have to be allowed to hunt down Moira Chasen? Did a part of the city have to go up in flames to cover the other vampires' crimes? There had to be a better way. If only because she couldn't let the man she loved have all those innocent deaths on his conscience.

"Not your species," she murmured, with her gaze unwaveringly on the eyes of the man in the photo. She tried to make her thoughts punch a hole in his strong shielding and his blithe amorality. "Not your problem, my ass, oh Lord of the Nile." She tapped her fingers impatiently once more. Her thoughts raced. So did the hours. When was he going to let them Hunt? How the hell was she going to get through to him in time?

Maybe she should break out her old crystal ball and

see if it could offer any advice. Or maybe she should just hit Selim over the head with it the next time she saw him and get him out of town until the urge to commit mass murder passed. "Whatever," she muttered, and she switched the channel back to the basketball game, just in case watching a lot of tall men running around in baggy shorts might help her think.

Chapter 13

SELIM SAT ON the roof of the two-story building and breathed in the night air. The heat absorbed in asphalt and concrete during the day had pretty much dissipated by now. The concentrated stench from car exhausts was no worse than usual in this part of town. There was still something refreshing in the atmosphere. There was the tension, of course. Concentrated anger and frustration boiled up from minds all around him. The emotional perfume was delicious, spiced by the fresh, tangy aroma of cilantro and sharpness of onion and garlic coming from the open kitchen window below him. All of it made his mouth water. Life would be perfect if he had a cup of coffee to go with everything else.

There was a meeting as well as cooking going on in the house below. Selim didn't try to concentrate hard enough to pick up the actual discussion. It was enough for him to recognize the hot emotions. Hot, but not hot enough. The people gathered inside the building were the cooler heads in the neighborhood, the ones looking for reasonable, long-term solutions. They knew that the death of the store owner was a tragic symptom of a deep, ongoing, complex problem. Selim admired and appreciated the responsible attitude of these community leaders, but responsible behavior wasn't going to do him any good.

The street was crowded with cars, many of them slowly patrolling police vehicles. People were clotted on the sidewalks. Mostly young men, their muscles bunched with tension, their words coming out in low-pitched growls. Many glared openly at the passing cop cars and made obscene gestures. The truly dangerous ones studied the enemy with long, coolly assessing looks. They understood hunters and prey. Selim marked them out and nodded with satisfaction at their reaction to the death of one of their own. There was danger brewing out on the street.

The young people gathered out in the street had a much better attitude about the whole situation than their elders in the house. Mad as hell and not going to take it anymore was the tenor of the conversation in the milling crowd down there. They wanted revenge. They wanted blood.

"We have a lot in common," Selim murmured.

Downstairs, someone added cumin to whatever they were cooking. That was what he was going to have to do, add spice to the mix on the street. He just didn't want it to boil over tonight. Soon, a few nights from now. Let it build, but keep it leashed, was his objective. Let the fever burn. Then either let the cops screw up on their arrogant own or engineer an incident. Either way, when the riot began, the vampires would have the hunting ground they needed to take at least a few of the six lives he'd promised them.

It was an elegant, simple, practical solution. Somehow, though, he had the sneaking suspicion that something was bound to fuck it up. It was just a feeling. One with Siri's name written on it, perhaps. Though what his companion—the one who was probably out somewhere with a blond right now—could do to change her master's plans, he had no idea.

Actually, he told himself, trying to make the best of

the situation, her involvement with someone else would distract her from interfering in the Hunt. It would distract her from him. Cool the intensity of their relationship. That was what he wanted.

"I want to kill somebody," he muttered. He looked down at all the dark heads below him. Not a chance of finding a natural blond in this neighborhood. "Maybe I should wander over to Malibu." He chuckled. "Like, there're natural blonds there?" Maybe he should try the Valley.

The real temptation was to head home, to go by Siri's place. Look in on her. See how she was. Find out what she was up to. Having grown used to fighting that particular temptation, Selim moved instead to a particularly shadowy corner at the side of the building and jumped down to the alley below. He moved onto the crowded street and took a slow walk up one side and then the other, reading minds and planting thoughts. The most important thing he did was keep the peace for tonight. He succeeded in stirring the anger without letting it boil over. It was tricky work, satisfying, but it left him with a headache as well a sense of amused irony after a few minutes.

What he needed, he decided once he was satisfied with his patrol of the area, was a triple-shot espresso. Then maybe he'd check some of the scavengers who made their homes by the concrete riverbanks. The city's beggars made for easy prey, but Kamaraju's nest would take only what Selim gave if they wanted to Hunt. Not that he wasn't a little ticked off by Jager going after Siri.

He stopped at a street corner and watched traffic pass by, dark metal shapes defined by the eyes of headlights and reflections of other light across their surface. He stopped paying attention to the people on the street. One part of his mind was aware of movement behind him, but he allowed most of his focus to wander as he watched the cars. It was a good way of getting back into himself after a trip inside strangers' heads. He thought cars were wondrous, beautiful things, for all the stench and heat and noise they threw off. Of course, they'd grown up with him, he'd watched so much technology evolve in the dizzying speed of the last two centuries.

When he first emerged from his daylight prison, the world was already a changing place. He was told that things were different once, that once upon a time eons went by without much changing. Just the usual wars, famines, and other apocalypses had marked the passing of the centuries back in the good old nights. He'd heard stories of vampires who'd fallen into the stagnation that sometimes afflicted their kind, who'd hidden themselves away, only to get run over by a train or some other modern monster when the need to Hunt finally drove them out of hiding. Vampire urban legends. No one really knew any vampires who'd died from lack of coping skills. Made good stories to tell the kids, though.

Selim smacked his lips together in imitation of a toothless old man. "Yep, things was different in my day, sonny," he mumbled. "Humans was easy pickins' then. Why, they roamed in vast herds, just naked monkeys as far at the eye could see." Despite the headache, he could hear Geoff Sterling coming up behind him. Selim had felt the young vampire's approach for blocks but hadn't been concerned about it. "Mighty good eatin'," he added as he turned to face the strig.

He was glad to see that Sterling had ditched the Goth look for the evening, just as Selim had ditched the Armani. It did not suit the surroundings. The jeans and T-shirts they both wore helped them blend much better into the crowd. Of course, the fact that they were both wearing black did give their choice of clothing a sort of uniform look.

Sterling glanced back at the humans, males for the most part, on the stoops and sidewalks and lingering in doorways. "I can't imagine all those monkeys naked," he said with a mock shudder. He held up his hands. "No. The thought's just too frightening."

Selim smiled. Could it be that the kid had a sense of humor? "What if they were naked girls? That's what interests you at the moment, isn't it? Girls?''

Sterling's eyes narrowed menacingly. ''You trying to insult me, *dhamphir*?''

Selim laughed. Not because he was the one who'd been insulted, but because Geoff Sterling, despite his threat display, was blushing. The heat of embarrassment that rose from his skin added to the surrounding temperature. ''All I asked was if you preferred naked girls. If you're a vanilla vampire.''

The term had actually been coined *about* Selim. He supposed it was his one contribution to vampire culture. Most vampires were bisexual. Selim was told that it wasn't gender that mattered for sex, but the strength of the human's gift. Selim didn't get it, never had, though he'd had his choice of partners—women, boys, animals, and eunuchs—from the moment he'd first shown an interest in sex. And that was *before* he was a vampire. He'd only lusted after women then; only lusted after them now. He was considered not only odd, but downright dull in his tastes by those who knew his preferenccs.

Sterling grew more belligerent. ''Vanilla? *You're* calling *me* a pervert?''

''Is that what it's considered now?'' Selim put his hand over his heart. Then, cobra-swift, he grabbed Sterling's throat and shook just a little before releasing him. No one else on the street noticed the brief assault. ''It was a simple question. Do you like naked girls?''

Sterling coughed. ''Yeah.'' He gave his characteristic shrug. ''Only one naked girl interests me at the moment.'' He sneered. ''I'd love to see a naked angel,'' he added, then frowned. ''That sounds like a porn title, doesn't it?''

''It certainly does.''

Sterling obviously didn't like that notion. ''I've watched at her window some nights. She always comes home alone, you know? Goes to bed by herself. She's gorgeous, could have any man she wants. But she's waiting . . . waiting for someone special.''

"You?"

He nodded. "I learned how to walk in her dreams today. In mine, I mean—shared her thoughts when I was—"

"I know what you did. So, you want to keep practicing?"

Sterling nodded. "I wouldn't let anyone else have her."

Looked like Sterling had made his decision about Moira Chasen. Selim didn't know whether to be happy for the young couple or annoyed at having to find some other prey for the strigs. He wondered if O. J. was in town.

"Let's talk," he said to the boy, who nodded.

Selim led Sterling to the nearest coffee shop, which was several miles away. Sterling had no trouble keeping up with the running pace Selim set. They dodged traffic and ran along the top of a gridlocked line of car roofs before turning off the freeway. Sterling was breathing hard by the time Selim led them into the coffee shop he had in mind. A psychological as much as physiological reaction. Selim let Sterling pay for the tall cardboard cups of espresso-loaded latte. They settled on a bench under the shop's outdoor awning. No one noticed they were there.

Selim leaned back on the bench with a contented sigh, breathed in the scent of night-blooming jasmine and exhaust fumes, and crossed his legs. Traffic cruised by, the headlights forming a thick stream of light that reminded Selim of lava. The coffee was still too hot for his taste. He concentrated on Sterling while he waited. The boy was staring straight ahead, reading the movie ad on the back of the bus stop across the street, perhaps. He glanced up at the sky and the outline of house-covered hills in the distance. He looked everywhere but at Selim, though he was very aware that Selim was looking at him.

Finally, Selim said, "Why'd you follow me?" Selim

carefully watched the conscious effort Sterling put into not shrugging.

The boy's voice was cool when he said, "Boredom?"

"You don't know why you followed me."

Sterling's head swiveled toward Selim. He leaned forward. "*Dhamphir*, I—"

Selim casually slammed him back against the bench. Normally he didn't explain. Normally, he didn't mind. "I am *not* a *dhamphir*. Vanilla is an insult I'll put up with, but do not ever call me that again. There's only one *dhamphir* in the whole damned world, and one is more than enough." Well, there was another. He almost smiled, thinking that if Siri were here, she'd add, "And we're not talking about Princess Leia." Siri wasn't here. She might never be again. The thought did not help Selim's mood. "Understood?" he growled at the young vampire.

Sterling swallowed. Nodded. Selim took his hand away from Sterling's chest. He hadn't realized his claws were out. There was no blood scent in the air, so at least he hadn't broken the boy's skin. The dream he'd had about Istvan was making him a little touchy on the subject of *dhamphirs*. "Sorry," he said. "Overreacted. You spilled your coffee."

Sterling ignored the hot liquid that poured out of the dropped cup and pooled on the sidewalk by his feet. "But—you're—you," he stammered. His eyes were wide and dark, but there was no other sign of the change in him. Hunger burned down inside him, but it was overshadowed by confusion, and another, growing need.

Oh. Selim began to see what was going on. *This punk kid? Oh, please!*

"I—don't—" Sterling gave up fumbling for words and scraped his fingers though his hair. He leaned forward, hands on his knees, and stared at the ground. He was breathing hard. "I'm burning up inside."

"Moira?" Selim questioned. Hoped.

Sterling shook his head. "I'm so hot and horny I can't stand it." He looked back at Selim, bleakly unhappy and infinitely confused. "Moira's not part of this. She was all that mattered . . . until."

"Until last night?"

Sterling nodded. "I don't know what's happening. Jager wasn't human . . . but his scent . . ." Sterling licked his lips, and a shudder wracked him. Revulsion and longing blended in him, and it hit Selim's senses with a carrion reek. "Feeling Jager's death hit me even stronger than when I witnessed the killing in Seattle. I thought that was just some freak reaction to trauma."

Selim gulped down the coffee. It was still hotter than he liked, but he barely noticed. He tossed the empty cup in a nearby trash bin as he asked, "How many have you killed?" Geoff Sterling looked around uncomfortably. "There's no one to hear," Selim told him. "Talk to me, boy."

"One." Sterling couldn't look at him.

The bleak pain in the young vampire's emotions was clear evidence to Selim. "One. The night you were born."

"It was disgusting."

"And it damned your soul forever yadayadayada. Or didn't your parent give you that speech?"

Sterling turned a fierce glare on Selim. "It's true! We're evil. Unnatural. Monsters. Damned. I thought being strig would make it easier to revel in the evil. I thought I was going to love being a vampire."

Selim put a hand on his shoulder. "You'll get used to it."

"Have you?" Sterling asked.

Selim found that he couldn't look the boy in the eye for a few moments. "Do you miss the daylight, Geoff?"

"No," Sterling answered. "That's not it. I don't miss being human."

"You don't want to hunt them."

"I don't—I enjoyed hunting Moira."

"Courtship. Not the same as hunting. You got a hard-on from Miriam's hunt."

"But it wasn't—" He had to take several deep breaths

before he could admit, "I had more of a hard-on from last night. When I felt you kill Jager."

The boy's shame stank to high heaven. His pained confusion burned against Selim's shields. "You sick pervert." Selim said the words kindly, with deep, unwilling understanding. "You're terrified that you're just like me."

Sterling's nod was a tight, pained movement, as though he were fighting against rigor mortis. *We're not dead, we're different,* Selim reminded himself as he watched the boy struggle with his emotions. *We don't die when we change, we jump species, like a disease that mutates from being able to infect one type of animal to infecting an entirely different species. Only we become the other. Become the disease? Vampirism as blood disease? Now there was a heretical thought. One never to be spoken aloud. The Strigoi Council had violently dismissed the notion. Like members of any fundamentalist religion, anything that might question their faith was rejected as sinful, evil, wrong. Sort of like vampires? Well, a sense of irony was never a qualification for membership on the Council.* He wasn't sure what was. *Age and wisdom, maybe? Really sharp teeth?*

"I don't want to be like you."

Selim was glad that Sterling had finally interrupted his rambling thoughts. The hours were passing. They were talking too much, and it looked like they had a lot more to say. It would be a shame if the sun came, and they were still sitting outside the coffee shop. They'd probably get mugged in their sleep or hauled off to a hospital. Possibly a morgue. Selim had no idea what he looked like when he slept; he only knew that he slept like the dead from sunrise to sunset.

"Like me how?" Selim questioned the younger vampire. "A vampire killer?" It was all a matter of what emphasis was put on the words, wasn't it? "Too late for that."

"I saw Istvan in Seattle."

Selim curbed the impulse to ask what Istvan was like.

He supposed the boy's remembered terror told him enough. "Oh?"

"I can feel myself turning into a *dhamphir* and I—"

Selim's laughter penetrated Sterling's painful confusion.

"What?" Sterling demanded in outrage.

Ignorance was considered something of a virtue among their kind. Vampires had developed concepts of compartmentalized knowledge and Need-to-Know long before humans had figured out that knowledge was power. Among the Strigoi the strictest law was one of silence. What one did not know could not be shared or sold, tortured from you by an Inquisitor, or read from your thoughts by some nosy psychic human. What one did know could only be bestowed on others one drop at a time. No human who didn't belong to a vampire could ever know any of the truth.

As Selim well knew, the young always felt they were dying of thirst. Those drops of knowledge, history, truth were never enough to quench the fever. It was inevitable that young ones adopt some of the legends humans made up about vampires. Even more inevitable that they invent their own vampire legends.

"You can't *become* like Istvan," Selim bestowed this important drop of truth on Sterling, after he'd stopped wheezing with laughter long enough to get the words out. "*Dhamphirs* are born hating vampires. It's not a disease that can be passed on or caught. Or a perversion. They're natural-born Hunters. Historically, most *dhamphirs* weren't even vampires."

Sterling looked at him like he was crazy, a typical reward for correcting a cherished misapprehension. "But . . . you're a vampire."

Selim waited in silence, wishing for another cup of coffee from the now-closed café, while Sterling sat back on the bench and tried to think through his confusion. Selim stretched his legs out before him and looked relaxed while he kept a careful watch on the sky. It was quite a few minutes closer to sunrise when Sterling asked, "What are Hunters if they're not . . . like him?"

"Enforcers of the Laws," Selim replied. "Shepherds of the blood-children. Cops. Like their mother or father before them. You have to be reborn in the Nighthawk line to begin with if you're going to have the fangs for the job."

Sterling touched his canine teeth as though he felt them growing already. "Oh."

"Then you have to be one of the few who feel the sacred call," Selim went on. He waved a hand casually. "And there's this . . . magic . . . thing . . . you have to do."

"Sacred call?"

"The hunger that's burning in your gut right now. Hurts like hell, doesn't it?"

Sterling laid a knotted fist on his abdomen. "I'm a Hunter?"

"Maybe." *If you live through the testing,* Selim added to himself. That was a drop of knowledge he wasn't ready to give the boy at the moment. Sterling was already unhappy enough at the urges growing in him and what answers Selim had offered. Selim checked his watch. "You like basketball?"

A puzzled Sterling nodded.

"I've got season tickets. Interested in the Lakers game tomorrow night?" Siri wasn't likely to be there. It was better than going alone.

Sterling looked flattered, then he shook his head. "Sorry. I have a date."

"A date?"

"With Moira."

"A date?" Selim repeated. Skepticism flowed off him in waves. "You're going to . . . ?" He drew back his lips suggestively.

"No!" Sterling was laughably appalled at this crude gesture. "Not yet. It's a real date. I went back to the club after I saw you last night. Got up the nerve to introduce myself to her. She said she'd noticed me."

Sterling sounded infinitely impressed by her discernment, even though he'd been stalking the girl for some time.

"Of course she's seen you."

Sterling was too intent on thoughts of his beloved to pay any attention to Selim. "She's nice. Lonely. I didn't have to use any psychic stuff. I asked. She said yes. I listened to her thinking about me last day, but I didn't telepathically intrude. I thought we should get to know each other before . . ." He drew back his lips suggestively. "You know."

Dating? "Get to know . . . ?"

"Develop a relationship. A rapport. What's wrong? Why are you staring at me like that?"

Develop a—Selim struggled with the concept. What was this modern generation of vampires coming to? "You're supposed to bite the girl, then get to know her," he pointed out.

"Why?"

"What do you mean? That's the way it's always been done. Never mind." They'd talked enough. It was late. He was tired. He stood. "I'm going home now," he said. He frowned at Sterling. "I'm going to catch you following me again, aren't I?"

Sterling shrugged in answer.

This was just wonderful, Selim thought angrily. He already had to control a city full of strung-out vampires overdue for a Hunt. Add to that the possibility that the companion he was trying to keep at arms' length was cheating on him. And there were those shadowy premonitions of the world's only *dhamphir* haunting his daydreams. Now it looked like he had to take on an apprentice Hunter to his list of responsibilities. What else could happen to complicate his world?

This is L.A, he reminded himself. *Things always get more complicated.*

If he was lucky, it would only be a major earthquake that he would have to contend with next.

Chapter 14

A SOFT HAND touched his naked thigh, then drew upward with infinite, teasing slowness. The hand belonged to no one he knew. The presence was unfamiliar, though it pressed lightly against the thin shell of his awareness. There was a strange woman in his bed. She did not belong to him nor to any of the brothers, uncles, and cousins who shared the palace within the palace that was their prison and home. He had no liking for strangers, for any new thing that disturbed his already addled wits. He was a mad prince, mad because they never understood that there were already too many of them. Too many thoughts he had to keep separate from his own.

You know me.

The thought did not drift in by accident, but it wasn't thrust inside him like a blade. It did not hit him or hurt him, though he knew this strange woman had the skill to do anything she chose with her thoughts. He knew this because she wanted him to know it. She took great pride in her skills. The unspoken words she sent him were simply there and gone, a bubble thought too fleeting and fragile to cause him any harm.

He sent a thought of his own: *Who are you?*

I've dreamed you.

She heard. No one had ever heard his thoughts before, though he had read the minds of others all his life. Worse, sometimes he couldn't tell where his thoughts ended and other people's began. He tried to think at her again, but her hands moved over his helpless, sensitized body, and thought fled before sensation.

His limbs were hot and heavy; he couldn't move. He could feel every thread, every stitch in the embroidery on the thin cotton bedshirt. The finely woven material weighed like lead against his skin. A breast brushed across his chest, soft promise, quickly withdrawn. His hands could not reach, though longing to cup lush roundness flared and burned. There was nothing but darkness before his open eyes. Nothing but mystery and brief, tantalizing touches. Things sensed, guessed at. A curve of hip grazed against his side. A musky perfume scented the air. A fingernail—or was it the tip of a steel blade?—traced a line of fire down his skin from over his heart to his navel, circled there, then was gone.

Sweat beaded on his forehead, at the base of his throat. Heat rose from him, and flesh scorched where she touched. Desire crashed into him, over him, grew inside him. A stranger's breath whispered across his lips, warm and sweet. There was a hand on his shoulders, then fingers ruffling through his sweat-curled hair, but it was the hand that had reached his groin that drew his complete attention. He hardened beneath that subtle touch; flesh swelled and grew. A throbbing ache filled his loins, tightened his balls, and blossomed up the length of his shaft. His hips bucked hard.

Patience, love. Have patience.

He had no choice in the matter. Hours passed in this darkness where desire flared, ebbed, throbbed, subsided, then grew ever stronger. He hurt. He hungered. There were hands on his cock, circling, massaging, stroking, until he wanted to come and die. A wet, suckling mouth covered him. Heat and pressure drove him mad. His length was engulfed, swallowed, laved, and licked. Then the stranger's mouth was gone again. Her laughter, affectionate but teasing, lingered inside him, all but unheard over his silent screams of frustration.

At first, he was barely aware of the mouth that settled on his. But the lips were so soft, so full, her tongue so gently insistent, he could do nothing but open his mouth for her. He tasted his own blood on her tongue, a hot copper saltiness, with underlying sweetness. He could feel the spot where she'd drawn the blood as he tasted himself. Until that instant, he'd been unaware of the sharp prick of pain on his throat.

You've dreamed about me.

He didn't remember.

We've known each other for a long time.

An image formed behind his closed eyes, of himself soaking tired muscles in a chest-deep pool of steaming water. There were eunuchs moving about, and a female slave approached, holding a cool sherbet he'd ordered. She had an extraordinarily beautiful mouth and a sharp, secretive smile. Other images formed and faded.

He knew the woman holding him prisoner in his own bed, though he'd never noticed her before. Known her for years. All his life. She'd been in the nursery when he was a babe. Among the women when he was brought to the Cage. She never changed or aged a day. Never spoke or caught anyone's attention. She was always just—there.

But never in the daylight.

No. He couldn't recall seeing her in the daylight.

I waited a long time for you to grow up, she told him. *It's been a long, sweet Hunt. Now you will be my companion.*

What a beautiful word. He wanted her to let him touch her. To bury himself in her. That was all that mattered.

My pleasure?

Yes.

He cried out in sudden terror. There was no stopping

the scream, though it had no chance to escape his throat. *What are you?*

Another image was thrust into his mind. He remembered the thick, syrupy mockery of a brother's laughter pouring over him. "They are all the same in the dark; soft, skilled mouths and wet heat between their thighs. Close your eyes as they pleasure you, and you can't tell them apart." He had tried that game more than once. His brother was right in some things. The palace women were all expertly trained in the same arts, all equally beautiful, all smiled or laughed or kept silent as the moment dictated. Their names did not matter, their lovely faces were interchangeable.

But they were not the same in the dark of his bedroom, or when his eyes were closed as he thrust into sleek, silky, surrounding flesh. It was then, when he was inside them, that he knew a woman best, when she was open and real, her mind as vulnerable for a moment as her body. It was only the ones who actually felt something toward him that he brought back to his bed more than once, even if what they felt was hate or contempt. Greed, ambition, those were familiar emotions, as well. He'd absorbed all of them in one mix or another, been aroused by them. Lived on them.

That was what she was. An emotional vampire.

Clever child.

This—*vampire*—lived on what he felt.

You're a skinny, underfed thing, but you'll do. Her amusement was silent, and terrifying.

Then she was lying with him. Small as she was, she filled the bed, the world. He felt the weight of her very real body, all lush, exciting curves, bare satin skin stretched out on top of him. The tips of her breasts were hot, hard points against his chest. His cock pressed against her belly. He had never been more aroused, even knowing she fed on what he was feeling.

"Not just emotions," she said, voice husky with her own need. Then she bit him.

•   •   •

She tasted hot, sweet blood and moaned in her sleep. *Turkish delight.* The thought rose to the surface like a champagne bubble, so bright and happy that she giggled out loud. It was the surprise of joy that brought her as close to awake as was possible in the middle of the day. Yevgeny wasn't beside her to account for the moistness between her thighs, the delicious ache deep inside her, or the languorous heaviness in her breasts. She felt the brush of cooled air across her hard nipples and actually heard herself moan. There was no blood in her mouth, but she tasted it there. Good Goddess but she was horny! That wasn't something that happened often, and certainly not in the dead of day when she ought to be still as a statue with every sense turned inward, walking the invisible paths of the old ones.

Or something like that.

Lady of Snakes, but she could fall into archaic language patterns with the best of them. Language evolved. It looked like vampires did, too, or she wouldn't be having trouble sleeping lately. Of course, if she was going to develop insomnia, it would be better if she was up writing instead of too aroused to think straight and too frozen to do anything about it. Was this some new punishment? Thou shalt not masturbate—because you can't. Nyah, nyah!

Valentine laughed again. She could actually hear herself laugh! Amazing. The first thing she could do in the daylight was laugh. And be turned on. She was having way too much fun lately. Wasn't she supposed to be old and wise and deep and decadent? A creature of spirit? A force of evil? To think deep thoughts well beyond the puny concepts that could be imagined by the minds of men? Well, screw that. She'd always been pretty shallow, come to think of it. She felt like a teenager. Giddy. She hadn't felt this good since—

Ah. That was it.

Valentine made a conscious effort to be unconscious, to sink back down to the level of awareness where she belonged, where the dreams lived. She had never resented anything so much in her long life, but the daylight world was *not* where she dwelled. It was not where her life was taking place. Down below the conscious level, someone she knew very well was walking in her dreams. Turnabout's fair play. She'd been walking in his for weeks.

Hello, little boy, she thought as she plunged through layers of swirling darkness. *Miss me?*

He strained toward her, hard and needy. Her light mood fled as she found herself rolled onto her back on a bed two hundred and fifty years in the past. Pillows scattered. Moonlight filtered gently from the latticework windows high overhead. The reflection of sunlight blinded her. She screamed and clawed at the light, until Selim pinned her hands with his, forced her to stare at the full, blazing moon. It was like being trapped in the center of a bright spotlight while sharply cut diamonds rained down, slashing her naked skin. For an instant the legend about vampires being burned by the sun became reality. Somehow the myth was part of Selim's dream about being with her. She adjusted her reality accordingly, and the light became normal, beautiful, without pain, once again.

She slipped out of his frenzied grasp. Touched him softly. Deft fingers smoothed over his face, through his hair, along the taut muscles of his back and down his flanks, while he panted and moaned. Sweat beaded on his skin. He glittered bronze in the moonlight. Pain radiated from him. And longing, loneliness worse than anything she'd ever felt from the lost boy raised in a luxurious prison.

"What are you on, sweetheart?" she asked him. "What hurts so bad?" She took his face in her hands. He was blind. Gone. Crying. "Tell Mama all about it." She put one arm around him, rocked him, stroked the pulsing length of his erection, and lifted her head when he nuzzled at her neck. His teeth found her pulse. Fire trailed clean, sweet pain down her throat. She threw her leg over his and guided them together. She buried her claws in his shoulder blades, felt the pop of skin and blood sticky on the palms of her hands as he filled her. She raked stinging trails swiftly down his back. His spine arched, head coming up with a sharp cry. She grabbed his buttocks as her inner muscles tightened around his shaft, wrapped her legs around his waist. When he tried to buck, she forced him to be still, and let him bleed. She kissed him while she tortured him, her mouth hot on his, their tongues dancing and twining through the barrier of primary fangs.

Fangs. She licked at them, ran her tongue slowly across them. The tip of his tongue touched first one and then the other deadly point of her extended canines. Electric shudders shot through her burning blood. *Sweet Goddess!* She thought, and returned the favor. It had never been like this before. Never, in thousands and thousands of years.

It was never supposed to be like this.
Forbidden! Forbidden! Forbidden!

Whether the thought was his or hers didn't matter. It was the shock of surprise that sent both of them over the edge. Vampires kissing. Impossible. Forbidden.

Selim screamed into her mouth and jerked frantically. The caged animal escaped her trap, pushed her thighs up against her chest, and drove into her with a mingled cry of terror and lust. She rose frantically to his thrusts in the same horrified fever, monster fucking monster. A scream of need escaped her torn throat, answered by a soul-deep bellow as he possessed her with pounding strokes, unleashing all his strength and force and need. Sun flares of orgasms burned up through her belly and blood and brain.

This is just a dream, she told herself when she could think again. One he unknowingly pulled her into. Neither of them were responsible for the shape of the dream. They might not even remember it come nightfall. The collapsed weight on top of her didn't feel like a dream. It felt like a warm, sweat-slick, sated, slack-muscled male. She didn't have to wonder if it had been good for him, too. *This did not happen,* she reminded herself again. She wasn't going to just lie there with a satisfied smile on her face and hold him in her arms until they both woke in their separate beds hours from now.

With great reluctance she made herself drift up out of the dream and walk into the mind that was doing the dreaming. Selim slept on in two different places: his body in Pasadena, and most of the rest of him created a dream that he was on a bed in Istanbul. *Where the sheets haven't been changed in over two centuries,* Valentine thought at the sleeping prince. *I've stayed in some motels like that.*

A part of Selim that wasn't in California or Turkey but somewhere much more distant, farther and deeper inside him, stirred, stretched, yawned. *So have I.*

This dreamer was blind, deaf, not really there. It had a voice, but not one Selim would hear when he was awake. This dreamer lived in the memories that couldn't quite be caught, within the vague fears, the most absent part of the mind. It came in very handy for those who knew how to talk to it. She had never been able to reach this part of him for more than a few moments at a time in all the weeks she'd been riding him.

She wanted to ask him what they'd just—dreamed— had been all about, but some things were better left unexplored. She did say, *Honey, you need to get back together with your companion.*

Siri.

It was a word, a name, and a prayer. It held all the love in the world. The boy had it bad, but then, she knew that. She admired his resolve, if not his methods, even if they were her own. She wanted to tell him to do what she said, not what she did, but this wasn't a part of him that could listen to her. Besides, she wanted to know about his life, not interfere with it.

Keeping that in mind, she probed gently deeper into his store of knowledge. She figured she might as well get some work done as long as she was here. *Tell me about the child,* she urged. *Tell me all the details—and I'll make you both famous.*

• • •

The ringing phone woke Selim up.

"Oh, boy," he said, staring blankly at the ceiling.

The discordant, jarring sound came again, and again. Staring didn't change anything. Blinking didn't help. There was no daylight coming in through the carved latticework of the roof. There was nothing but a blank white ceiling over his head. What had happened to the blue and white tiles on the walls? He stretched his hands across the width of the mattress, but no body shared this bed with him. Where was she?

"Siri?" he asked.

Who?

A vision of another face floated across his mind, blotting out the dull white ceiling. Black curls half obscured her big, dark eyes. His hands grasped with aching longing to hold the slenderest waist in all the world. The cursed noise kept calling to him. He reached out toward the big-eyed phantom even as she faded. Her rich, warm mouth was the last thing to fade, curved in a teasing smile, fangs pressed seductively against her full lower lip.

"Damn," he muttered. Selim sat up, scrubbed sleep and the dead past out of his eyes. His soul weighed a ton. He felt like he'd been outside his skin but hadn't put it back on right. The merciless telephone kept ringing. He grabbed the receiver. "What?" He was barely aware that he asked the question in Turkish.

"You left a message to meet you at Dar Maghreb." The sound of Middle Eastern music underlay the harsh tone of Don Tomas's voice. "Where are you?"

Not where he was supposed to be. Selim looked at the clock on the table beside the telephone. "Overslept. Rough day," he answered. Bad dreams. Good dreams? He wasn't sure. "Tom, do you ever—? Do you and Cassandra—?"

"What?" It was more of an annoyed growl than a word. Spoken in Spanish.

Selim shook away the last of sleep, the last of memory. Some things were better not to think about or to know. Especially when the answers could bring death. "Nothing."

"Why did you want to see me?"

The hard voice, the tautly strung together words, reminded Selim of this week's reality. He told Don Tomas about the rising tension from the shooting. "What do you think?"

After a considerable silence, he received only a single-word answer. "When?"

Selim stretched and scratched his chest. The bedclothes were not rumpled. The room did not smell of sex. There was no sticky dryness of sweat and semen or blood on his body. There were no visible marks. No proof. But he was empty, physically, psychically, all the way to his soul. He needed—

What he hadn't gotten last night. Needed those strong, sharp emotions that speared into him and kept him going. *We live on emotion,* was the first lesson he'd learned. *Blood is just for sex.* He didn't want blood—liar!—he wanted to not be alone. That was what last day's dream had been telling him. *She'd* risen up out of his subconscious to deliver the message he wanted to hear.

"I'll get back to you, Tomas." He stood up, looked wildly around. He checked the clock again. There was still time. "I have somewhere I have to be."

"You wanted to meet with me."

"I've changed my mind." Don Tomas was not used to being put off or hung up on. Selim did both.

He hurried to get dressed and get out of the house. He could make it, running hard all the way to the Forum. Maybe afterward he could get Siri to give him a ride to his late-night appointment. Maybe she'd be there. If she wasn't out with her blond. Maybe she wouldn't show up, but he had a strong feeling she would. Sometimes he had to go with his feelings where Siri was concerned. Besides, Hunt or no Hunt, he hated missing a home game.

Chapter 15

HE DIDN'T HAVE time for domestic drama. He didn't have time to indulge his hobbies. He should be working right now. Time was short. The world around him was howlingly tense and short-tempered. He should be out patrolling the streets, keeping death-starved strigs and nesters in line. *Where's Buffy the Vampire Slayer when I need to take a night off?* Selim wondered as he glanced at the empty seat beside him.

Where was Siri when he wanted to see her? He always wanted to, damn it! That was the whole point of having a companion: companionship. Plus sex. Damn, he missed the sex. A bit from last day's dream floated to the surface, sending a shock wave of lust and remembered lust through him. Whatever he'd dreamed wasn't quite clear. It had been intense, off, wrong. Not Siri.

What was he going to do if she showed up, drag her under the seating area? Why not just make love to her right here in the third row center court seats? Because he wasn't going to make love to her. He just wanted to see her, be with her. That was all. He bunched his fists tightly as a reminder against sprouting claws. He kept his mouth firmly closed, didn't run his tongue over his teeth. He kept his temper under control and tried not to contemplate how much he had enjoyed killing Jager and how much he was going to enjoy running down the next one who got out of line. It wasn't sex, but it was something.

"Please," he murmured. "Let the next one be blond."

She wasn't going to come. Why should she? He'd started this. She was doing what he wanted. Who said he wanted it? What made him think he could live alone? He was a selfish bastard. He was sick of worrying about her. He could call her. He would. No he wouldn't. He wouldn't break his vow of abstinence. He gave her free will, as much as possible. Free mind. Free choice in everything but when and how they made love.

It was still early, he reminded himself. The game was only in the first quarter. The crowd energy hadn't gotten going yet. He'd lose himself in the energy soon. It would ease the lonely ache a little. It was Siri who brought him to his first game. He'd caught her addiction immediately. There was a psychic art as well as athletic skill to this sport, like chess in motion, like war as ballet. And when the teams' and the audience's excitement took off—delicious!

Basketball, the sport of vampires, he thought and sank glumly down in his seat. Siri was off somewhere enjoying the freedom he'd pushed on her. *Who cared about some stupid game?*

You do, she answered, and sat down beside him. "You missed me," she stated as Selim sat up straight with more than human speed. Heads turned their way, but no one could look away from the playing for long. She put a warning hand on his arm. He stared at it. She wore a black pearl ring he'd given her on their first anniversary. Did she always wear it? He couldn't remember. Females noticed jewelry. Males noticed . . . women.

"You're beautiful," he told her, but the sudden roaring of the crowd blew the words away. "It's only been a couple of nights," he reminded himself, as much as her. "But I missed you more than I thought."

Her smile was slight but fierce. Her tone smug. "Good."

Selim caught himself and considered biting his tongue. Biting her breasts would be better. The insides of her thighs. The tiny scar on her back where her waist began to flare into the lovely round curve of her ass— the scar she'd had the clasped hands and heart of a *claddagh* tattooed around. The Irish marriage symbol was a memento of the first time he'd tasted her, though neither of them were Irish. The scar would remain, there was magic in that, called a witchmark by ancient witch hunters who knew what they were talking about. Pity the tattoo was beginning to fade as her immune system strengthened. There was something sexy about a woman having a tattoo in a spot where only her lover could see it.

The crowd's excitement was getting through his shields, rattling him, making it easy to let his own emotions out. A year of restraint had just blown out the window, and here he and Siri were, grinning at each other like a pair of newlyweds. He noticed that they were holding hands. He reminded himself why there'd been a year of restraint, though the reminder didn't help much.

"So," he said, trying to chill the mood—and because he was jealous. "Who's this blond you've been seeing?"

Siri snatched her hand out of his. She waved it airily, "Oh, just a guy." She sounded unconcerned, but she radiated confusion, uncertainty, sudden fear. She leaned close to his ear to whisper. "Watch your eyes."

Not just his eyes. His senses shifted. It was too bright under the lights. He saw too much: body heat, and emotions that rose like coloredflavored steam off the people around them. His hearing was keener as well. Hunger was a leashed need. And the Hunting instinct—

An image formed in his mind of jumping onto the court, of taking the players down one at a time before the gaping crowd. The pale, polished wood ran with red, circles of paint were covered with slippery blood. He threw back his head and laughed.

Siri hit him, a hard smack on the shoulder. "Down boy."

Selim blinked. What happened? Oh, yes, a fit of jealousy threw him over the thin edge of sanity a moment ago. He was back now. A quick check of play on the court reassured him that he'd only been hallucinating. Good. Eating the players was no way for a fan to behave during the playoffs.

Selim pressed his palms against his temples as he heard Siri say to someone nearby, "He'll be fine. He got into some bad acid in the sixties."

The someone laughed. "He wasn't born in the sixties."

Selim lifted his head and looked deeply into the concerned citizen's eyes. "I'm older than I look. Go away."

Siri was equal parts frightened and flattered by Selim's erratic behavior. "Yevgeny," she promptly answered his no-nonsense look once they were as alone as it was possible to be in a crowd of many thousands. "It was business," she promised as he continued to glare. "I think he was with Jager. He was pissed about being cut loose, wanted to talk about it but couldn't quite bring himself to trust me. I've seen him twice."

"Twice?"

"In public both times—if that's any of your business."

"It is."

"I met him at a strig hangout on Sunset the second time, when Jager came after me. It wasn't a date."

"You were wearing something sexy."

"I'm glad you noticed. I had to blend in, didn't I?"

Selim's eyes were large and dark, but in a normal way as he listened to her explanation. The expression in them was stern and suspicious, but there was nothing otherworldly about it. She was just glad to have his attention. "I almost didn't come tonight," she told him.

"I did my best to stay away from you. I thought that's what you wanted."

His hand closed over hers again. "I need you with me."

"As personal assistant?" She bit her tongue after the bitter question was out. Damn. She hadn't come here to get into a discussion of their problems. But if he wanted to get into a discussion—

"You feel like a woman with a grim purpose," he said, as the quarter ended.

The Laker Girls came out to gyrate briefly to loud electronic music. Siri sat forward, pretending to pay attention to the cheerleaders while trying to decide how to answer, how to begin. She couldn't come right out and say, 'I know what you're up to, and I'm not letting you get away with it.' He wouldn't listen to her arguments in favor of her species—even though he should.

The players came back on the court for the second quarter, and the music faded from heavy to a dull roar. The sound system was drowned by the crowd noise anyway. Selim leaned forward beside her. He ruffled through her expensively cut short hair. She hated when he messed with it in public, and he knew it. She didn't complain. She certainly didn't object as his hand came to rest on the back of her neck. It was warm there, comforting. She arched against his palm, like a cat. She didn't need to think to react to his touch. She couldn't help but react, she couldn't close her eyes and do anything but react, even if she wanted to.

He whispered, half aloud, half in her mind. "There's something important you want to discuss."

Even though she knew it was the wrong tack to take, she couldn't help but think back, *You don't want to kill people.*

No, I don't.

A jolt of pleasure went through her. Relief. Hope. She knew he hadn't meant to let her hear the thought, but there it was, out in the open. He had something she

could work with. It was called a conscience. She turned
to look at him.

He struck at her hope before she could say anything.
"This isn't about me, Siri."

She ground her teeth in frustration. "I understand
that." She didn't. Not quite. There were lots of things
she didn't understand, even though she'd thought she
knew so much. She had to try once more. "I know *it*
has to happen. But . . ." Blunt words were impossible.
She didn't have time to worry about this being the
wrong place to talk. He was willing to start a riot to
cover his ass—the hunting vampires' asses. She had to
talk him out of it, find alternatives. "Couldn't you make
them take the bad ones?"

Selim scratched his jaw and pretended to look like he
was thinking about it. She could tell by the anger in his
narrowed eyes that he wasn't interested in her opinions,
didn't want to hear them. As far as he was concerned,
they'd had this argument, and he'd already won it. Bastard.

"There's no need for good people to die," she
pleaded.

"Why not? Martha, my love?" His voice was soft,
sarcastic, and cutting. "Good people die all the time."

She bridled for the usual reason. No one called her
Martha, especially Selim. She could hear an echo of
Larry Jager's mocking voice with Selim's use of her
name. Jager had called her Martha a moment before she
ran from him. Was Selim trying to rattle her with the
reminder? If so, she tried not to let it work.

"Do in drug dealers, murderers. No need for innocents to suffer. No need for families to have to mourn,"
she said, mindful of how odd the conversation would
sound if anyone was listening. Then again, maybe not.
What was odd in Los Angeles? Especially here in the
courtside, expensive season ticket seats? They could be
talking over a script idea more easily than discussing the
real events of the future. Which reminded her.

"Who do you want to play you in the movie?"

That got his attention. Every muscle in Selim's body tensed. The terrified energy that shot from him gave her a brief, blistering headache. After a moment, the pain in her head cleared, but the grip he had on her arm was crushing. She squirmed. "Selim!"

He relaxed and carefully stroked her bruised arm while she looked at him anxiously. After a deep breath, he said, "Sorry." He shook his head and offered a lame smile. "It was like somebody walked over my grave."

"Which is somewhere in Egypt, right?" she asked jokingly.

"Somewhere in the Middle East," he agreed. "What do you mean, 'play me in the movie'?" Siri felt the strain of worry beneath his light tone.

"New vampire movie in the works," she answered. "Tentatively titled *If Truth Be Told*. Preproduction press release said that it's about real vampires. Who do you want to play you?"

Selim looked at the court as a player came to the free-throw line. Siri watched Selim rather than the shot. He was pale. Living at night tended to make vampires that way naturally, but a tanning booth helped give a certain healthy glow to his honey gold complexion. Right now he was pale beneath the tan. Siri found this most worrying. His reaction to her mention of a movie was very, very interesting. Siri smiled to herself and eagerly grabbed onto the chance of diverting him from causing a very real riot.

"Well?" she persisted.

His laughed was forced. He looked around and pointed. "How about that scary-looking guy in the sunglasses?"

She peered across the court and spotted a balding man wearing sunglasses. He was on his feet, shouting at the iniquity of Shaq missing an easy layup. "Jack Nicholson?"

Selim looked offended when she made a gagging noise. But it was just an act. He was acting human, making faces, while other senses raced and played inside his head. He was good, but she could feel the difference. No one else who looked at him would see anything odd about the slender man in the seat beside her. He was dying for details and afraid to ask. Siri was not used to Selim fearing anything, hadn't even thought it was possible. This was very interesting and scary.

"What do they mean, 'real'?" he asked after a considerable silence. Then he relaxed a little. Enough to sigh and put his arm around her shoulders. "You're not the only one who does the vision thing, Siri, my love."

Tingling electricity ran up her spine. The Danger Will Robinson warning went off in her head, but her reality didn't shift into events happening elsewhere or when. The vision had already occurred, but to Selim, not her. She wasn't used to that, either. It seemed unfair, somehow, that someone sitting right next to her would have a vision, and she'd be unaffected by it. "Isn't that my job?"

"It's your gift. Mine, too," he added. "Sometimes. You know that."

She'd forgotten. "What did you see?"

He shook his head. "Can't talk about it. Probably not important. Daydreaming while I'm awake."

She didn't think so. "Oh."

She didn't push it. After a few minutes of being held by him, she didn't want to talk at all. It felt good to have him touching her. She wanted to concentrate on the hard-muscled feel of him against her side. She wanted to enjoy being wrapped in his embrace, to go with the pleasure of physical closeness and never mind his plans for the future. Lives were at stake. Souls, too, including her own. She couldn't stand by and let innocents die. So, if he was freaked by the possibility of another schlocky vampire movie getting made, it behooved her to encourage his interest in the project.

"Do you want me to find out more about this film deal? Maybe Joseph can get his hands on a fax of a working script."

"Can he do that?"

She nodded. "He says he gets scripts all the time. Kamaraju's companion works for a big agency, too. Lisa handles a lot of scripts when they go into circulation. Shall I contact them?"

He rubbed his jaw, still pretending only casual interest. "Sure. It might be fun to see what Hollywood means by 'real.' " With his arm still around her, he urged her to her feet. "There's somewhere I have to be," he told her. "Can you give me a ride?"

Like she was going to let him out of her sight if she could help it. She kept her tone as casual as his. "Sure. Your wish is my command and all that."

"Well, I'll be damned," Valentine breathed as she stared at the television screen.

"What?" Yevgeny asked, without taking his attention off the printout in his hands.

"He saw me." She laughed breathlessly. The old, leather-bound book she'd been reading slipped off her lap. It fell to the floor with a heavy thud that startled Valentine. Yevgeny didn't pay it, or her, any mind. She shivered and searched the crowd at the Lakers game for another glimpse of Selim. The camera was more interested in play on the floor right now than panning past the celebrity-filled front seats. A moment before, Selim's face flashed by on the screen just as an impulse told her to look up. Their eyes met, though miles separated them. His expression froze, the big dark eyes set in his long, triangular face widened. Maybe he didn't see her, not the woman sitting on a couch with a book in her lap and a companion curled up beside her. But Selim *saw* something.

"This is not good," she murmured.

Maybe it was the book that brought them together. There was magic in the book, and she didn't mean just written-down spells. Words had their own power. Every writer knew that. Some magicians did, too. Selim's name was in the book. The name of every Enforcer of the Law was in the book. And how they were made.

How all vampires were made, though there was more than the one, traditional way. Very few vampires knew that.

Yevgeny put the script onto the coffee table. "I like the part with the kid. It's intense. Fast." He blinked and rubbed a hand across his face. "Why are you frightened?"

"Frightened? Me?"

He nodded.

She glared at him. "What are you doing here?" she asked. "Why did I let you come back? When did I give you a key to my apartment?"

"Fifteen years ago."

"I should have the locks changed."

"You never let anything change."

She slammed a fist into the softly cushioned back of the couch. He ignored her burst of temper. He bent over and picked up the dropped book instead. He ran his thumbs along the thick, cracked leather of the cover. "What's this?"

"It's a romance novel," she snapped. She reached for it.

He moved it out of her reach.

"Give me that. I was just getting to a good sex scene."

His smirked and tilted his chin toward the bedroom. "If you want a sex scene—" He let the book fall open to the page she'd been reading. He squinted at the squiggled marks made in ancient, faded ink. "What language is this?"

"Linear A." Though that wasn't what they'd called it where she came from.

"Ah." He continued to stare at the page. Yevgeny had a gift for languages. Rather, a Gift. He picked knowledge of a language he'd never seen before out of her head while staring at the words, though she tried to block him. Either she was getting thoroughly senile, or his mind-reading talent had grown lately. Within moments he said, "Interesting."

She didn't know whether to be panicked or amused. "That's forbidden knowledge, you know."

He looked up briefly. "I guessed." He went back to reading.

His finger moved down the page while she leaned back and watched. She really ought to take the book from him, make him forget what he'd read. She should never have unpacked it from the safe where she normally kept it locked. She thought of it as a diary of sorts. Others might call it history or define it as a grimoire if they were into the study of magic. She'd taken it out to do a little research for the script, to refresh her memory a little, only to discover that memory had served. She'd gotten the details of the ritual right to begin with. She had gotten caught up reading, in being reminded of things she had forgotten, many of them best left forgotten. She'd barely noticed when Yevgeny arrived, only frowned at his intrusion when he settled beside her. He was the one who turned on the basketball game she'd been looking forward to, and then he promptly become engrossed in the first official working draft of *If Truth Be Told*. She barely paid any attention to the game until Selim's awareness had called to her. Now, here was her estranged companion absorbing facts no mortal, and very few vampires, were ever supposed to know. Some things she was willing to share with the world. Others—no. No way.

Valentine shook herself out of her wandering thoughts. She held her hands out toward Yevgeny. "Give me that," she said in a tone that wasn't to be denied.

He glared, blue eyes sharp as lasers, but did as he was told. His resentment was an acrid, smoky stench against her vampire senses. No, giving this man secret knowledge was not a good thing. She put the book on the table in front of the couch and concentrated on her angry companion. "You feel like a volcano ready to blow."

He nodded tightly. "Let me go," he begged. "It's time. We both know it."

"I shouldn't have let you come back." She sighed and twined her fingers tightly together in her lap. "It's being with me that makes you so—"

"Hungry!" he snarled. He grabbed her by the shoulders, and she let him shake her like a terrier with a rat. "It's not being with you that makes me burn. It's just as bad living in the exile you forced on me."

"For your own good, my love. You don't want to be like me."

He gave a harsh, pained laugh. He stopped shaking her, but his grip on her shoulders tightened. "You never asked what I wanted. One night I found myself in your bed. I don't belong there anymore."

His bitter heartache scalded her. Valentine felt tears burning in her throat and behind her eyes. How long had it been since she'd cried? "I know. I'm sorry. I tried not to. The loneliness—we have to take companions. If I could live completely alone, I would."

"You've lived alone for the last three years. Made me live alone."

"I—I thought it might help. That if we could exist apart, you'd get better."

"Better?"

"There have been a few times when the spell's broken. When it's worn off," she explained. "A few people have recovered from vampire bites."

His laugh was loud, raucous, and furious. The sound was as harsh as if he'd stirred a flock of angry crows out of the shadows of the room. "After fifty years?"

"It was worth a shot!" she shouted back. Her voice was as piercing as crystal and as cold as arctic ice in contrast to his dark fury.

Ice and crystal didn't pierce him, didn't calm him. "Not to me! I need the change, Valentine. I need the magic to make the change. I need your spell. I *need* to be born, Valentine."

"Someone has to die for you to be born. I don't kill

people anymore. I don't bring killers into the world. You should be thankful that I won't make you into a serial murderer.''

He made the sharp, cutting gesture that was a symbol a companion shouldn't know. ''Break the damn cord and let me go!''

She pushed him away with the slightest touch of a hand against his chest. ''No.'' There was no arguing with her tone. She saw in his eyes that he knew that. He stood, turned away. She let him. ''Get out,'' she added for good measure. Just in case he was in any doubt that this conversation was definitively over.

''It's over,'' he agreed as he went to the door. ''But believe me, Valentine. I'll find a way.''

He'd read the book, she realized after he was gone, and she'd done nothing about it. ''Oh, shit.''

Maybe he would find a way.

Chapter 16

SELIM DIDN'T TELL her where he wanted to go, and Siri didn't ask. She drove away from the Forum and let the connection between them take care of the rest. It felt good, right. Like old times. Except that the car smelled and felt new. *Like an omen of a new beginning?* Siri wondered. Somehow, she doubted it. Selim sat back in the plush leather seat and closed his eyes against the glare of oncoming traffic—or maybe against the glare of the annoyed, frustrated thoughts of people caught in the heavy traffic—and she maneuvered them through the streets and overcrowded freeways.

They were heading west from Inglewood when Selim sat up and looked at her. "You don't have to worry about Moira Chasen anymore. Sterling's keeping her."

It was a peace offering, and they both knew it. Like he was offering her one life so she wouldn't protest the loss of more. "Keep her?" she asked skeptically. "You mean forcing her to become his companion?"

"You don't sound pleased."

"Should I be? Should you?"

"She'll live."

Siri waited until she'd moved the car across three

lanes of thick traffic before she responded to his harassed curiosity. "What about the media?" she asked him sweetly. "Moira lives in the public eye. Aren't you worried about somebody finding out our little secret?"

The silence that greeted her question was thick, shot through with surprise and embarrassment. She suspected he'd forgotten about the pesky little detail of privacy being very hard for a popular actress to come by. Privacy was imperative for their culture's survival. Anticipating details and difficulties was his job. Ensuring the survival of the community was his job. He was usually very, very good at it. Something was distracting him when he should be more on top of things than usual. Siri wasn't vain enough to think that he was being distracted by troubles in their relationship.

"Oh," Selim said at last. "Shit."

"Change of plan?" she asked, unable to shake the treacle-sweet venom from her voice. "Going to have to Hunt the girl after all?"

"No," he answered, adamant as stone. "Sterling's made his choice. He'll have to cope." Selim sighed. "Once upon a time, I had it bad for Maureen O'Hara." Another sigh. A romantic one.

Siri snarled.

"Never laid a fang on the girl," Selim went on. "Followed her a few times. Daydreamed a little. But I decided it was too risky. She was too famous. Movie stars." He shook his head. "One of the risks of living in this town is getting involved with actors. And when actors get famous . . ." His fatalistic shrug drew a soft, shushing sound from the leather upholstery. "We've avoided famous people until now, but I was going to have to let it happen sometime."

"So Moira Chasen gets to be the guinea pig?"

"You would rather she was the main course?"

Siri's stomach turned as a graphic memory of Miriam's Hunt replayed in her mind. "I get the point."

Selim stared out the windshield and kept his worry to himself. He didn't know why he was bothering to hide it from Siri. Maybe he hated letting her think he wasn't completely on top of every situation. Maybe he was trying to hide the sick feeling of his world spiraling out of control from himself. If he was, he wasn't doing a very good job of it. Selim felt alone in a completely dark place. Cut off. Out of touch. At the same time, he *knew* he was being watched. He *felt* himself being manipulated, moved about like a puppet. Yet, it was different. Like an actor taking direction? No, he felt like the part, not the player. Like a role being played? That made no sense. He groped blindly for understanding, tried desperately to make sense of the vision that had stabbed into him like a lightning strike earlier, leaving white noise and shadow images behind.

He was thinking too hard. Selim closed his eyes and tried to empty his mind.

"What about that guy in Burbank?"

He heard Siri's words but made them be only noise. He let the yawning darkness have him. Maybe that was what he needed it to do. He went to the blackness with the hope that it wasn't a threat but a retreat, a haven. In the darkness, he hunted, aware finally that he wasn't alone.

Someone's been riding me, he thought. He whispered, "Holy shit."

"You'd be doing everyone a favor if you got rid of the serial killer that's dumping bodies in Griffith Park."

Watching me. Asking questions. Turning me into a documentary.

"Don't think of it as a public service to humans. Think of it as protecting your hunting territory from another predator."

But who? Why? The how he understood. But it had to be somebody who was very, very good. Very old. He found no trace, no psychic trail of the old vampire who'd been mindraping him.

"And just what did you see in this vision you're currently so freaked about?" Siri demanded.

He heard the concern and dread beneath her annoyed

curiosity. He responded to her voice this time. ''I saw myself in a fight.'' That was all he was going to say. Except to add, ''There were angels in it.''

''Angels?''

Selim opened his eyes. Siri'd pulled off the freeway and was slowly cruising along a side street. Dry, drooping palm trees lined the sidewalks. Beyond them, Selim glimpsed rows of tall, chain-link fencing topped with spiraling razor wire. He could smell the ocean not too far away. ''Pull in here,'' he directed, pointed at the entrance of a parking lot on the left.

They weren't too far off Rose Avenue, meaning they weren't in the worst part of Venice, but certainly not the safest, either. Siri didn't like it. She didn't know why, considering who she was with. ''I've got a bad feeling about this,'' she muttered as she pulled into the empty lot. Empty, that is, except for the long, black stretch limo that was already there.

''That's just Kamaraju's vibe,'' Selim told her as she stopped the car. ''He always smells bad.''

Selim didn't have to tell Siri to stay in the car, and she didn't protest his leaving her, even though Kamaraju emerged from the back of the limo accompanied by his companion and the three other vampires in his household. Kama liked traveling with a posse. Selim was glad to see he hadn't brought any of the two dozen nest slaves with him. Kamaraju was a true parasite, the sort of person who gave vampires a bad name. Kamaraju could protest that he broke no Law with the number of humans he kept in his service, since he had the age and strength to keep tight leashes on all of them. Skirting the Laws without actually breaking them was Kamaraju's way. Easily bored, he did what he wanted, knowing how to duck when trouble threatened.

Selim projected his usual coolly brisk and business-like facade as he approached the vampire in the center of the group. He looked over Kamaraju's companion critically as he approached. Lisa, dressed in a very short, strapless white dress clung devotedly to her vampire lover, her gaze worshipfully on him alone. Typical two-year-old behavior. The girl couldn't get enough of the one who took her blood and gave his blood and magic in return. It was the most sacred, most important relationship of their kind. Kamaraju didn't seem aware the girl was clinging to his arm. If he felt anything toward her at this moment, it was boredom. Selim didn't see how Kamaraju could live with himself. He turned his attention to the trio of young ones to keep from spitting contemptuously in Kamaraju's face.

There were two males and one female in the group—Siri would know them all by name. All were dressed in black, stark and obvious contrast to Lisa's white, all outwardly as bored as the vampire who fostered them. Each of them looked him over with cold, flat eyes as he approached, feigned disinterest doing a poor job of covering their curiosity, hunger, and fear. Selim didn't pretend any disinterest in them; he met each one's gaze until they looked away, each one convinced that the Enforcer was aware of their every thought of transgression. The whole process took maybe five seconds.

"It is good to be king," he murmured and turned his attention back to the fuming Kamaraju. Selim swept a hand to indicate the parking lot. "You people look like we're involved in a drug deal in a John Woo movie." There he went again. Why did he keep comparing real life to a movie?

Kamaraju ignored his comment. He pushed Lisa aside and strode forward, putting himself nose to nose with Selim. "Pervert!" The Hunting urge burned through his normally finely honed sense of self-preservation. "Murderer!"

"Your point?" Selim asked calmly.

"I know all about how you murdered Jager. He was my child."

"Which makes you a piss-poor father."

"I loved Jager."

"Briefly."

"It's not the time we have with our companions that

matters with our kind, Hunter, it's the intensity of the moment.''

Selim laughed. He didn't look at Kamaraju as he answered. Selim looked over the other vampire's black-clad shoulder, addressing the girl in white. ''Time seems to get shorter and shorter for you with every companion, Kama. Stop taking slaves and start a harem.''

Lisa was shocked and frightened by this advice. Her pain lashed at Selim; her silent plea for reassurance was ignored by Kamaraju, who was looking thoughtful. It wasn't as if he hadn't heard the suggestion before; it was an acceptable treatment for the ennui vampires frequently suffered. Lisa was a modern American girl who wasn't as decadent as she thought. She was shocked at the notion of polygamy, but also totally unaware of the type of divorce Kamaraju practiced.

Selim could only hope that she would think about the chances for her survival after she overheard this conversation. Maybe she didn't know she was destined to turn into a vampire herself one day; awareness of the change came slowly, comprehension even slower, and it all needed to be savored. It took years of preparation. He knew too well the madness that came with being born too soon. He never wanted to see another creature put through the hell he'd barely survived.

''That Jager lived ten years amazes me. He might have made it if you'd bothered to find him a good home. If anyone would have taken in a fledgling made after only a few years in your bed.''

''He wanted the freedom to fly. It was his right. Not all of us need the Council and Laws.''

''Making him my rightful prey even before he tried to kill my companion. Never mind all the other crap he learned from you.''

''He learned to indulge his appetites. All my children do.''

The young vampires had disappeared into the darkness of the parking lot, showing that Kamaraju had helped them master at least some of the basic tricks of

the trade. Selim could still feel the trace of their heartbeats, but faintly, with his blood hunger more than with
his psychic senses. Their hearts called to his, but the
Law kept them safe for now.

Kamaraju had enough control to back off, to fight his
anger and urge to attack, but Selim read Karmaraju's
longing to do some damage, to prove his dominance
over the city's Enforcer. Vampires frequently battled
each other, though not in Selim's town. Selim caught a
quickly fading but explicit and vivid image from Kamaraju's mind.

He was a step closer to the other vampire before he
could stop himself, claws out and hands raised. He spat
in Kamaraju's face. "You call me a pervert?"

"I don't eat my own kind."

"I don't fuck mine."

Kamaraju smiled. "There are times when it is allowed, Hunter. You said I should start a harem." He
gave a slight shrug and tried to make it sound like a
joke. His eyes were dead flat and serious as he added,
"I know you'd never volunteer, but—"

"No challenges," Selim said coldly. "You wouldn't
even think of it if the Hunger wasn't getting to you."

"I'm sure you're right." Kamaraju mouthed the
words. "It's just hormones talking. That time of the decade." He took a step backward. Lisa came to him, and
he put his arm around her waist. His three fosterlings
came out of the shadows. "What did you want to see
me about, Hunter?"

Selim took great pleasure in informing Kamaraju just
who and where his nest was going to Hunt. Kamaraju's
temper boiled while he listened. Selim looked forward
to the coming protest. The fledglings stirred restlessly
but limited their objections to tense muscles and dirty
looks. They kept most of their attention on Kamaraju,
waiting to see how he'd respond. Selim waited as well,
hoping the nest leader would react badly. But before
Kamaraju could even manage to start swearing at him,

they were caught by the headlights of another car as it turned into the parking lot.

Cars had been going by on the street during the conversation, but this was first one that had penetrated the psychic warning barrier that kept the space free of everyone but vampire kind. The fledglings disappeared once more; Lisa retreated to the backseat of the limo. Siri opened the tinted driver's-side window of her Mercedes to get a better view. Selim could feel her fingers hovering tensely over the ignition of the new car, ready to bring the engine to life if Selim signaled her to leave. Selim turned, arms crossed on his chest, to face the intruder's blazing headlights. Kamaraju stepped up beside him, showing uncommon solidarity. Selim figured he was trying to impress the young vampires in his nest.

"Why am I not surprised?" Selim said when the newcomer cut the lights and the engine and stepped out of the car. "Did I invite you to this party?" he added as Geoff Sterling approached him.

Sterling shrugged sheepishly. "Couldn't stop myself." He didn't look particularly happy about being here. He was wearing a tuxedo jacket over a tab-collared shirt. He was gestured back toward his car. "I was driving Moira to Crazy Girls for a drink. She's never been there, so after this premiere we were at—"

"Cut to the chase," Selim suggested.

"Moira?" Kamaraju asked. His gaze shifted from the young intruder to Sterling's car. "Tasty." Selim could feel her there as well, bright, curious, virginal. What was the boy thinking to bring an unbitten human to a meeting of vampires? What was *he* doing here?

Selim took Sterling by the arm and led him to stand next to the Mercedes. "Got a bad feeling, did you?"

Sterling nodded. "From you. I felt this compulsion— Don't you just hate when that happens?" He looked unhappy. "We're connected."

Selim didn't feel it. Unless, of course, some of his fashion sense had rubbed off on the strig. Sterling looked very different since he'd recovered from his leather and torn lace phase. "Three days ago, you hated and feared me. I miss that."

"Me, too. I'd rather concentrate on Moira, but I've also got this need to—" He shook his head. Sterling looked across the lot at the scowling vampire standing by the limo. "Who's the asshole? Jager's ex?"

It occurred to Selim that this kid from Seattle who'd lived as a loner since he came to L.A. could use a briefing on the town's players if he planned to become one himself. "My companion knows all and sees all," he told Sterling. "Have a long talk with her." He glanced at Sterling's car; it was something in a low-slung speed machine. Ferrari, maybe? "New wheels?"

Shrug, followed by a wry smile and a wistful look toward the passenger of the sports car. "I'm trying to impress a girl."

"Courtship rituals elude me. Speaking of eluding," Selim went on. "Did it occur to you that paparazzi might tail you to this—private—meeting? Please tell me you've got that covered." Selim could feel Kamaraju sneaking around his shielding, attempting to listen in on the conversation. The other vampire's curiosity had a very unpleasant feel to it; nothing new in that. Selim ignored Kamaraju while he waited for Sterling's answer.

"It's covered," Sterling assured him. He wiggled his fingers and rolled his eyes. He grinned. "People will ignore you if you just know how to ask properly. Telepathy has its uses. I got used to telling the media to go away when I was stalking her. She'll have privacy with me," he added, with a loving glance toward the woman in his car.

Selim was happy to hear that the young vampire was already well aware of security precautions. He still wished Sterling hadn't brought his—fiancée for lack of a better term—with him tonight. Selim decided that it wouldn't serve any purpose to give Kamaraju a chance to complain about homeless hunting along the concrete river or question what a human was doing here. Selim opened the passenger door of the Mercedes with one hand, pointed Sterling toward the sports car with the other. "You don't have to come running every time you feel something from me."

"But—"

"I'll call you."

"What if you need my help?"

"I'll call you," Selim repeated, slowly and distinctly. Sterling returned to his car, and Selim settled into the seat beside Siri. Her curiosity filled his senses. "Drive," he told her.

"Fine."

He silently put up with her annoyance until they were well on their way to Pasadena. Finally, he asked her, "What's Crazy Girls?"

She spared him a brief glance. "It's a strip club. Why?"

He threw his head back against the thickly padded seat and laughed. "Thank goodness. The boy isn't turning into Eddie Haskell on me after all."

"Who?"

"You're too young. Never mind."

"Fine." Siri had many, many questions, but she could tell that Selim wasn't going to answer any of them. "I don't know why I put up with you."

"Chemistry," he answered. Then he sighed and got serious. "Sometimes," he told her. "I wish—"

He was thinking about Kamaraju and Lisa and about Geoff and Moira. She didn't catch the images, but she knew that's what was bothering him all of a sudden, coloring his feelings toward her. "We aren't like either couple," Siri pointed out.

"Maybe I should have courted you first," he said, looking out the windshield instead of at her. "Maybe I should let you go."

"Maybe you should shut up," she answered. "Maybe you should stop worrying," she added as his pain pricked her. "We are. Why worry about past or future?"

He still didn't look at her. She felt his reluctance to

talk. She'd been feeling this reluctance for over a year. She was surprised when he fought his way past it. "Maybe I should tell you—"

"Why you haven't made love to me for over a year?" Maybe she should wait for him to go on, but she asked, "Is it because you don't want me to change into a bloodsucking fiend? Because—"

"I'm a selfish bastard," he cut in. "Who doesn't want to live without you."

It was Siri's turn to stare silently out the windshield for a while. "What we're doing now isn't living," she managed after a while.

"I knew you'd say that. Drop me off at my place," he added, "Don't ask to come in."

"Bastard."

"Yes."

"Fine." The miles passed, but she heard not another word or thought from him. "This place has been turned into a senior's residence, you know," she pointed out when he got out of the car in front of his building. "Someone's going to notice that you don't look like you belong here sometime. You could move in with me." It was an old discussion, one he didn't bother to respond to. He just waved her away and went inside.

Siri drove home too fast in the light, late-night traffic of Pasadena. She didn't know if there had been any progress between them tonight. On any front. She concluded that she should get some rest, then maybe she could think. She wanted to sleep but dreaded once again retiring to an empty bed. Checking her voice mail helped put the moment off a few minutes more. There was only one message.

"Girlfriend, I need a big, big, huge favor. You're his godmother, an aunt, really. And the only one I can trust," Cassie's voice told her. "It's about Sebastian's birthday party. Yes, I said party. Don't tell Tom this, but—"

Cassie went on. And on. Siri listened. Then replayed the message. "I don't believe this," she said. She believed it, all right. She just didn't want to think about it. Siri decided that going to bed, even alone, and getting some sleep was the only sensible way of dealing with vampire dramas, domestic and otherwise. "My next boyfriend will not have fangs," she muttered as she settled her head on the pillows. "And neither will his relatives."

Chapter 17

THE BACKGROUND MUSIC on the shop's sound system was fashionably retro. Dire Straits' *Portobello Belle*. From the early eighties, she thought, maybe the late seventies. Siri wasn't quite sure which decade was currently being regurgitated as style. The stores in Pasadena's Old Town were a nice mix of traditional and trendy, so maybe the owner of this high-end toy store wasn't trying to prove a point. It was possible that she just liked Mark Knopfler's insidiously insistent singing style. Siri did know that she found the music far more soothing than seeing the prices of the items she picked up.

What did one get for a five-year-old who had everything, anyway? She wondered. Including fangs. Now, that wasn't fair. Joking about Sebastian was one thing. She and Selim always did. But the truth was, Cassie and Tomas's son showed no outward signs of being anything other than a normal, precocious, telepathic, overprotected, spoiled little rich boy. He didn't exactly live in a normal environment, what with both of his parents being vampires, but they loved him and did the best they could to provide a stable, caring home life. At least Cassie did. Tom provided protection from the other vampires.

Those few vampires who knew about Sebastian's existence would be happy to see the child dead. There was a fear—irrational, Selim assured her—that someday Sebastian Avella would destroy vampire kind. Or become king of vampires. Or replace Istvan as the most feared Hunter of them all. There were several conflicting prophecies. Siri had no opinion on Sebastian's future and no visions of it, either. She did know that Cassandra worked very hard on keeping Sebastian human. Sometimes Cassandra called on her to help.

Right now, she didn't want to. Siri had had only four hours of sleep and had plenty of other concerns to do with Hunting vampires. She was shopping when she was supposed to meet Joe at his office because Cassie's long voice mail message had been the plea of a woman trying hard not to lose her mind and take her baby with her. Cassie was feeling the heat of growing Hunger. She wanted to keep Sebastian out of it, to distract him, protect him, keep him human. How could Siri turn away from the needs of a child? How could she deny her best friend, even though her best friend was now someone she hardly ever saw? Cassie was a different person now, something *other*. Okay, by Selim's definition, Cassie was a member of a different species, but she was still Siri's best friend.

"Damn it," she muttered and released her death grip on the stuffed tiger she found she was holding. What to get a kid for his birthday? She thought again. She put the stuffed animal back on the shelf. Maybe he'd like a real tiger. Maybe the young *dhamphir* and the dangerous hunting cat would hit it off, have a lot in common. *Speaking of dangerous cats . . .* she thought, and looked toward the door. Yevgeny stood there. Big, blond, unshaven. He didn't look like he'd slept in weeks. He looked more like a hungry wolf, actually, than a tiger. Or like a hungry vampire. That was the energy he projected, even without the physical changes that came with the hunting mode.

His broad shoulders blocked the doorway, his very

presence blocked the morning light that poured in
through the plate glass window. Siri looked around for
another exit. She did not want to be here with him.
"You don't look so pretty in the daylight," she told
him, putting on a brave front as he stalked up to her.

"That's because I don't belong in the daylight."

"And you need a shower," she added as his big hand
closed over her arm.

"Let's go," he said and drew her toward the door.

Siri looked frantically around the busy toy store, but
went with him without protest. The man felt even more
on the edge of violence than he looked. She didn't dare
put anyone but herself at risk by calling for help. She
sighed and dug her sunglasses out of her purse as they
stepped out onto the sidewalk.

The morning was bright and hot, the desert sun fierce
this close to noon, and she was more used to the cool
California nights. She glanced at the sky, her gaze following Yevgeny's. There were no clouds in the blueness
overhead, but plenty of straight white jet exhaust plumes
crossed the sky above barely visible tendrils of smog.
He stood very still for a few moments, while people
passed around them on the sidewalk.

Despite having a death grip on her, Siri didn't think
he was aware of her. "You're saying good-bye to the
light, aren't you?" she guessed.

He brought his intense attention back to her. Looking
into his wild, blue eyes, Siri wished she'd kept her
mouth shut. "I won't miss this," he told her.

"California?" she mocked sweetly. "You're leaving
town? Came to say farewell?" She tried to pull away.
"I'm touched. Have a nice trip."

"Shut up."

There was a small park at the end of the block, with
hibiscus bushes and shade trees and flowerbeds set in a
brick walkway. A tiled fountain bubbled in the middle
of this mini-plaza, and there were benches set under the
trees. Siri was relieved when Yevgeny took her to the
park. The people already there, a woman with a baby in

a stroller, a couple romantically holding hands by the fountain, walked away from the park when Yevgeny pulled her down beside him on one of the benches. Siri was glad of the privacy. Also slightly reassured that they were, technically, in public. The more she was with this companion, the less she liked being with him.

"You're nuts, aren't you?" she said when they had the peaceful area to themselves. She looked him over critically, with her psychic as well as her ordinary senses. "Flat-out crazy."

He nodded. "Yes. Quite mad. I admit it." He released his hold on her, at least the physical one. She knew she couldn't get up and walk away if she tried. "I am trying to get better."

"Define 'better.' " she urged. Then, "You know, I thought you must have something to do with Jager, but now I see that's impossible."

"I'm too old," he agreed. "Too good to have belonged to a putz like Larry Jager." He smiled, and there was something slightly sane in his expression for the moment. "I'd be offended that you thought I was involved with Jager—if I hadn't planted the suggestion in your head to begin with."

"Planted—"

"My lady is a strig," he went on over her stunned protest that anyone could control her thoughts. "If such a crude term can be used for what she is." Love pulsed through him as he spoke of his vampire. Hate as well, and frustration that fed the madness, but the love was the strongest. "She's special. Unique. You couldn't begin to comprehend her. But she's wrong about me. I hate it that she's wrong. I hate having to defy her. I would do this differently if I could. I swear to you that I would."

Siri's fear escalated as Yevgeny spoke. Noon sunlight or not, the plaza darkened around them. The hot air turned icy cold. The cold darkness belonged to Yevgeny. It was where he lived. She felt his struggle to get out, knew that it was the source of his madness. His pain was strong enough to cover the world. Siri almost felt sorry for him.

She had trouble breathing in the darkness but stubbornly struggled to find her voice. "Do what?"

He took her face between his big hands. The touch was gentle, warm, alien. She wasn't used to being touched so intimately by anyone but Selim. She hated it when the force of his will made her lift her gaze to look into his eyes.

"You're very good, Siri," he told her. His voice was gentle, insistent, impossible not to listen to. "But you will obey my will."

I belong to Selim. She couldn't speak the words aloud, but she knew he heard them because of his soft, mocking laugh.

"Your devotion isn't that strong," he told her. "Not after what he's been doing to you lately." He laughed again, but there was sympathy in it this time. She felt him inside her head, learning things, reading her. "It's like I'm reading your diary," he said. "Isn't it, little girl?" That was exactly how it felt. "The secrets you keep inside you aren't any different than mine. Your beloved is putting you through the same things my lady's done to me. They do it for our own good when they should let the choice be ours."

Yes, Siri heard herself think, though she fought off the spark of rebellion a moment later. Was the rebellion hers? Was it absorbed from Yevgeny? She prayed for help, for—

"Selim's sleeping. Do you know what's happening while he sleeps? She's riding him, walking with him while he dreams. Your beloved is with another woman right now. My woman, to be precise. She's so good that he'll never know she's mindraping him, taking his life and turning it into her fiction."

What do you mean? The "real" story? The script?

"Precisely. She's with Selim for the sake of her art. She needs to get out and live, but she won't listen to me when I tell her that's what will help her storytelling. She won't live. And she won't let me have the life I need. But the story she's stealing from you and Selim will change all that. It'll change everything. She has a hunting instinct she doesn't even recognize anymore. She's hunting vampires with words. Naming names and times of death." He laughed again, bitterly.

Somewhere from a great distance yet only a few feet above in the tree over their heads, Siri heard the soft call of a dove. She used the sound as a beacon and tried to catch onto even more reality, but Yevgeny caught her consciousness too quickly, forced her to focus completely on him. "This is a taste of mindrape, darling," he whispered. "But don't worry, you won't remember any of this. I promise you that Selim won't suspect a thing. You haven't suspected she's been with him, now, have you?"

No. No, she hadn't. *If I'd known someone was hurting him—*

"Such delicious anger! But what could you have done, a child companion like you? I couldn't stop her. Couldn't even bring myself to talk to her about it."

Siri felt sorry for Yevgeny, while at the same time hating his guts.

"She doesn't think I should be jealous of her being with Selim for some reason, just because he doesn't know," he went on. "She's as mad as I've come to be. She couldn't get to you, though. Couldn't read your mind, waking or sleeping. But you had your part to play in this story of hers. She wanted to know you. For character development. So she sent me to find you." His awful, sad, mad laugh tore through Siri's mind again. But there was triumph in his personal darkness now, as well. "It was through you that I found out about the little boy." He paused. She felt him savoring her shock and fear. "She put a vision of what's going to happen to him in her story."

What? What's going to happen to Sebastian? What future did she see?

"It's very sad."

The name *Istvan* floated up out of her own store of visions, past the barriers set on her by Yevgeny. *Istvan wanted Sebastian. Cassie and Don Tomas would die trying to stop him. And Selim—There were angels in it.*

Siri didn't see anymore.

She couldn't feel her tears. She couldn't feel his thumbs wiping them off her face, but Siri knew that's what was happening. The very sound of his gloating voice was obscene, but she couldn't stop it. "And the magic is going to be real. She won't need a special effects team, because it's going to be real. Except it isn't going to happen the way she envisions it. I hate to disappoint her, but she's going to have to write a new ending."

Hope shot up through Siri's pain. *You're going to help Sebastian?*

He sighed. "I'd like to. I really would. I hate the thought of a child having to die, but I'm afraid it can't be helped. I read her secret book, you see. I know there's another way. It told me what I have to do to be born. There's a spell, one that needs the blood of a *dhamphir.* I don't think Istvan would voluntarily give anyone a transfusion, do you? Or his heart? Better to receive than to give is his creed." Siri almost laughed at this lame joke, except that her soul completely froze a moment later as Yevgeny said, "I'm going to have to use young Sebastian in the ritual, and you're going to help me."

"What do you mean there isn't any more of this?" The little office reverberated with her angry words. Siri waved the paper in her hand at Joseph.

He'd just returned from throwing up in the faculty's shared bathroom. His office was on the third floor of a quiet older building on the UCLA campus, surrounded by blooming jacaranda trees. The bare hardwood floor sagged a little. The walls of the small office were decorated with framed posters from *Casablanca* and *Duck Soup.* There was a framed photo of Joe with Jerry Bruckheimer on the wall as well. Siri knew the picture had been taken at some seminar both Joseph and the producer spoke at, but it looked impressive.

"How does it end? Where's the rest of it?"

"I told you the fax machine broke down! What to you want me to do?" he shouted back. "I've left a voice mail with my contact at Arc Light. All I can do is wait for her to get back to me."

"How long will that be?"

"I don't know!" He thought for a moment. "Wait— I could call Lisa. The casting director at Arc Light would have—"

"Not Lisa!" A red light was going off in Siri's senses as she remembered the hostility between Kamaraju and Selim the night before. Siri shook her head. "No. Don't bring it to her attention." Joe had received a one-page outline that didn't go into much detail, and a partial of the script of *If Truth Be Told* that gave far too much. The truth, indeed. Damning truth. They were screwed. "How many people have seen this?" she asked. "How many are going to?"

"How would I know?"

"You're in the business!"

"I'm not a player. I'm a teacher."

Joe's frantic worry hit hard against Siri's bruised psychic senses. For a moment the office disappeared, the crisis disappeared. For a moment she was somehow in the dark at midday with the sound of a dove cooing over her head. Her stomach knotted in terror that had nothing to do with this moment; then she was back in real time, with Joseph holding her by the shoulders and looking at her strangely.

"Vision?" he asked.

Siri blinked. "I guess." The nausea faded. "I don't usually want to throw up from visions, though." She sat on the edge of Joe's desk and fanned herself with the paper. She shivered.

"You don't have time for visions right now," Joseph complained. "You have to do something."

"Me?" She felt her temper escalating again. At least

it helped focus her on the vampire community's very real problem. "Me?" she asked again. "What about you? You're the one who's involved with the film industry. Did one of your students write this script?"

"How? Read my mind?"

"You or I could do it."

Joe laughed. He pointed angrily at the paper she clutched. Paper she wasn't going to let out of her hands. "Not in that much detail. Real detail. Would I have told anybody any of that shit? Besides, it's not *my* name that's mentioned in that scene."

Siri took another look at the wrinkled pages. She didn't want to look at the words. Only a faint hope that it wasn't as bad as she remembered let her get into the experience a second time. False hope, as it, unsurprisingly, turned out.

SIRI:
You called me here! You were waiting for me!

SELIM:
No, you weren't bait. What the hell are you doing here? Never mind.
(Siri reaches out, but Selim is not there.)
Angle
Jager moves along Sunset. People in crowd react to the sight of fangs and claws as he moves between streetlights and shadows. He is intent on hunting Siri.

JAGER:
Where are you, owl bait?
Angle
Selim steps from shadows behind Jager.

SELIM (Sardonic whisper):
Owl bait?
Selim taps Jager on shoulder with hilt of silver dagger.

SELIM:
Yo, Hannibal Lechter. Your turn to run, little boy.

It went on for several more pages, ending just as Selim stuffed Jager's body in the trunk of her car. While she hadn't witnessed Larry Jager's demise, she was certain every detail was absolutely correct, that it had happened just as the spare words of the script laid it out. She didn't know how this could have happened. She didn't know what to do about it.

She looked unhappily at Joseph. "I wish to God I'd never started this.".

His confusion was a palpable throb against her senses. "You admitting to writing that—heresy?"

"Break the First Law? Are you crazy? Of course I didn't write it! I mean I wish I hadn't told Selim about this script just because I thought it might distract him. I didn't dream it would really be about our community. I just thought—"

"Doesn't matter what you thought. Reality matters. What the Strigoi Council does about it matters."

Siri held up a warning hand. "Never mind the Council. It's Selim we have to worry about."

"Selim's going to be in trouble over this. What if the script mentions Miriam? How can I protect her?"

"You can't, companion."

"We're all dead." Joe paled. "We're not supposed to be in movies!"

"We aren't," she pointed out. "Not yet. This film hasn't been made yet."

"But it's been green lighted. It's going to get made."

"What does that mean?"

"Nobody Buffalo sixty-sixes an Arc Light production."

Siri grabbed Joe by the front of his shirt and shook him like a terrier. "Speak English! What the hell are you talking about?"

"Power," he responded, with a calm succinctness that was terrifying. "Money. Influence. Clout. Knowing where the bodies are buried,'' Joe added with a twisted grin. She let him go and stepped back as he went on. ''Most importantly, the people at Arc Light have a moneymaking track record with the studios. They get what they want.''

''Money talks.'' Siri breathed a despondent sigh. Joe nodded. She wanted to pound her head against the wall. She wanted to pack up all her belongings, stuff Selim's unconscious body in the trunk of her car, and get the hell out of town. Possibly off the planet. Everything was bleak and hopeless and confused—and there was something inside her she couldn't reach that was very, very important. It hurt to even try to think about it. She gave a hollow, aching laugh. ''Yesterday I was only worried about all of East L.A. going up in flames. Now I have to deal with the whole town exploding.'' Her temples throbbed with the mother of all headaches. ''What the hell am I going to do?''

Joe put a hand on her shoulder. ''You're not going to do anything, companion.''

He was right. She was going to have to take this to Selim. It was for him to deal with. Officially. Oh, God.

Siri swallowed hard and looked out the window at the late-afternoon light outside. It wasn't that long until sunset. She just didn't know whether to welcome or dread the coming of night.

Chapter 18

"You seem to be taking this remarkably calmly."

"Do I?"

Selim stood in the center of his living room and looked at the smashed chaos around him. He didn't quite remember the last several minutes, but the evidence of how he'd spent the time was abundantly clear. He tried to smile at Siri. She was wide-eyed with terror, her back pressed into the corner farthest away from where he stood. He would like to tell her that it was the sound of her voice, calmly sarcastic with an underpinning of terror, that brought him back from the edge of madness. He would like to reassure her.

He said, "We're dead."

This wasn't what she expected to hear. "Selim!"

He picked up a sheet of paper that had come to rest on some ripped-out stuffing from the couch. The broken glass of a framed picture crunched under his shoe soles as he approached his companion. Selim waved the paper under her nose. "How do I fight this? How do I save the world from the truth?"

Siri's hands balled into fists. "Think of something!" she spat the words at him.

The last thing she'd expected from Selim was this fit of temper. It had been impressive to watch as he first read the script pages, then tossed them in the air and set about ripping, rending, and tearing apart everything he could get his hands on. Hands, not claws or fangs. That he reacted with a human fit of temper surprised her, and the sickening waves of hopeless futility that mixed with his fury sickened her. She felt small, fragile, and afraid, witnessing the swift destruction of so many old, treasured possessions, but somehow *she* actually felt better when he was finished.

"You've been needing to redecorate, anyway," she said as he continued to stare at her from inches away.

Selim's mouth opened and closed several times, like a landed fish.

Selim let the page fall to the floor between them. It landed on the torn sepia-tinted photograph of an old girl-friend. A really old girlfriend. They'd met in 1880. Maybe he tried to remember the past too much.

"Sometimes I think you have more souvenirs and relics than the old lady in *Titanic*," Siri said, picking up his thought.

"Don't," he told her grimly, "talk to me about movies."

Siri couldn't bear to look into the cold fire in his eyes. She was looking at the floor when she spoke again. "What are you going to do about *If Truth Be Told*? You have to do something!" she added loudly, after he was silent for a long time.

He put his hands on her shoulders and drew her away from her safe corner. "I know." He sounded remarkably reassuring for a person who was utterly clueless. "I'll think of something."

"What?"

Selim was momentarily blinded by an image of himself—only taller—all right, himself as played by, say, Keanu, struggling back and forth across an underlit billboard catwalk with an absurdly muscular, tattooed, and pierced Larry Jager. He couldn't help but laugh at the absurdity of it all. Other images played through his mind, and he just kept on laughing. Better to laugh than cry over a mindrape he couldn't and didn't want to remember. He'd already had his tantrum over that.

When he stopped laughing, he was sitting atop a layer of debris on the living room floor. Siri was seated in front of him, legs crossed, her expression a cross between worry and exasperation. "Sorry," he told her. "It's just—" He chuckled. "I rented *Blade* once. It was the funniest movie I ever saw."

"It wasn't a comedy."

"You aren't a vampire." He chuckled. "You remember the opening scene? Where the hero kills off more movie vampires than there are real ones on the whole West Coast in the first five minutes? With garlic? And silver bullets? Vampires aren't allergic to silver, that's werewolves."

"I don't believe this. You said not to talk to you about movies."

"I did, didn't I? Guess there's no escaping pop culture."

"Vampires don't go to vampire movies."

"Who told you that?"

"You did."

"I lied. We don't sleep in coffins, either. Actually, some do, but that's just youthful pretension."

She crossed her arms. He thought it was to keep from throwing something at him. "You frequently lie to me." He watched her force the urge to sling recriminations aside. Her tone was bracing and abrasive. "Stop talking so much, Selim. Verbal hysteria isn't going to save our asses. Let's deal with one problem at a time, shall we?"

"I love you." They looked at each other for a few moments. He was ebullient, feeling light as a feather. Happy to have let himself say those words, even if he was babbling about everything else. He supposed this mood, this *love* they shared while they gazed into each other's eyes, was also mostly hysteria, born of crisis. So what? It was still the truth. "Because I love you," Selim went on, and a laugh bubbled out of him again, "I am going to tell you a true thing." It was not a big thing. Not the names of the members of the Council or the way to destroy a six-hundred-year-old vampire or how even a mortal could easily kill a fledgling or that wooden stakes through the heart hurt like hell. It was simply, "Enforcers love vampire movies. Always have."

"You're kidding."

Selim shook his head. "It's just that we always identify with the Van Helsing character." He picked up and read one of the script pages again. "But those movies aren't real. They have nothing to do with our banal, middle-class existence." A flash of hope from Siri speared through him. It felt pleasant, but he rejected it in an instant. "This is real."

"But—it'll just be another movie. It won't seem any more real than any other horror film to the people in the theaters. Will it?"

"Won't it? What if somebody is outing us, Siri? Using the media to break open thousands of years of silence? A vampire is deliberately breaking the first and most important Law of our kind and using the entertainment industry to do it. This script is probably only the first blow."

"A vampire?"

"Has to be. A strig? Or maybe a very, very powerful human psychic. I'd prefer if it was human."

"Why would a vampire break the First Law? Even strigs aren't that suicidal, are they?"

"I don't know. Every vampire knows that human awareness of our existence will end in our extinction. Every time its happened in the past—" A stab of fear went through him, though the memories that played in his mind were not his own. His kind had their own mental film archive, he supposed, passing warning images on to the fledglings. "Humans don't allow any predators to be equal to them on the food chain. Lions and tigers and bears haven't fared very well, have they, against those damn, smart apes? A creature that feeds on those apes doesn't stand a chance if they find out about it. Us," he amended. "Or it could be a power play of some kind. The Council won't stand for it, of course. No mortal will know of our existence. Everyone who has come into contact with this script will die to cover our existence, and that includes all of us characters in this little drama."

She nodded miserably. "That's what I thought would happen. But there has to be a way out. We have to think of something. Maybe something else is going on, and all we have to do is . . ." Her gaze was on him, but she sighed as her sight went inward, and outward, leaving the room and him behind.

Selim waited a few moments before quietly asking, "What do you see?"

"I'm not seeing anything."

He scuttled across the floor to put his arms around her. She was stiff in his embrace as he drew her onto his lap. Selim tapped Siri's temple with his forefinger. "There's something going on there."

"Hearing something," she mumbled.

He softly kissed the spot he'd touched. "What do you hear, sweetheart?" His voice was an insistent, compelling whisper.

"Music." Confusion radiated from her. And faint indignation that brought an affectionate smile to Selim's lips.

"What kind of music?"

"An oldies radio station?"

He didn't blame her for being indignant. This was hardly the time for her psychic talent to switch into some kind of radio receiver. He couldn't bring her out of her vision state, no matter how trivial the experience, no matter how much time it took away from their life-and-death crisis. All he could do was be patient and help her through it. "What song's playing on the radio, Siri?" he coaxed gently.

"Jefferson Starship—no, Airplane."

Meant nothing to him, but there was a sixties sound

to the band's name. He'd bypassed that era and gone from Tommy Dorsey to Ziggy Stardust and the Spiders from Mars in his musical tastes. "Oh?" he said, more to make reassuring noise than anything else.

"Something else before that. Something about sultans." Now, here was something interesting, but before he could make delicate inquiries, Siri stiffened and pushed away from him. "It's gone now. And I have a headache," she added as he helped her to her feet.

She didn't normally suffer side effects from the gift any more than she normally heard rather than saw. He didn't like her reactions, but he didn't have time to explore them. "Stress?" he suggested.

"Sure." She shrugged. "Why not? Plenty to be stressed over." She turned a bleak gaze on him once more, breaking his heart. "Selim, what are we going to do about *If Truth Be Told*?"

"I'll think of something," he promised, just to be saying something. He had no ideas. He noticed the photo on the floor once more. It reminded him that there was somewhere he had to be, an appointment to keep. Business as usual. Might as well pretend everything was normal for the moment. He took Siri's hand. "Give me a ride, please? I have to see Alice."

Siri would wait in the car when he went anywhere else, but never on the rare occasions when she drove him to this large colonial-style house on a quiet, well-groomed street in Burbank. She claimed that the neighborhood made her nervous. Truth was, she was jealous. Although tonight she made a point of reminding Selim that a human murderer could well be lurking in the bushes.

"Not around this house," he answered.

"Yeah, maybe," she grudgingly agreed, but she came in with him anyway.

He shouldn't have brought her with him in the first place, but it was good to have her company, even though they hadn't spoken much during the drive. Rene looked delighted to see them when he opened the door. Kind and courteous, this particular one of Alice's several companions was a world-famous French chef. He invited Siri into his kitchen after telling Selim that Madam was waiting for him upstairs. There was no irony in Rene's use of the word. Selim noticed Siri's faint, nasty smile behind Rene's back, though he knew she would never actually make a rude comment about Alice Fraser. "Alice," he had once told his companion, "was a successful madam when I met her. Why should she change a profession she's good at just because she became a vampire?" Siri had just sniffed disdainfully. He didn't think it was at Alice's business, but because he was responsible for the madam becoming a vampire.

Alice opened her office door before he could knock. She gave him a quick hug as she drew him inside. The office was decorated in dark wood and antiques, yet the computer on the rolltop desk didn't look out of place. The room smelled of roses and fresh coffee. Selim took a seat in a wing chair. The fragrant roses, a mix of red and yellow blossoms, were in a cut-crystal vase on a small table beside his chair.

"There's darkness downstairs," Alice greeted him. She poured coffee from a tall carafe on a sideboard and handed a cup to him. "Somebody's in great pain. Siri, I think." He nodded but didn't try to explain. She went on, "Rene's doing something with a dessert. Maybe *crème brûlée* will help cheer her up. You don't look very good yourself, darling." She took a seat on the footstool in front of his chair and looked up at him through her long eyelashes. Her voice was rich and husky. "Tell me all about it."

There was always something persuasive about Alice, in her tone, her manner. It was the vibe she naturally put off, gentle, caring, comforting, and insistent, even when she wasn't trying.

"Actually," she said before he could tell her anything, "it's going to take more than a *crème brûlée* to cheer me up." She drained the hot coffee and set the cup on the floor. "I hate feeling like this, Selim."

"It'll be over soon. That's what we need to discuss." He reached out and touched her cheek. "You're the calmest vampire in town," he told her. "I appreciate that."

He wanted very much to tell her about his recent encounter with Kamaraju, to explain that even Don Tomas was edgy and reckless. He wanted to tell her a lot of things, but one simply didn't. Couldn't. The nests already knew more about each other than they should, communicated with each other more than the Council liked. It was hard enough to keep secrets in their very psychic little world. He also blamed himself for letting Siri establish so many friendships, no matter how useful he found the information she brought him. Even a week ago, all the community's communications links had seemed harmless, very modern. Now he thought that the Council was right, vampires *belonged* firmly entrenched in the fourteenth century. They should keep their mouths shut and their nests secret from each other if they wanted to survive.

Alice brought him out of his reverie as she held out a hand that shook faintly. "If this is calm—" She touched her canines. "Fangs are so unattractive, Selim."

"Not on you, Alice."

"I very nearly bit a customer last night," she complained. "I don't even normally take customers. For some reason I thought sex with a stranger might be interesting, fun. It wasn't a distraction; I need the cure."

"Can you hold out a couple more nights?" She gave a reluctant nod. "Good. I have someone in mind for you."

He was lying, trying to act like he was in control. When he'd woken up this evening, his plan had been to inquire of Alice who she'd like to hunt. He was going through the motions, acting normal to keep anyone from getting suspicious that the city's Enforcer had totally screwed up and been screwed over, and that they were all going to die because he wasn't strong enough to keep his mind from being invaded. He couldn't afford their finding out his weaknesses, his inexperience, his age, and turning on him.

Her demeanor brightened considerably. "Anyone I know?"

He forced a laugh. "I doubt it, nest leader."

"You're mad about our hit list, aren't you, babe? That was Mike and Kama," Alice assured him, and smiled at his sardonic lift of an eyebrow. "Mostly. They knew that Miriam wouldn't mix business with Hunting. They did call me. Tom knew about it because I called him, but he kept out of it. I thought he'd tell you." Selim shook his head. "Foolish of him. Man isn't guarding his back as well as he thinks he is. Kama and Mike would gang up on Don Tomas if they thought they could get away with it, you know."

"I know. They're scared of rumors and shadows. They talk too much, think they can make alliances."

Alice smiled faintly, and quoted, "Alliances lead to rivalries, rivalries lead to reckless behavior. Recklessness leads to discovery. Discovery leads to extinction."

Extinction was definitely something they had to look forward to. His guts clenched with fear, but he fought the temptation to tell her. "I've heard that somewhere."

"First thing I learned as a fledgling. Miriam's a good teacher. Taught me the difference between a friend and a coconspirator, certainly. We are friends, you and I," she added, punctuating the words with a brief brush of her hand against his thigh. "I didn't see any harm in making the list, Selim. I wasn't going against your authority. If you're going to kill someone anyway, it might as well serve a purpose."

"Why?" In a way, her argument reminded him of Siri's pleas to hunt only bad guys. "Never mind. I don't feel like debating the matter. Our only purpose is to survive." Not that they were going to survive much longer, if truth be told. He sighed.

"There's something very nasty eating you, Selim."

"Anyone I know?" he joked back.

Alice got up and stood before him. "What is it?"

"Nothing." He put the coffee he hadn't touched next to the crystal vase and also stood. Alice pressed herself close to him, her arms going around his neck. An old, sweet, sensation shot through him at the feel of her. His hands went around her waist, but he had no intention of baring his soul, no matter how good Alice felt against him. "Let's not play this game, shall we?"

She rubbed her cheek against his. Her breath brushed his lips, then she whispered in his ear, "It's not wicked if it feels good. Or maybe it feels good because it's wicked. Talk to me, Selim."

He was going to say no. He was going to push her away. He was going to lecture her sternly. Warn her. Leave. He was going to do all those things. But the door was flung open and Siri rushed in to find them embracing before he could move.

Selim's first impulse was to fling himself halfway across the room from Alice. His second was to hurriedly explain that they hadn't been doing anything! He didn't get the chance to do either. In fact, Siri didn't even seem to notice that he and Alice Fraser were in a somewhat compromising position when she came running in. Rene came in a few steps behind her, and Alice's companion's eyes did narrow jealously when he saw them together. It was Alice who moved away from Selim at that look from Rene.

Siri came to a halt in the middle of the room and flung out her arms. "Alice!" she shouted.

His companion wasn't radiating jealousy or anger but was nearly bursting with fevered excitement. "What?" Selim shouted back.

"Go ask Alice."

"What?"

"Ask Alice," Siri repeated. She pointed at the other vampire. "That's the song's title."

" 'White Rabbit,' actually," Rene interjected.

"I think we better leave, Siri."

"No way."

"What does he have to ask me, Siri?"

"Nothing, Alice." He reached for Siri's arm. "We're leaving now."

Siri grabbed the front of his shirt and shook. "Listen to me, you paranoid idiot! You have to trust me on this. You have to trust her. You have to talk to Alice. We're all going to die if you don't *'go ask Alice'*!"

"Jefferson Starship?" Alice asked.

"Airplane," Siri and Rene both answered.

"What are you supposed to ask me?" Alice asked Selim.

Everyone's attention focused on him. Alice and Rene were worried and curious. Siri was frantic, angry, hopeful. All Selim could do was shrug and answer, "I have no idea."

Chapter 19

"IT WAS YOUR vision," Selim told Siri. "You tell me what I'm supposed to ask her."

She didn't flinch from the fury he aimed at her. She ignored the bitter sarcasm as well. She took a deep breath and then spoke as quickly as she could. "Rene and I were in the kitchen talking, and I mentioned hearing old songs and he mentioned that he used to live in San Francisco and went to the Filmore, but that was before he met Alice, and I suddenly knew what the vision had been trying to tell me earlier." She blinked and took another breath.

Selim spoke before she could go off again. "You don't have cryptic visions. You either know something, or you don't."

"I've been having a bad day, all right?" she snapped back. She touched her temples gingerly. "I feel weird."

"What do you mean?"

"It's like my subconscious is trying to talk to me, but is having to sneak things past this . . . dark curtain. I'm stressed out," she went on. She looked earnestly between Selim and Alice. "How I know something isn't important. I just do."

"You have to trust Siri's instincts," Rene chimed in. "I do."

"And I trust Rene's gift," Alice added.

Selim gave them all an exasperated look, but he helped Siri to sit in the wing chair when he should have taken her by the arm and gone home. She clutched at his hand and gave him a pleading look. "You look terrible," he told his companion. The fact that she was going through hell in an effort to help was a deciding factor in what he said next. "If it was anyone but you, Alice—" He looked at the woman who had once been his companion but had long been a nest leader in her own right. He was completely unsure how to go on.

She looked back. Rene, tall and slender and far from handsome, had his arm protectively around her waist. "I'm not in very good shape myself," she reminded Selim. "I need a Hunt more than whatever this crisis is. Still . . ." She managed one of her soft, inviting smiles. She projected a very good facsimile of her usual counseling demeanor. "Maybe you should first explain to me why we're all going to die."

Selim rubbed the back of his neck. "Oh, boy." He opened his mouth, but no words came out. At least not on the first try, but after several false starts, and much prompting from Siri, Selim eventually explained as much as he knew.

"A script?" Rene asked when Selim was done. "Am I in it?"

The companion's enthusiastic curiosity was galling. "I don't think you understand the seriousness of the matter," Selim told him. He had wanted Alice to send her companion away, but Alice had balked when he suggested it. She'd said she needed Rene's strength, and that since he already knew there was trouble, he might as well know what it was.

"It's just another vampire movie," Rene answered. Selim had the impression Rene was trying to be reassuring. Trust Alice to have companions that were as

sympathetic as she was. "Who's going to notice if it's
the truth?"

Selim thought that perhaps he hadn't explained quite
as lucidly as he hoped. Then he looked into Alice's eyes
and saw death reflected there. She understood. "You
don't know where this script came from? Who wrote it?
The whole story?"

He nodded. "That's right. What I feel . . . and I trust
my feelings," he added, "is that the story isn't over yet.
Some of it has happened, but the vampire writing it has
a vision of the end that . . ." Selim was going to say that
he wasn't going to be alive when the credits rolled, but
the sick look on Siri's face and the frightened specula-
tion on Alice's kept him from going that far. "Maybe
it is just a feeling," he added. "Maybe I'm being too
paranoid."

"What you need is a copy of the complete script,"
said Rene. "I'm sure Joe—"

"What he needs is the person responsible," Alice
interrupted. "You have to cut off the head." She
laughed. "It wouldn't hurt to kill every human involved
as well." She rubbed her hands together briskly. "I've
given blow jobs to many a studio executive, but I've
never actually eaten one." Her eyes sparkled brightly.
"This could be fun, Hunter."

The true meaning of Siri's vision came suddenly to
Selim, so suddenly that he had to sit down. The thick
carpet proved to be quite comfortable as he settled cross-
legged onto the floor beside where Siri sat. He ran his
hands through his hair. "Studio executive." He smiled
at his companion. "Studio executive," he repeated to
Alice. "You're a madam. A Hollywood madam? Like
that Heidi—Lewinski girl?"

"Fleiss," Siri corrected. "Or Madam Alex."

Alice raised her gaze toward the ceiling. "Oh, please.
I much prefer out-of-town businessmen as my clientele."

Selim was disheartened. "Oh. But you said—"

"Years ago, darling. The current Hollywood fad is

for driving SUVs and going to PTA meetings. Decadence is passé.''

"There has to be *somebody*," Siri said. "Or my vision wouldn't have—"

Alice waved her to silence. "There's something there, all right, dear. Let me think." She drew away from Rene to pace the room.

While the humans watched Alice, Selim found himself drawn to one of the room's two windows. He pulled back a sheer curtain and stood very still, holding the soft material bunched tightly in one hand. There was a brick terrace below the window. Beyond the terrace was a lit pool where several young people were swimming laps. No sexy cavorting for the members of Alice's household. These were her "specials," he supposed, those with the incredibly rare gift of being able to give or take blood without forming any permanent connection to the other person involved but who always loved the one they were with. Alice searched long and hard for such "transients" as she'd dubbed them. It sickened him to think that he'd actually considering renting the services of one of the women below recently.

He glanced over his shoulder at Siri, almost furtive, definitely guilty. Her attention was on Alice, on the problem. There were dark circles under her eyes, a darkness in her aura. His fault, even if it was for the best. *If I'm going to die anyway,* he thought now, *I want to make love to Siri once more before I go.* Then again, that kind of selfishness could get her killed. He shouldn't think about his own needs but about getting her to somewhere safe while there was still time. If there was still time.

Something about the night called to him, and he turned back to the window to gaze at the sky. He couldn't see many stars overhead even if he let his vision change, not with all the light thrown up by the city. Danger moved in the darkness. It grabbed Selim's attention away from other problems for a moment. He felt it like a strong, hot, sand-laden wind on his skin, as a pulling, pulsing rush of blood in his veins. There was always danger in the darkness; he always felt it. Selim spent much of his waking life analyzing the rich, thick, electric currents of intent, emotion, and action that impacted against his special senses. Most of what he detected was the residue of the violence humans perpetrated on each other. Most of it didn't have a damn thing to do with him or his kind.

Take the rushing red tendrils of hate and fear and lust that were as visible to him right now as lights of the city. He concentrated on them and pinpointed the cause of the distracting disturbance. There was a killer stalking Griffith Park, not that far away. If Selim were a betting man, and he was, he would put money that the source of his discomfort was six blocks away; an arrogant, sexually dysfunctional human male with a great deal of imagination and intelligence, putting off a trail of white-hot mental energy.

"Ugly," Selim murmured. He turned back toward Alice. "How can you put up with that?"

"What?" Rene asked.

Alice didn't answer him. She stopped pacing and smiled. "Got it!" She laughed. "I'm getting old, Selim. I should have remembered him right away."

Selim moved to Alice's side. "Who?"

"We have a plot on our hands all right, darling," Alice announced. "A conspiracy. Or at least a very powerful man has been made into somebody's brand-new toy. If we're lucky, it's just one." She gave him a hard look. "You betting on your luck?"

"Just tell me what you're talking about," he said. "Who?"

"Yeah," Siri chimed in. "Who's the slave? Who owns him?"

Selim flashed a quick smile at his companion. Siri, thank the Goddess, had cut to the chase. "Names," Selim said. "Who do I hunt?"

"Art Rasmussen, of course," Alice said. "The man who runs Arc Light. It should have already been obvious that whoever provided the script is controlling the production our way.''

"Enslaving a studio?'' Rene asked. "Is that possible?''

"It wouldn't have to be everybody,'' Siri pointed out. "Besides, there have to be a few artistic people left in the film industry. Most artists have a certain degree of the gift.''

"I passed a call from Rasmussen on to Angela a day or two ago,'' Alice went on.

Angela was Alice's other companion, though they wouldn't be together much longer. "And this is important how?'' Selim asked.

"Angela handles community affairs,'' Siri explained to Selim. "So to speak.''

"She told me he was looking for something in a dominatrix scene. Told her he loved his wife and kids, wasn't into kink, but had this new connection that was stronger.''

"Sounds like a new slave,'' Selim agreed. A distracting ripple of fear wavered through him as he spoke. It was an outside sensation. Probably something to do with the murderer nearby. He attempted to shut it out and concentrate on his own problems. "How did Rasmussen find you?'' he asked Alice. "Who does he belong to?''

Alice gave him a skeptical look. "A slave is going to give one of my girls more than the necessary buzzwords to get what he needs? I don't think so.''

"Fine. I'll have a talk with him,'' Selim said decisively. Here was something he could work with. Something he could do to start putting his world back in order. Go ask Alice, indeed. "I need an address for this guy.''

Siri stood up, quivering with anxiety. Her eyes flashed at Selim. "He has a wife and children. I doubt if he's a volunteer slave.''

"Most are, these days,'' Alice agreed. "We should find out how he came to be enslaved before deciding what to do about him.''

Selim found that his claws were slightly extended.

He wondered how long he'd been puncturing and shredding the fine cloth of Alice's drapery. He let the curtain go and stepped away from the window. He fought to focus completely on the women. "I don't care how he got involved with our kind," he informed them. "I just want to know what he knows."

"And we all know how you plan to do that," Siri answered belligerently.

Alice put her hands on her hips and lifted her chin stubbornly. "I won't have it, Selim."

"Won't have what?" Red rage filtered into his consciousness, but it had nothing to do with these foolish females. Nothing to do with his reaction to their foolishness. It came from outside, from far away. Not aimed at him, but he was part of it. He fought off confusion. "Won't have what?" he repeated to Alice.

"Won't have you torturing an innocent man just because it's the quickest, easiest way. Let me find him," she urged with her usual persuasiveness. "Talk to him. It may take a little longer, but no harm will be done."

Before Selim could argue, another rush of terror hit him. He staggered forward. Siri was by his side instantly. Alice a step behind her. He felt like he was being hit on the head with a hammer. His blood started to burn. He stared at the concerned women. "Do you feel that?" They shook their heads. To Selim it looked as if they were puppets moved by the same string. A laugh ripped out of him at the sight.

They tried to help him to a chair, but he pulled away. Wildness built in him.

Help! Please! Geoff! Someone help me!

Laughter answered. He laughed with them. He joined with *them*. Running footsteps, pounding heartbeats, bloodfire.

Not too close. Not too fast. Play the game. Play it out. Make it last. Feel her? Close your eyes and follow the fear. Taste her terror on the air. Taste her hope. Sexy sweet and hot. She doesn't see us, thinks she's free of us. Slow down. Stalk the bitch.

Selim shook his head. Freed himself from the vision. It was happening right now. Should have felt it sooner. The human murderer's vibes covered over signs of the Hunt. Hunting without his permission.

With an animal cry, Selim tore away from the clutching grasps of the women. The change came. Wild. Freeing. He laughed again, loudly, the sound issuing from a mouth full of monstrous fangs. He could feel who now. He was drawn to where it began. Not far. He didn't have much time.

Selim turned and ran. He leapt through the window, paying no mind to shattering glass or to any nearby shouts and cries of alarm. He concentrated on the screams for help coming from miles away as he hit the ground running.

There was a wall surrounding the grounds. Inside the wall he found an odd combination of long, low, functional-looking structures punctuating street after street of facades from every era and style of architecture. These buildings showed painted faces in front, with nothing behind them. Not a real place at all; a front; a mask. A television studio, he realized as he rushed down empty, dark streets. These were simply outdoor sets. Reality wasn't to be found outside. The grounds went on and on, mostly dark and deserted. It was still early in the evening, though, and there were people working in some of the buildings. Selim slowed as he neared one that was surrounded by parked vehicles. He came to a halt not far from an open doorway, waited and watched for a few precious seconds in shadows he made even deeper. People moved around inside, puzzled, afraid. The sound of questioning, shrilly angry voices came to him on the air, and in his thoughts.

Damn.

Someone had been damn sloppy, leaving a mess for him to clean up. Deliberate. A distraction for him. A diversion.

"Son of a bitch," Selim snarled and reached out to

touch the most receptive nearby mind. In a few moments, a petite young woman came out of the studio and walked into Selim's shadow. Selim took her by the hand, tilted her chin up and they gazed into each other's eyes. "Tell me what you saw."

After one brief sigh, the girl answered. "A blond. A skinny, pale, hard-eyed woman. She came onto the set and stared at Moira. *Stared.* It was scary. I don't know why, but it was. Tony was going over to tell her to leave, but Moira said it was okay, that she knew her. That the intruder was from her agent's office."

Kamaraju's Lisa, Selim thought without surprise. "And?"

"Moira left with the woman. She shouldn't have left the set, but she went. Without a word. She looked dazed. I thought the woman must have given her some bad news, but I don't think the blond said a thing. They didn't speak to each other. It was very eerie. We waited, but Moira didn't come back. Tony sent someone out to look for Moira, and he didn't come back. And we thought we heard screaming in the distance, but it was like we couldn't move. Nobody wanted to, really. Then in a few minutes this crazed . . . creature. Some guy in a vampire mask, I guess. He came running in screaming for Moira. Then he ran out again. It was like—well, he looked at me and I got a headache. Just from his looking at me—into me." She blinked. "I threw up after he left."

"What did he look like?"

"Like a vampire—or a werewolf. Something with fangs and gigantic, glowing eyes. Great makeup and prosthetics."

For once Selim blessed any and all involvement between his kind and the entertainment industry. His work with these people was already half done. They didn't believe in the supernatural, but they were intimately involved with makeup artists. Within a few moments he'd have them recalling seeing someone that looked like a vampire somewhere on the studio lot, but not here, not only a few minutes before. It wouldn't have anything to do with Moira's disappearance.

He could feel the Hunt once more. Prey and hunters were on the other side of the studio's walls, well away from people now. He had an image of Moira's black hair flying behind her in the moonlight. She was running across an open, grassy area. Stumbling, gasping. Surrounded. The prey's terror ripped through him. Instinct was to give chase, but not after the girl being hunted. Instinct was fought down in the face of duty, in the face of the Law. None could know of their existence, no human could remember what they'd really seen here tonight. He had to do damage control.

"He had dark hair," the girl recalled of the vampire she'd seen. "And a great ass." She smirked at the memory. "He was wearing tight jeans and a white shirt. No cape. Not a proper vampire costume without a cape."

Geoff Sterling, Selim supposed. The girl's description suited the young vampire well enough. Why the hell couldn't it have been one of Kama's nest that showed himself so openly to the humans? "Damn," he grumbled, and then proceeded to ease deeper into the girl's mind. Once inside, he switched her memories around a bit, told her a story she was happier believing, anyway. There were no vampires, real or fake, in the version she knew when he pulled out a moment later.

It took him a precious five minutes more to implant similar recollections in as many of the others inside the studio as he could reach, and that was most of the actors and crew on the set of the television series about angels.

It wouldn't have taken quite so long if he hadn't felt Moira Chasen's final horror as Kamaraju's nest surrounded her. If he hadn't heard her pleas and prayers and screams. If he hadn't felt the rape. The pain. The death.

He was crying when his job was done. He hadn't shed tears in years. He didn't like them, didn't want them. But for the Law, he could have saved her. But for him, she wouldn't be dead. That she was dead shouldn't affect him. But it did.

Chapter 20

THE LAUGHTER WAS the ugliest of several ugly sounds that filled the night. Cruel, menacing. Worst of all, dispassionate.

The voice that shouted in response was far too passionate. "You're dead! You're fucking dead, you bastard!"

More laughter followed the shout, but it didn't hide the meaty sounds of flesh impacting flesh or the grunts of pain. Selim smelled blood on the air, tasted it with a quick flick of his tongue. Not just mortal blood, but the special sweetness of his own kind settled on his taste buds. "Fuckers!" he muttered, and increased his speed uphill, across springy, sprinkler-moistened grass.

He found them at the bottom of the hill, on the edge of a playing field somewhere deep inside the large park. Kamaraju's limo sat squarely in the center of a parking area next to the field. Two of Kama's fosterlings had Sterling pinned against the hood of the car, beating the shit out of him. As Selim drew closer, Sterling let out a howl like a banshee. The pain that reverberated with the sound had nothing to do with the physical punishment he was taking. Everything to do with grief.

Selim was on Sterling's attackers by the time the young vampire's cry faded in the night. One he tossed over the top of the car. The crack of the fledgling's spine breaking as he hit the concrete on the far side of the limo ensured that he wouldn't be getting up for a while. Selim heard Kamaraju's cry of protest, was aware of the nest leader rushing to his fallen fosterling, but paid the touching little drama no mind. Sterling was splayed out on top of the wide hood, his shirt ripped open. The exposed skin on his chest was shredded by long claw marks, his clothes were soaked in the bright blood welling up from the wounds. His face was bruised pulp. Selim reached for Sterling's other assailant.

The second of Kama's pups tried to run. Selim didn't bother with the silver dagger, he just ripped the bitch's heart out and tossed the body aside. The heart he pitched over his shoulder, to Sterling. If the boy didn't know what to do with it, he didn't have it in him to be an Enforcer. Selim paid no more attention to Sterling. He was totally focused on Kamaraju as he leapt over the top of the limo and stalked toward the kneeling nest leader.

Kamaraju rose angrily to his feet as Selim approached, and he backed away from the injured fledgling. "What's the matter with you!" he demanded. Selim was blood-spattered, the hot liquid on his skin cooling already in the chilly night air. There was no blood on Kamaraju. He didn't even look like a vampire at the moment. He was impeccably dressed in a dark suit and a tab-collared silk shirt. There was no blaze of hunger in him. But there was outrage, fury, and smug satisfaction. He swept an arm around the parking lot. "Are you crazy, Selim?" he demanded. "Leave my people alone."

"You moved fast after the murder," Selim said, looking the other vampire over disdainfully. "Didn't want any blood on your hands?" He sniffed. "I can smell it on you, though."

"Murder? What murder?" Kamaraju gave an elegant

shrug. "There was a Hunt." He backed a step as Selim continued to walk forward. Fear flashed through his controlled facade.

"You were letting them kill Sterling."

Kamaraju held his hands up before him. "The strig? We were just playing with him. Teaching him a lesson for trying to interfere with a nest's rightful Hunt."

"A lesson?" The words were spoken with soft menace. Sterling's almost mindless pain, the anguish of his loss, spread like fog across the night. The very *real* knowledge of it seeped into Selim's being. It twisted in his guts, turned into a pool of molten lead in his conscience. "It looks like the lesson could kill him, to me," he spoke to Kamaraju.

He was answered with a fulsome laugh. "Nonsense. It'll be good for the strig. Teach him to respect his betters. I even thought I'd take the boy home on a leash. He'd make a good pet." There was answering laughter—albeit with an undertone of deep nervousness—from the rest of Kamaraju's household. Selim silenced them all with a deadly look as Kama added, *"We* don't kill our own kind, Hunter."

"No." Selim smiled. "That's my job."

Kamaraju's answering smile was equally nasty, yet also conciliatory. "You're not threatening me, are you, Hunter?" He looked around, his pose all innocence. "What have I done to offend?"

Selim advanced smoothly, stopping within an inch of the nest leader before Kamaraju could retreat further. Selim put a hand on Kamaraju's shoulder, staining the nest leader's clothes with the blood of the vampire he had killed. Kamaraju wasn't going anywhere except into a meat locker before too much more time passed. Selim didn't know why he bothered to continue the conversation. "There was no need for Moira to die. No need at all."

Kamaraju pretended not to be intimidated by Selim's proximity. "She was prey. Prey *you* designated."

How had Kamaraju found out about that? Sterling

must have talked to another strig about Selim's offer for their hunt, and Kamaraju had found out from the strig grapevine. Or Kama had been good enough to pluck the information out of Sterling's mind last night. Was it only last night? How didn't matter now that the damage was done.

He tightened his grip on Kamaraju's shoulder. He heard Sterling scrabbling to get to his feet behind him. "I changed my mind," Selim told the nest leader.

Kamaraju contrived to look and feel innocently outraged. "Nobody told me."

Selim shook him. "It wasn't your Hunt!"

"What the hell difference does that make!" Kamaraju shouted back. "Your job is to name the victims. That's all the Law requires of you! I only had to agree to Hunt someone you chose."

"Don't talk to me about the Law, you bastard! There was no reason for that girl to die!"

"What difference does it make to you? Prey is prey. Meat is meat."

Selim heard Sterling's silent cry of pain in his bones. It was only a little worse than his own. "This one had a name. A face. She was chosen!"

Kamaraju gave a scathing, grating laugh. "By a strig? Who cares? He hadn't tasted her yet. She wasn't chosen. She was meat." Kamaraju licked his lips. "Damn good meat, too."

He was going to rip off Kama's face first, Selim decided. Then he was going to tear him limb from limb, pluck off every extremity slowly, like taking the wings off a fly. Then he was going to make him eat his own balls. Then he was going to kill him. Maybe in a month or two.

"You've had this coming for a long time." Selim raised his arm, claws extended, ready to sweep them down across Kamaraju's eyes. Kamaraju tried to break from Selim's grip. Someone screamed a protest. Selim struck.

Or would have if a hand as strong as iron hadn't

closed over his extended wrist. "Not so fast, Hunter!" a breathless voice shouted in his ear.

Selim didn't know where Mike Tancredi came from, but there he was, big as a bull, wide as a wall, his grip as tight as a vise. His bulk shut out the sight of the rest of the parking lot. For a moment, the only thing that filled Selim's vision was the sight of a beige sports jacket, then his gaze shifted to Mike's face. He looked scared, but stubbornly rebellious as well.

Selim kept his hold on Kamaraju as he looked calmly at the other nest leader. "I would suggest," he said quietly, "that you take you take your hand off me."

Mike swallowed hard but didn't move. "Take you hand off Kama first."

"No."

"He hasn't done anything wrong."

"He's a murderer."

"Since when is that a crime?"

"Listen to Michael," Kamaraju said. His tone was soft, insidiously reasonable. The Snake in the Garden's voice. "I asked him to be here. A witness. I knew you wouldn't like my Hunting without supervision, but you know it wasn't unlawful."

"He's right," Mike said. His grip was hard on Selim's wrist. Selim made his muscles relax, but Mike didn't let him go. He released his grip on Kamaraju and took a step back. Mike gave him a half-apologetic, thoroughly nervous grin, but he didn't release Selim. "You're tricky, Hunter. I'll let you go when you're really calm. We're all empaths here, remember?" His tone was soothing, persuasive. The Snake as a Car Salesman. "Let's talk this out like reasonable adults."

"We aren't reasonable adults," Selim told them. "We're vampires. Kamaraju's a vicious killer," he added. "He deserves to die."

"Maybe he does," Mike said, with a quick glance at Kamaraju. "By the human definitions of what we are, he's a monster of the worst sort. Decadent, cruel, sadistic—just like we all are. But, Hunter," Mike continued reasonably. "You don't enforce human laws. No Law was broken tonight. None. Bent a little, maybe," he hurried on. "I'll agree that Kamaraju took more independent action than you like, but he didn't break the Law. The prey was of your choosing. He didn't reveal his people to the humans. The Hunt was in an area where the humans are looking for a mortal murderer, so any suspicion will bleed onto this human monster."

It all sounded so logical. So true. "And you did what?" Selim asked. "Waited in the car with these excuses all ready for when I showed up?"

Mike nodded emphatically. "Yes. Precisely. Kama knew you'd give him trouble for simply doing what he needed to do. For taking care of his people the way he saw fit."

"We need more autonomy," Kamaraju said. "It's time you saw that, Selim."

Mike said, "I agree with Kama."

"Nobody asked you." A groan close behind him briefly caught Selim's attention. He shifted his gaze to see Sterling kneeling on the concrete nearby. "You all right, Geoff?" He received another groan in answer.

When Sterling lifted his head, Selim saw that the young vampire's bruised mouth was covered with blood not his own. He struggled to his feet, clutching his belly like he wanted to claw out the fire he'd swallowed. Good. He was getting the hang of what it took to be a Nighthawk. Good? What was good about being a Hunter? What good could possibly come out of this night? And why did he have a persistent, nagging, insane belief that strigoi needed or deserved a concept of "good"?

A vision of Moira Chasen's pale face filled his mind, though he realized the vision wasn't his own. He couldn't recall having ever seen the girl in person. Hadn't even seen her on television. It didn't matter. She deserved better than the death he was responsible for bringing to her.

"Fuck the Law," he said to the nest leaders. He pulled his arm away from Mike's grip. Bones broke in his wrist, but the clean sharp pain was worth the effort. "This is about justice."

Kamaraju laughed, even as he turned to run. The injured fledgling grabbed Selim's leg. Mike planted himself between the fleeing Kamaraju and Selim as Selim tried to shake off the young vampire's grip. Lisa emerged out of the shadows to scream, "No!" Sterling stumbled to his feet with a roar of pain and rage. The limo driver started the car's engine. Everything happened in an instant, though time stretched and slowed to Selim's senses. He knocked Mike down. Sterling kicked the broken-backed vampire off of him. He was still kicking him when Selim dashed after Kamaraju.

All the interference gave Kamaraju enough time to make it to his limo. For the limo to pull away from the parking lot. Selim laughed wildly, knowing that Kamaraju could have gotten away faster on foot. The long car picked up speed as Selim headed back the way he'd come, back up the hill above the playing field. There was only one road out of here. The was a sharp turn the limo had to negotiate to reach the streets beyond the park. Selim intended to be waiting at that turn.

The night quieted around him. The smell of blood faded from his nostrils. The moon looked down and probably saw nothing for the light pollution and the air pollution and didn't give a damn about what little it could make out. It was just a rock in the sky, anyway, not the all-seeing eye of the Goddess Reborn. Except— he felt as though she were watching him, that her cool, moon gaze was firmly centered on his back. He was half-tempted to glance over his shoulder or to whisper a prayer into the night. It was a strange feeling, but just another strange feeling in what had, so far, been the strangest night of his life.

There was a clump of bushes and some decorative-looking boulders at the spot where the roads met. Selim scrambled down a steep, gravelly slope to reach the bushes. He sat down on one of the jutting rocks and took a deep breath. He tried not to think but emptied his mind as he looked in the direction the limo had to come. He wanted to take Kama alive, that was the plan. To take him in a showy way, let everybody else in the limo live to spread the word. Then he'd take Kamaraju with him. He saw headlights approaching but decided he had time enough. He took his cell phone out of an inner jacket pocket.

"Selim? Where are you?" Siri's shrill voice demanded in his ear a moment later. "Never mind. I'm on my way." She sounded harassed, frantic. Accusing.

He wanted to ask what he'd done this time, but only had time to say, "Kamaraj—"

"This is *important!* Stay right where you are and don't move a muscle."

"I have to stop him. I want you to meet me at—"

"You're at a crossroads with a hibiscus flower sticking in your ear. I've *seen* you. I have a movie producer in my backseat," she went on. "You want to talk to him more than you do Kama."

"That can wait." Selim pushed away the flowering branch that was tickling his ear. He could hear the big car's powerful engine, quiet though the limo was. Headlights approached from the main road as well. Siri on her way to pick him up. "Stop where you are," he ordered his companion. "Wait until I say." He put the phone back in his pocket, turned, and tensed for the leap onto the limo roof.

Siri's voice in his head said, *Rasmussen's more important right now than killing Kama. There are only so many hours in the night. Only so much time to save the world.*

"Shit!" Selim snarled the word and stepped back, hiding in the bushes while Kamaraju's long car glided past and made the turn. "Damn! Hell! Son of a—!"

He was still swearing when Siri's Mercedes pulled to a stop a few moments later. He slammed the passenger door shut when he got inside. He glared at her furiously. "Damn it, woman! I hate when you're right. Kamaraju deserves to *die!*"

She gave a curt nod, unfazed by his fury. She patted him on the arm. Her touch was a calming balm. She let out her breath in a sad sigh. "I know what he did. We'll get him." She glanced toward the backseat. Selim turned his head and saw a large, smiling man seated next to Alice in the back.

Alice smoothed a hand across the man's cheek. He arched, and practically purred at her touch. "Say hello to the nice man, Art."

"Hello," Art Rasmussen said to Selim, though his gaze didn't leave Alice's face. "I have things to tell you," he went on, and smiled hopefully at her. "Alice says so."

Selim was amazed. He was in awe of Alice Fraser's talent, of her power, her gift. His heart raced with excitement, fear, maybe a little hope. He gave Alice a grateful look. To the slave who should be a mindless vegetable at having his bloodbond broken, he said, "I'm listening."

Valentine sat crossed-legged on the cool Spanish tiles of her balcony floor, a mug of cold coffee cradled in her hands. Her gaze was turned up to the moon, but she wasn't looking at it. Her vision floated for a while, then settled down, not necessarily on purpose, not necessarily with who she wanted to be, but even she sometimes had to go where the gift of the Goddess took her.

The parking lot was illuminated by a couple of moth-encircled streetlights that gave a faintly gold tint to the tableau she watched. She recognized the older ones, and the sight of them left a sour taste in her mind. Oh, Michael Tancredi wasn't so bad. She remembered him as a Byzantine mercenary who'd sold his fighting skills all over the Mediterranean for hundreds of years. Smart enough, but happier following orders than he'd like to think he was. He looked taller than she remembered. But Kamaraju wasn't pleasant to look upon, certainly not to think about. He'd been a follower of Kali in his mortal life, only hadn't gotten it, not the sacred meaning of what he'd done. Kama got off on killing people, and the day should be cursed when somebody decided that meant he'd make a good vampire.

"Humph," she snorted disdainfully into the night. "Riffraff." *Is it any wonder the sensible ones end up recluse? Who wants to associate with such scum?*

She asked herself the questions, then settled back into watching events unfold. Dark, tragic events, but she had to admit she enjoyed the drama. At this distance it was like watching a movie; a low-budget indie done with a handheld camera and in need of a serious script doctoring, but it held the attention nonetheless.

Valentine's eyes flew open when Selim said, *"Fuck the Law, this is about justice."*

She winced, and rose to her feet. "No, no, no," she complained. "Too easy. Too melodramatic. Nobody really talks like that. You should have said—" No, wait. This wasn't a movie. "Well, it should be," she pouted.

She shook herself all over, gave the moon a sardonic shrug, and went inside to get more coffee. Once there, she went to her desk, sat down at the keyboard and started to write. She didn't lose track of the time. She was waiting for a phone call, and it was late in coming. The notion that her slave hadn't yet gotten in touch with her sent a thread of nervousness up her spine, but she was willing to make excuses for now. He was a busy man in a busy town. This was Wednesday; he was probably caught up in a dinner meeting at Morton's. He wanted to iron out a few more details before bringing her news that would make her happy. All would be well, she told herself. He'd grovel. She'd forgive him. No biggie.

What she felt for Rasmussen was only a faint, surface anxiety anyway. A mask, a Band-Aid, useful for covering her worry for Yevgeny. She looked up from the screen and stared across the dark room. Where was he? What was he doing? Would he come home?

"Idiot!" she muttered. "You're the one who drove him out."

Desperation was the last thing she'd felt from him, and it frightened her. She tried closing her eyes and reaching him, not for the first time. And, not for the first time, all she encountered was a wide, thick, black wall. She was good. She was the best, but he knew her too well. She'd blocked him out for years, and now he'd turned her tricks on her. Tricks he'd learned in the last several years of trying to breach the defenses she put around her mind.

I did it for you! she thought as loudly as she could at him. She knew he neither heard nor cared. It was too late to get through. "Damn."

She buried her fears by working. She typed quickly, the words pouring onto the screen. Not a new screenplay, or more revisions for *If Truth Be Told*. That was history for the moment. She'd have suggestions for rewrites on that soon enough, now that the script was making the rounds. She'd deal with those suggestions when she had to. For now, she'd decided to try her hand at a novel. Something historical. No dragons, no elves, no spaceships, no superheroes or secret agents. No vampires. Definitely no vampires.

She carefully avoided looking at the clock on the bottom of the screen. She stood up to stretch and turned toward the terrace doors as she did so. She pushed her chair back, but that wasn't what made the sound that came, faintly, to her ears. *Yevgeny?*

The indistinct sound of movement on the balcony came again. *Not Yevgeny,* she decided, not admitting that she'd had a moment's hope. Yevgeny had a key.

Art Rasmussen? Hardly.

Valentine sighed with exasperation. She heard a footstep. The intruder thought he was moving silently, and to anyone else, even another vampire, he would be. She'd always had very good hearing. Another step. To her he sounded like a bull elephant clomping around, trying to avoid her patio furniture and potted plants.

Valentine marched to the terrace door and threw it

open. "I have a front door," she said to the intruder on the terrace. "You could ring the bell."

Selim froze in place, just next to the blossoms of a topiary rose tree. He was pale, bloodstained, and looking very much the worse for wear. His big dark eyes stared at her in utter shock. A wave of cold disbelief poured off him; a wave of hot anger followed. He took a breath. He reached out a hand but stopped an inch away from touching her. His mouth moved, lips forming the word once, then again. The third time, he managed to make sound. The word came out as a croak.

"Valentia?"

"Valentine," she answered tartly, and boxed him on the ear. "And is that any way to address your mother?"

Chapter 21

SELIM CLOSED HIS eyes. It was simply all he could think of to do. He took a deep breath, but Valentia's very real, vibrant scent betrayed any attempt to claim this as a hallucination. He may not have been engulfed by the distinct physical and mental perfume that was her in centuries, but her essence was as familiar to him as on the last night they'd been together. It masked whatever else waited in the apartment beyond the terrace.

When he opened his eyes, she was still there, leaning against the doorway, watching him. Small, delicate, beautiful, faintly smiling, one hand resting on the luscious curve of her hip. In her other hand, she held a blue ceramic mug decorated with a gold embossed logo from some movie. She was utterly real. As real as the aroma of coffee that also wafted to him on the evening breeze. His ear stung, and that was real, too. She lifted the mug to her lips and took a long gulp. If she had any deep feelings at seeing him again, her casual attitude and mental strength masked them neatly.

"You can't be here," he told her, finally finding his voice, if not his brain. He touched his ear. "That hurt."

"That's my spoiled little princeling," she said. "You

never were any good at taking discipline.''

"Why should I be?" he answered automatically. "When I never did anything wrong?" More memories than he wanted to pull out and examine crowded into the moment; more years than he wanted to think about. Most of them spent alone—or, at least, without her.

She laughed. He drank in the sound. He wanted to drown in her laughter, die in the blaze of her smile. She hadn't changed. Not one little bit. Except now she was wearing faded jeans and a sweatshirt with a movie star's face on it. He was used to her in more elegant attire.

"And why should I change? I like me just the way I am.''

Her mouth was as lush as ever, her hair as thick and long and curling. He wanted to run his fingers through it, to taste those full, red, smiling lips. Of course he did. She was everything to him: life and love and the first person who'd ever given a damn whether he lived or died or was even a little bit sane. She was everything beautiful in the world.

"I'm your mother," she reminded him. "Your lover. Your maker.'' There was infinite understanding in her aura, as well as chilling tartness in her voice.

"Not my mother," he answered. "My mother was—"

He barely remembered her, the one who had given first birth to him. She had been a true Egyptian, not a daughter of the Mameluke Arab conquerors, but a Coptic Christian girl sent along with other tribute to the sultan in Istanbul. One did not catch a sultan's attention without beauty, not in a seraglio full of the most beautiful women in the world. Beautiful, with at least a dash of intelligence, he supposed. One did not avoid the visit from the palace abortionist without a certain amount of cleverness after attracting the sultan's attention resulted in pregnancy. She had been a favored one, a *khadin*, long enough for her son to be born, at least. Then she'd fallen out of favor. He'd been sent to the luxurious prison where spare princes spent their days at a young age. He could not remember the Egyptian woman's name.

"While you lived in the Cage," Valentia reminded him. "I came to you." He nodded, throat tight with agony—of love, and loss, and remembering. "We tasted each other. I made you what you are." Her voice purred and spun magic webs around him.

"No." He blinked at the pain. *You went away! It happened too soon!* He tried to push the thoughts away. To forget.

"I know you have abandonment issues, dear," Valentia told him. "But I'm still the one who made you what you are today."

He shook his head. He slashed his hand down diagonally between them. "You—you didn't—" Selim spread his arms wide, helplessly trying to take in everything he'd ever been and done.

Valentia did not look impressed. She looked him over critically, though. "I didn't make you a Hunter, you mean? Who was she, then, this third mother of yours? I assume it was a woman, knowing your narrow tastes," she went on after a short silence where he stood in front of her like a stubborn child, gaze on the Spanish tiles of the balcony floor rather than her, his first lover, his second mother. "I'm gratified you'll admit to even that much, Selim, even if you won't say it." Jealousy curled around her words like wispy smoke, faint but there.

Selim couldn't help but meet her gaze. He couldn't help but feel faint amusement at her attitude, faint pride in his answer. "Olympias. It was Olympias herself who brought me to the Hunt."

Valentia raised an eyebrow sarcastically. She crossed her arms beneath her full breasts, letting the empty coffee mug dangle from one finger. "Am I supposed to be impressed?"

He mirrored her gestures, though it was a silver dagger that dangled from his fingers when he spoke. "I certainly was."

"I never thought that square jaw of hers was attractive. And the girl's too tall for my taste. More Xena Warrior Princess than Epirean Temple Priestess. Of course, you didn't know her when she was young." Valentia glanced at the dagger and neither showed nor felt concern. At least he sensed no contempt at his bravado, though her amusement was strong. "Is there something you plan on doing with that, dear?" She grinned at him. "I really wish you hadn't felt the need to draw it so soon."

"Why? Do you have something to fear?" Damn right, she did. Or, more likely, he hoped, someone in her household had something to fear. And how did Valentia come to have a household in his town without his knowing about it? How long had she been here?

"Something to fear? From you?" She shook her head. "No. I was just hoping to use a version of the old Mae West line on you."

"Mae West line?"

Her grin widened. She took a slow, sexy, step toward him. "You know the one. Is that a knife in your pocket, or are you just happy—"

"Don't!" He was blushing when he put the dagger back in its sheath. He held his hands up before him. He didn't know how this conversation had gotten out of control. That's right, it had never been in control in the first place. He barely remembered how he'd gotten here or why he'd come. Right now, he knew he wanted her, though he knew wanting her was impossible. Forbidden. And—he remembered the dream of making love to her a few days ago.

"To see me," she finished, her gaze on the growing bulge at his crotch. She was still smiling sexily, but she didn't come any closer. In fact, she backed up and gestured him inside the apartment. "Want some coffee? Want some answers?" she added when he hesitated, and then she sauntered, hips swinging, inside.

Selim stared after her, pure masculine response overpowering him. It took a few moments to get the reaction under control. He didn't do it by reminding himself of the seriousness of the matter, of the heresy of wanting the one who had made him, that it was his duty to punish whoever had broken the First Law. He managed to get his hormones under control by remembering how Siri would react if the little spitfire ever found him fooling around with somebody else. "Never mind the Strigoi Council," he murmured, and made himself step inside the spider's lair. "My wife would kill me."

The room he entered was large, but multifunctional. There was an office setup near the balcony doorway. Beyond that was a living area with a leather couch, a wide-screen television, a glass and iron coffee table, and tall bookcases. There were some large, colorful, art glass pieces in a lighted cabinet, but no paintings on the walls. There were no photos, no knickknacks, no mementos.

"I travel light," she said, watching him look around. She tapped her temple with a forefinger. "Got everything I need right here. There's no one in the bedroom," she added as she went into the kitchen, a narrow open space between the living and office areas. Selim followed her and listened with dread. "I know you sense that I'm alone, but I thought I'd make it perfectly clear before we continue that I'm the one you're looking for. No household." She refilled her mug and poured a second cup for him. "Do you still take it sweet?"

"Black," he answered automatically.

His mind tried to process information while his hands reached for the cup she politely held out to him. He went into the living room with her and took a seat on the couch beside her. They were silent for a while. Not an awkward silence, not an antagonistic one. He felt her withdrawal, her patience, the familiar, comforting compassion while she gave him time to order his thoughts. He drank boiling-hot coffee without tasting it. He stared at the blank television screen. He put the cup down on the table when he realized that the liquid remaining was now cold, and noticed the cover of a coffee table book resting on the middle of the coffee table. Michael Jordan's face looked back at him, and Selim's thoughts, such as they were, turned to basketball.

"You have season tickets for the Lakers," Valentia said. He turned his head to look at her. She was curled up on the opposite end of the couch, legs tucked beneath her, the blue mug cradled in her hands, a small woman not taking up much space. Her power filled the room, his mind. He blinked and could do nothing but listen. "That's where I first spotted you," she went on. "You and Siri. I was watching the game one night and spotted you in the crowd. Fascinating child, Siri. You really must take her back to your bed."

He shook his head, held out a hand, started to explain. Valentia didn't let him get in a word.

"Is it because of what I did to you? Because we had such a short time as lovers? Are you trying to draw out your time together because of what happened to you?"

"She needs time," he heard himself say. The pain in his voice humiliated him. He knew, and Valentia knew, that he wasn't talking about Siri, but himself. He wanted to shut up, but couldn't. "She has to be ready. It takes years to prepare a companion. Decades."

"And you'll miss her when she's gone?"

He nodded miserably. "That, too."

"Denying what you need won't work." She gave a soft, bitter laugh. "Believe me, I know. Abstinence isn't doing either of you any good. It's wounding her and distracting you. An Enforcer can't afford to be distracted. The distraction helped me get inside your head without your noticing. Of course, it didn't hurt that I was already there, in your memories, at least."

He tried to stave off those memories, but they rose with bruising, battering intensity. As she intended, he realized. She was doing a very good job of keeping him off balance.

It was Valentia who put words to memory. "A brother you almost cared about died that night, and I made you take his life. You really didn't know what was happening as I made you take his blood and mine one after the other, spoke the words of the spell, and forced you to love me on his dying corpse as I spoke them. The magic was strong and hit you hard; so did his fear and pain as you absorbed his dying. It sickened you. But, then, a curse should sicken those who are trapped in it. I truly believed eternal life was a curse not a gift then, and you were infused with what I felt along with everything else. I've never known another fledgling to be as ill and disoriented as you were that night—but you lived. Your brother would have died anyway. Court politics, and not a vampire, would have put an end to his existence before the night was out. You were already dying. The Janissaries sent to assassinate the princes in the Cage started with you. You don't recall that, do you? The palace coup? I saw it as I slept and could do nothing to stop it. I saw the knives go in, my love, and couldn't even scream. The stab wounds bled you nearly to death before I was able to reach you just after sunset. I found you surrounded by dead palace guards. You didn't go under the knife easily, but you went. You were still mortal, but changed enough from four years with me to survive longer than those who left you for dead could imagine. I forced some of my blood down your throat when I reached you, but I knew you wouldn't survive as a human. So I ran to fetch you the first mortal I could. I found your brother hiding in the bathhouse. It would have been better if you could have Hunted, would have made your birth easier, but there was no time. You survived, changed. We escaped the seraglio," she finished.

He looked at her, in as much pain as if he'd lived through that awful night and the nights after, once again. "And you left me," he added. "After all that—horror— you disappeared."

Valentia crossed her arms. "I did no such thing, Selim. I left you with the first nest I could find. You know I couldn't stay with you, and why. I'm sorry, but I was still very religious in those days, no matter how harsh and old-fashioned it seems now."

It was years before he recovered from that night, if

he'd ever recovered at all. He barely remembered the vampire that fostered him, other than he'd had no love for an Ottoman Turk and hadn't made Selim's new life easy. One night he'd sensed something very *different* than he'd ever known, and followed the sensation with growing excitement to Olympias, who'd eventually made him a Hunter of hunters.

Selim forced his thoughts to the current century, glad that memory had cycled him back into awareness of his purpose in life. It would be so easy to stay lost in the past with Valentia, to find out where she'd gone, what had led her to Los Angeles, to tell her all about his life since their abrupt, still-aching, parting. So easy to sit at her feet and pretend to be companion and mistress once more. Then he wouldn't have to even think about killing her. About holding her heart in his hands and—

"What have you done?" he asked her. "Why?"

"How long have you lived in California?" she questioned back. "I've gotten a sense that it's been quite a while from walking in your dreams, but I never sensed you before I saw you on television. Not that I'd been trying, of course," she added with a musical laugh. "The only vampire I knew about was Don Tomas, but then, I didn't want to know about any others. Been there, done that, had the body bags to prove it. I met Tomas once when I first came to town. That was in 1932, by the way. He sensed my presence by accident. It was pure coincidence that I moved into the same building where one of his companions lived. I convinced him to forget about ever seeing me, and I convinced his current lady to move across town. You were already in Los Angeles then, weren't you?" she guessed.

He nodded. "I asked you why you're attempting to destroy our way of life," he reminded her. "Not for your autobiography."

"I'm getting to that. It's really very simple, in a complicated way," she added. "Long story. Or maybe I should say it's one story too many. I'm a creature of Hollywood far more than I am a creature of the night, my dear. You see, I was living with an American writer in Paris, and he got an offer to work in the movies. We lived at the Garden of Allah and I moved in that circle for a while. Caught the screenwriting bug from some of the best writers in the world. My boyfriend—not a companion, just a boyfriend who drank too much and was not a day person—didn't do too well in Hollywood. Decadence suited him, but the studio system didn't. I ended up doing all his work. He made a very good front for me for the next fifteen years. By the time his liver gave out, I was established, quietly, in my own right. I survived the death of the studio system, corporate takeovers, *auteurs,* and high-concept artists. They all come to Valentine—not Valentia, dear—Valentine. You came looking for Valentine, I expect.''

He nodded reluctantly. ''That's the name Rasmussen gave me. I wish it wasn't you.''

''Art told you.'' She wasn't surprised at her slave's betrayal. ''Nobody can keep a secret in this town.'' She sighed. ''I'm sorry for his family.''

''He's not dead.''

She looked impressed. ''You are good.''

''I have friends.''

''I know. They're all in the script. Enemies, too,'' she added. ''There's some really good action scenes in *If Truth Be Told.*''

Fear curdled in Selim's stomach. He smashed a fist down on the glass-topped coffee table. Cracks starred out around the point of impact, but the thick glass didn't shatter. ''You know everything that's happened,'' he snarled the accusation at her. ''Everything that's going to happen, and you put it all into a script! You're showing it all over Hollywood. Why?''

''Because I couldn't think of anything else!'' she shouted back.

Selim stared. He felt her agitation, but he didn't comprehend her words. He tried asking his question again. ''Why are you trying to destroy your own species?''

''I'm not.''

"But . . ."

"If by species you mean vampires, that is." She leaned forward on the couch. "I'm not trying to destroy anybody. You know me better than that," she added, with a haughty lift of her chin.

"Then what are you trying to do, out us?"

"Maybe," she answered. "But only if the marketing people think it will help promote the movie. I mean, what harm could it do?"

"What harm? Valentia—Valentine—we're real!"

"Yes," she replied. She looked at him, with a faint, altogether infuriating smile. Her dark eyes laughed at him. "Your point?"

He understood now. Of course. "You're crazy. Insane. Mad." She didn't look it, didn't feel it, but what else could it be? Why else would she betray everything they were? "Didn't you care that the Strigoi Council would come after you?"

Her mouth twisted in a disdainful frown. "Honey, I've been on the Council. They think far too highly of themselves."

"What about the Law?"

"What about it? Who cares? Selim, have you looked at a calendar lately?"

"There are reasons we have laws. Reasons we live underground. Reasons no mortal may ever—"

"Ever heard of Thomas Jefferson?"

He snarled at her interruption of his speech. A speech they'd both heard too many times before, he supposed. He tried to drop the party line and concentrate on what she really wanted, what she was really doing. He ran a hand frantically through his hair while she waited patiently at the other end of the couch. "What about Thomas Jefferson?"

"He said, at least I believe it was Jefferson, that a little revolution now and then is a good thing." Her bright and pleasant smile returned. "I'm fomenting a little one-strig revolution. Care to join me?"

Selim watched her carefully. All of her, probing as

deep as he could. On the surface, in fact far deeper than the surface, he found a woman who meant every cheerful, irreverent word she said. What else he found was hard to decipher, but there were deeply disturbed currents below the surface. There was a throb of hunger deep down inside her, boxed away, but straining for freedom. There were several kinds of fear, a great deal of worry. He concentrated on the fear, probed, with no subtlety. She sat there and let him, as though allowing his effort to mindrape her was some sort of reparation for invading his dreamworld and taking whatever she wanted.

"What do you feel?" she asked him after a while, as though she were overseeing the lesson of a newborn fledgling.

"Desperation," he answered her. "Desolation. Emptiness. Wild, hopeless terror. Fear that nothing will ever be right in your world again. Self-loathing. Doubt. Living hell."

"That sums it up nicely."

He longed to reach out to her in compassion. The void inside her frightened him. "What is it?"

"Writer's block."

Selim opened his eyes. He hadn't known they'd been closed. He glared at the woman on the other end of the couch. "Writer's block?"

She nodded and shivered.

The fear of this thing was very real for her; he sensed that it went deep down into her spirit, that it burned and tortured her. He'd come here to rip out a Lawbreaker's heart. Many things made him hesitate to do his duty. One of them was curiosity. "I don't get it."

"Of course not," she replied. "You're not a storyteller. But I'm feeling much better now. Writing *If Truth Be Told* broke a lot of creative energy free in me."

He believed he began to, perhaps, make a little sense out of her words, her feelings. No, not sense. There was nothing sensible here. He tried to put words to what he pieced together. He said slowly, "You're telling me that you are going to get me killed—me, you, Siri, every nest and strig and every human that comes into contact with this story of yours—because you couldn't think of anything else to write? Is that what you're saying, Valentia?"

"Valentine. Valentine has been in Hollywood for over sixty years. Valentine isn't a vampire. She isn't of the strigoi, she isn't a blood-mother, she doesn't Hunt, she uses the magic only when she has to. She certainly doesn't believe in the old religion. In fact she—I—didn't realize anyone still did until I went wandering inside your head. What are you people doing living in the dark ages?"

"Surviving!" he shot back. "The only way we can. And how dare you," he snarled at her, "blaspheme against everything we are for the sake of—what?" He searched for concepts, words through a bloodred haze of outrage. She merely watched Selim as he sputtered, then finally shouted, "What made you do it? Money? Prestige? Screen credit?"

She was on her feet. Shadows gathered and coalesced around her. Her eyes blazed, hot and red, burned into and through him. She shed all shielding. Power flowed out of her. Selim very nearly slid from the couch to fall to his knees. He barely managed to get to his feet and stay there, knees shaking in the presence of such sudden, raw energy.

It lasted only a moment, then was gone as quickly as she'd summoned it. She was a small, beautiful, vulnerable woman again. One who lived alone in a small apartment and dressed in ragged clothes. "My imagination remains," she told him. "That's all I need or want. But—" She blinked on tears. "It was going. I was lost, empty—and my agent had just gotten me a deal for a horror movie. I had to do something."

"Did you have to break the First Law?"

"It's a old Law."

"But still a good one."

She gazed at him, tears shining in her eyes. She

looked more childishly stubborn than like a being of incredible power. He felt more like an indulgent, if outraged, parent than a betrayed child or an Enforcer of the Law. "You broke faith with us, and I really can't understand why."

"How can I make you understand?" Her anger and outrage returned. "Have you *ever* had writer's block?" She stabbed a finger at him. "You think the fever to Hunt is bad?" Her harsh laugh rang through the room. "You have no idea what hell is until you sit down in front of a blank screen and it stays blank day after day after fucking day! Or worse, have every word you wrench out of your soul be nothing but pure crap. I'm Valentine." She jabbed her finger at herself. "It doesn't happen to *me.*" She collapsed back on the cushions and sat back against the arm of the deep couch with an explosive sigh, her anger dissipating. "But it happened to me," she went on, speaking as calmly as before. "I was supposed to be writing a horror story . . . so I wrote a real one. You want to read it?" she asked eagerly. "No, Rasmussen must have given you a copy. What did you think? I'm so glad you got into that fight with Jager. It's just so pivotal to the—"

"I haven't read it," he told her. "Not the whole thing."

"Oh." She looked disappointed for a moment, then got to her feet. He watched her pad gracefully, bare feet silent on the carpet, to her desk. She brought back a stack of paper and handed it to him. "Let me know what you think. I'll put on more coffee."

The pages were heavy in his hands. He didn't want to read any more than he already had, but his gaze was inexorably drawn to the words she'd written. "Fine," he muttered, and began to read.

Valentine headed toward the kitchen. When the doorbell sounded, she stopped, and Selim's head came up. She looked over her shoulder at him. The buzzer sounded stridently again.

"What did you do?" she asked Selim accusingly, clearly not expecting or welcoming an interruption. "Call for a side order of pizza to go along with my heart?"

Chapter 22

VALENTINE KNEW THAT Selim didn't feel the emotions coming from the other side of the door. She had barely felt the young vampire's approach herself, something registered on the edge of her senses while she'd concentrated very, very hard on keeping Selim's attention where she wanted it. He was good, though. Very good, very strong in person and wide awake. He kept escaping from the mental traps she wove, kept coming back to his purpose for coming here. She hadn't had the energy to spare to warn the youngster off, she had thought that he wouldn't be foolish or brave or desperate or needy enough to follow Selim wherever he led. She'd been wrong.

Well, it wasn't the first time lately.

Valentine sighed and opened the door. "Hello, Geoff," she said to the bruised and battered child at her door. Tear streaks had washed through some of the blood on his face. The bruises were already starting to heal, but he still looked a fright. Selim didn't look much better, she realized. It was just that the blood crusted under his nails and on his clothes wasn't his. Somehow that made it easier to ignore.

She took the boy's arm and led him into her living room. "I believe this is yours," she said to Selim, but he only glanced up briefly with a quick, annoyed glare and went immediately back to reading. Well, at least her story was holding his interest. She concentrated her attention on the lost creature that had dragged itself to them for—what? Succor? Sanctuary? He stared at her, dazed, grieving, hurt, and helpless, and she wanted to hug him, to give him a nice warm cup of blood, tell him a story, and tuck him into bed. She pointed toward the bedroom.

"Shower's through there," she told him. "There's some clothes in the closet that will be too big for you, but they'll do. Get cleaned up; then we'll talk."

He stared past her, gaze hungrily reaching for Selim. "I—she . . ."

Valentine put herself squarely in Geoff's line of vision, blocking off Selim's existence with her own mental energy. She forced the boy to look into her eyes. "Moira is dead." She said the words gently but made him listen with all her will. "Go take a shower." He sighed, a breath that shook him down to his bones, and shuffled off the way she'd pointed.

Valentine watched him go, then glanced at Selim, then out the open terrace door as she went into the kitchen. In the distance she could make out the graceful outline of the World Center, and she realized that sunlight would soon be returning to the world. Odd, it felt like the night was just starting, when in fact it was nearly over. She felt refreshed, invigorated . . . maternal. She frowned at that and took a steak out of the freezer. When she had it defrosting in the microwave, she returned to the couch. Selim was holding a loose page in his hands, staring at the words as though his glare would be enough to make them go away.

She took a seat beside him and pried the page out of his clenched fists. "You've gotten to the fight with Istvan, haven't you?" she asked without bothering to look at the paper. Selim turned a stunned look on her. "Of

course, I changed his name to Corsare. It was necessary
to make some compromises, but you recognized the
source material.'' She patted Selim on the knee, aware
that she didn't have his full attention, even when he
blinked and his eyes focused once more. ''What are you
going to do about Geoff?'' she asked. ''The boy needs
a lot of help.''

''Istvan.'' Selim took a sharp breath. ''Istvan is coming. I have to fight the *Dhamphir.''* He shook his head,
glared at her. ''I felt this coming, hoped I was imagining
things.''

''You were.''

Selim drew away from her comforting touch, sprang
to his feet to look down at her accusingly. ''How am I
supposed to protect Sebastian against something like
him? Damn it, Valentia, how could you draw that hell
down on the child? Sebastian's a baby. A human
baby—''

''Born of vampire parents. Well, one vampire parent.'' She sat back and drew her legs up, wrapping her
arms around her knees. ''Amazing, isn't it? He's only
the second one I've ever heard of. I was delighted to
find out about the boy. Gave me just the focus for the
conflict I needed. A real reason for the audience to sym-
pathize with a vampire hero. You have to save the child
from Istvan, who doesn't want him to grow up to challenge his rule of the strigoi, and then you and Siri kiss,
and credits roll over the romantic ballad on the soundtrack. We break twenty million on opening weekend, no
sweat.'' She smiled up at him. ''Am I good, or what?''

''I have to fight Istvan,'' Selim repeated. Then, very
slowly. ''I. Have. To. Fight. Istvan.'' He spread his arms
out to the world and sent out a silent howl of tortured,
fatalistic pain.

Valentine looked upon her bloodchild uncompre-
hendingly for a moment; then she took in the pages of
the manuscript that were scattered in no order on the
table, the couch, and the floor. She put her feet down
with a sharp thud and crossed her arms beneath her

breasts. "Oh." After a pause, she added, "I think I see your point."

Before she could say any more, the microwave chimed loudly, and Geoff Sterling shuffled out of the bedroom. She chose to deal with the more important crisis first. Going to Geoff, she took his hand and led him to the counter that separated the kitchen from her office. She pushed him into one of the two kitchen chairs. She put a plate of warm meat in front of him a moment later and handed him a knife and fork. He looked at them as though he'd never seen silverware before. He looked at her as though he had nothing to live for. Geoff was wearing one of Yevgeny's tailored white shirts, with the too-long sleeves rolled up.

Valentine considered a great deal of advice for the boy, but Selim was waiting. She settled on, "That steak's rare. Don't get any blood on your shirt." She left Geoff staring at his plate and went back to the vampire by the couch. "Stop acting like we're all going to die," she ordered him. "It's just a movie."

Selim put his hands heavily on her shoulders. "Woman, you are *so* crazy." She stepped back, and Selim hands fell to his sides. His gaze was on her, but she felt his thoughts race, searching for answers, plotting, all his senses reaching out, hunting.

"For something that isn't there," she told him. "For trouble that isn't coming."

"You've *seen* it," he accused her. "I've *felt* it. We see and feel and know the future, Valentia—"

"Valentine."

"Don't you remember what you really are?"

"I try to forget as much as possible, actually." She waved a contemptuous hand toward the night, the world beyond her window. "Who needs all that crap? Especially at my age?"

He stared at her, those big, dark, beautiful eyes full of worry, full of the conviction that she was mad, full of dread and concern for the child. She wasn't going to argue about her sanity, maybe she would even admit that her definitions of reality were slightly askew. It went with the job. Goddess knew, it went with the business. Who was truly sane in Hollywood?

She took Selim's hands in hers. She felt how different they were from human hands only because it had been so long since she'd touched one of her own kind. Body temperature was a little higher, skin that was soft, yet subtly tougher than human, a faint ridge at the base of fingernails that masked the sheathed claws. The differences from human were no more pronounced in Nighthawks; it was mind-set and magic that set them that further step apart from human. Or maybe it was a step closer. Valentine liked to think so. In fact, she liked to think that there was really very little that separated them from the people they used to be. The proof that drinking the Goddess's blood didn't really take them away from humanity was in the occasional birth of vampire children.

"Sebastian's a miracle child," she told Selim. "So was Istvan. Istvan would never want to harm another *dhamphir*. I just made that up." She didn't tell him that the spells referred to in the script were real. Why admit to even more crimes against the dictatorship he served? "I've been mucking around in your subconscious for weeks, my dear." And that was crime enough, against a person, not antiquated Laws, and for that she was sorry. "You just picked up the idea that Istvan was involved from me." She squeezed his hands. "You're really good for such a kid. You almost caught me a couple of times. I'm quite proud of you."

Selim didn't seem to absorb her praise, but he did listen to her explanation. He twined his fingers with hers, drawing her closer to him. He radiated danger, but Valentine was unafraid as he looked down at her, his expression gone still and blank. "Maybe he isn't coming for Sebastian," he agreed with her. "But what about the rest of us when he finds out what you've done?"

"You aren't going to kill me," Valentine answered

him. "You aren't going to stop me. We both know that."

"If I don't take care of it, they will send him."

"He's a good boy. I can reason with him."

Geoff Sterling's wild laughter interrupted whatever they would have said next. Valentine pulled her hands from Selim's and went to the grieving strig. Geoff's laughter shifted to shuddering sobs as she crossed the room, then turned to a thundering howl of pain. Selim was but a step behind her. It was Selim who took the boy by the shoulders and shook him hard.

"He's seen Istvan work. I think that's what set him off," Selim explained to her. "But not what this is about."

"I know. I saw you with Kamaraju."

"I'm not sure who I'm going to kill first," Selim said. "You or Kama."

Selim looked for her reaction as he put his arms around the young vampire and drew him into a tight embrace. Sterling quieted and held onto Selim for all he was worth, whispering over and over the name of the girl he'd lost.

Valentine stood back with her arms crossed. She glanced from Selim and Sterling to the balcony and back. "You'll have to decide on that tomorrow," she told him. She got between the two men and took Sterling's arm. She wiped tears off his face, put her hand over his heart, and waited until his ragged breathing had calmed a bit. She urged him toward the couch. "Sleep there," she told him. "We'll talk when we wake up. No dreams," she added softly, looking deeply into his eyes and his mind. "No dreams at all today. Just rest."

Dawn was just a few moments away when Geoff headed toward the couch. Valentine took Selim's hand. He was looking at the lightening sky, watching for the sun that was about to trap them together with their unfinished business until night fell once more. "Come on, princeling," she said. "You can sleep with me."

He didn't protest. You couldn't argue against daylight. He went with her, the enemy of the Law, into the bedroom and settled down beside her to sleep.

"Tell me about the child."

Siri looked at the man driving her car, and couldn't recall how he came to be in the Mercedes or behind the wheel. She didn't like to let anyone else drive. She smiled dreamily at Yevgeny. "What do you want to know?"

He shrugged. "I don't know. Everything. What happened to his mother?"

The air-conditioning was on too high, chilling her down to a shivering mass. Siri looked at her watch. It told her that the time was 10:25; the sunlight glinting off concrete, chrome, and shiny metal skins of the cars all around them on the freeway told her that it was morning. She welcomed the heat of the sun, but couldn't get to it, not even to roll down a window. She tried hard to remember where the night had gotten to, how she had come to be where she was, and with who, but the compulsion to respond to whatever Yevgeny wanted overrode every concern and question.

"Oh, she's a vampire now," she told Yevgeny.

"Really? How interesting." He changed lanes and speeded up. "Shouldn't giving birth to the little monster have killed her? Shouldn't he have killed her when he tore out of her womb?"

"That's a myth," Siri responded tartly. "Legend. Modern medicine intervened, actually. Cassie had the best ob/gyn in town. Sebastian was delivered C-section, a few weeks early. That was Selim's idea, just in case the myth proved to have some basis in fact. He wasn't born with fangs and claws, so it probably wasn't. Cassie did almost die, though, from complications to do with a blood transfusion she wasn't supposed to have. Someone at the hospital screwed up."

Siri still got angry at the memory. She was convinced it had been an attempt by someone, possibly Kamaraju, to kill off the *dhamphir*. Except the murderer was already too late when the attempt was made. There was no proof, though. Neither Selim nor Tom had ever found the technician to question him. To Siri's suspicious mind, this was proof that it hadn't been a screwup or accident. She had enough control over her own thoughts not to offer this information, though she couldn't help but continue giving Yevgeny what he asked for.

"You know a companion can't take anyone but their vampire's blood?" she went on. Yevgeny nodded. "After some technician pumped about a pint of the wrong type of blood into a woman too drugged to stop him, she went into convulsions. To keep her alive, Tom had to take her Hunting, do the makeover thing. She was *so* pissed off."

Yevgeny took his eyes off the road long enough to give her a very curious glance. "She didn't rejoice in her rebirth?"

"Hell no."

"Why not?"

"She'd just had a baby! She didn't want to leave her husband and house. She especially didn't want to leave her child, and there was no way Tom was going to send his son to someone else's household. In the end, she didn't leave, which has caused all sorts of friction in the community, but she'd rather stay at home with Sebastian than do the vampire thing, anyway."

"The child is more important to her than becoming immortal?"

"Of course!"

"Why 'of course'?"

"You've obviously never been a parent."

Yevgeny went very still, his thoughts going far from the car he was driving. "I have, actually," he said after she'd watched him for a long while. He gave a soft laugh. "I'd forgotten. Two sons and a daughter. I loved them very much before I was taken from them." He shuddered, and the determined look came back to his face. "It doesn't matter. Tell me more about Sebastian. No," he stopped her before she could go on. He held up a hand. "Maybe it's better not to know."

Silence settled in the cold car as he turned onto Mul-
holland and drove up the steep, curving road. Siri stared
out the windshield. Every now and then, a thought tried
to break through the darkness that blanketed her. She
caught glimpses of memory, of Yevgeny rousing her out
of a fitful morning's sleep. She was certain awful things
had happened in the night, but she could only grasp at
shadows. Yevgeny kept whispering in her mind that all
that mattered was her taking him to Sebastian. Music
tried to hum inside her head, but she caught no chords
she could put together. Yevgeny's determination kept
getting in their way.

By the time they reached the gated drive of the Avella
estate, she had a terrible headache.

"It will be over soon," Yevgeny said gently and put
a hand on her shoulder. He switched off the car engine.
"I'll wait here. Go to the door," he instructed Siri carefully. "The slave's waiting there for you with little Sebastian."

This was not good. This was not right. Panic lanced
through her. "I—"

Yevgeny's grip on her shoulder turned harsh. He
caught her gaze with his, bored the necessity to obey
into her as he said the words. "Go to the door, Siri.
Bring back the child. Bring him to me right now." He
repeated his commands over and over, until Siri nodded
at last.

She got out of the car and went to the door. Two
members of Don Tomas's household were waiting with
Sebastian by the door. The adults, a man and a woman,
didn't look happy. Sebastian, dark curls combed neatly,
bright amber eyes shining with excitement, had never
been happier. He threw his arms around Siri when she
reached him. His enthusiastic embrace, reaching somewhere above her knees, threw her off balance. She had
to grab hold of the adobe arch over the doorway to keep
her feet. Siri gave Sebastian's nanny a grateful look as
the woman pried the little boy off of her.

"Behave," the woman admonished and was ignored.

"I'm having a birthday party!" Sebastian crowed as he looked up at Siri's face. He punched the air with a small fist. "Yes!"

She took Sebastian's hand. "Yes, indeed," she agreed. "We're going to Andy's place. He's closed it for the day, and decorated it with dinosaurs and balloons. It's going to be great."

"I know," Sebastian said. He tugged hard on her hand. "Let's go."

She started toward the car with Sebastian, the two slaves following close at her heels. Yevgeny stepped in front of them before they could get in the backseat, though. He caught and held their attention while Siri continued on to the Mercedes. Sebastian paid the man with her no mind. As she settled the little boy in the backseat and adjusted the seat belt for him, she heard Yevgeny talking to Don Tomas's people. "That's all right," he told them, in his soft, persuasive way. "You won't be coming with us. In fact," he went on, friendly, confident, magnanimous. "I'm giving you the day off."

Siri opened the passenger door. By the time Siri had her own seat belt fastened, the servants had started back toward the house. Yevgeny slid into the driver's seat. The car started.

"Won't this be fun?" he said and guided the car smoothly back down the driveway.

Chapter 23

SEBASTIAN TUGGED ON Siri's hand as they walked away from the car. "Why do we have to go here?" he asked her. "Why can't my party be near where I live? How will my friends find me?"

Siri had been waiting for these questions. "Your mama told you why, didn't she, owlet?" She waited until Sebastian nodded twice, to acknowledge that Siri had spoken the secret word that told him they couldn't talk about the subject right now. He chafed against it, but, young as he was, most of the time he was good about keeping their secrets. "We'll talk about it when we get where we're going."

Sebastian fidgeted and looked worried but kept quiet. He held her hand and was careful to look both ways as they crossed the street. Siri sighed at the burden this life put on a child and was glad that she could do little things, like arrange birthday parties, even under tight security conditions, that helped ease the stress of growing up strigoi for Sebastian.

She glanced back once, worriedly, at Yevgeny. He walked behind them as they started up the hill. The sight of him disturbed her, but only for a moment. He put out his hand to caress the back of her neck, and she was soothed, calmed. She walked on without any worries.

The noontime traffic was light, but there were plenty of pedestrians on the sidewalks, with college students and shoppers heading for cafés and coffeehouses in the central area of the town known as the Village. The street was lined with trees and flower beds, with an old-fashioned pharmacy on one corner and benches under the trees. The benches were full of young people eating quick take-out meals. Siri noticed the aroma of fresh, warm chocolate from a handmade candy store mingled with the hot, spicy smell of the curry being eaten by someone on the bench outside the candy store as they walked past.

They'd left the Mercedes in the train station parking lot, the closest parking space they found to their destination on the far edge of Claremont's old-fashioned downtown. It was a two-block walk to Andy's, a small, hole-in-the-wall place wedged between a dress shop and a store full of Tibetan art and jewelry. The coffeehouse was always very busy during the evenings but normally open for the lunch crowd, as well, offering sandwiches and desserts along with lattes and espressos. Now it was closed, the day help replaced by Gary and Joseph. At least, that was the arrangement Siri had made with them. The idea had been Cassie's, to give Sebastian a party out in the real world, but in a spot that was quiet and safe, among people who could be trusted. It wouldn't be as much fun as taking the kids to Disneyland or even the party room of a McDonald's, but Sebastian had been convinced that it would be fun, and it was his only shot at normal at the moment. Sebastian wanted a normal life desperately enough to go along with anything—after the requisite hours of tantrums.

"Where are my dinosaurs?" Sebastian asked as the door closed behind them.

Yevgeny's wide shoulders effectively blocked out the light from the half-moon window in the thick wooden door. *Blocking any exit,* Siri thought with a shiver. He

smiled reassuringly, and she returned her attention to
Sebastian, who tugged his hand out of hers, and Gary,
who came rushing toward her from around the counter.

"What is this all about?" he asked, sparing an anxious look at Yevgeny. "Who's he?"

"Where are the decorations?" she asked the slave.
"We've got six kids and their parents showing up for
the party in less than an hour."

The tables squeezed into the long, narrow room were
bare. The overhead lights hardly shed any light on the
room. There was a shadowy, claustrophobic feel to the
surroundings that Siri had never noticed at night. It sent
a cold chill through her. No balloons were in evidence,
no presents. Definitely no dinosaurs.

"What party?" Gary asked as she turned an angry
look on him. "You called this morning and told me the
party'd been called off but to meet you here at noon.
You had me call all the children's parents."

"I did no such thing! Where's Joe?"

"At home with Miriam, of course. Do you think he'd
leave her side when the whole community's in danger?"

"What danger? We're having a birthday party."

"You canceled it. I assumed it had something to do
with . . ." He glanced furtively at the man by the door,
before whispering, "What Joe told us about."

"Don't I get a party?" Sebastian spoke up loudly.
"Why not? It's my birthday," he added as Siri turned
to him. "It's an owlet thing, isn't it? Why does everything have to be owlet stuff? Why now?"

Siri looked at Gary. "I never called you."

"You did." He was adamant, and he cast a nervous
glance at Yevgeny. "He doesn't belong here, does he?
You don't belong to Don Tomas, do you?"

"No," Yevgeny answered. He didn't move from the
doorway but surveyed them all, one by one, with a cold
blue stare. Ice stabbed through Siri's heart as his gaze
passed over her. She looked at him as though she'd
never seen him before, as though she'd never noticed

how *large* he was, how dangerous. What was he doing here?

"You're the guy from the Viper Room."

"You're crazy," Gary breathed. "Crazy sick. You better leave, I'm calling—"

"Shut up, slave," Yevgeny replied. He smiled, chilling the room down even more.

Gary grabbed Siri's arm. "Why did you bring a madman here?"

She blinked, tried to summon some sense to the morning's actions, tried to even remember the morning's actions. So much was darkness. For a moment, all she got was music running through her head. "What is that song?" she said. "I can almost make it out."

"Can you?" Yevgeny asked, soft and menacing.

He took a step forward. Siri wanted to turn and run, but his cold gaze held her in place. What she'd almost remembered slipped back into darkness. Beside her, Gary made a strangled noise, as though a protest was being pushed down his throat. Yevgeny snatched Sebastian off his feet. His hold on her and Gary broke somewhat as he held Sebastian up at eye level. Gary ran for the back of the building.

"It's almost noon," Yevgeny told the little boy. "We haven't got much time."

Siri hurried forward to see Sebastian gazing calmly back at the big, menacing man. She stopped, shivered, and did no more. Yevgeny brushed a hand through Sebastian's hair. The soft curls clung to his fingers, and he drew his hand away as though he'd been burned.

"You're going to kill me," the young *dhamphir* announced calmly.

Yevgeny looked surprised. It was several seconds before he could answer. "Yes, little one." He didn't sound gleeful about it. He didn't look evil but tired and desperate.

"My daddy won't let you," Sebastian told him, not showing the least fear. "Or Uncle Selim."

"They're sleeping. You have to die at high noon.

That it's your birthday is a fortunate coincidence, but it will add strength to the spell.''

"Are you going to drink my blood?" Sebastian showed all the curious interest in this mayhem that any five-year-old male would when discussing cartoon and action figure violence. "So you can become a vampire like Daddy?"

"Are you reading my mind, young man?"

Sebastian nodded, his expression turning sullen, furtive, and sheepish in quick succession. "I'm not supposed to. Don't tell my mom, okay?"

Siri rubbed the back of her neck and fought hard to get her memory back, to get her reflexes working, to think of a way out of this situation. She knew there were things she should be feeling, things she should be doing, but . . . what? Yevgeny set Sebastian down on one of the small tables. He brought out a knife, a moon-sickle curve of sharpened silver, the hilt studded with milky gems.

Sebastian reached for the blade. "Can I touch it?"

"No. It's very sharp."

"Sharp as my dad's fangs?"

"Sharper."

"Cool."

"Aren't you afraid, little one?" Yevgeny asked Sebastian.

"Yes," Sebastian answered with a proud lift of his chin. "But I can't show it."

"Why not?" Yevgeny ruffled the boy's hair again.

"My father says not to. Ever."

"Because you're *dhamphir*?"

Sebastian was puzzled at the word no one had ever spoken in front of him. "My name's Avella. Avellas don't show fear. We're brave and strong and leaders of men."

"Your father told you that?"

Sebastian nodded. "My father won't let you hurt me."

"He would help you if he could, I'm sure," Yevgeny

answered. "If he were here." Yevgeny's hold tightened on Sebastian as the boy tried to leap off the table.

She had an urge to rush to the boy's side, to throw herself between danger and her best friend's child. Siri took a step forward and stumbled, nearly falling over one of the chairs crowded around the small tables. Yevgeny gave her a look that brought her to a halt. She found herself thinking, *Why does Selim have to be asleep now?* And concentrated on Selim, on calling up his face and touch and voice in her mind, recalled the scent of him to block out the awareness of the big blond in front of her. *I never went for blonds, anyway,* she thought.

Then Yevgeny said, "I'll need your help, Siri."

Sebastian started to cry. She fought the urge to take the boy in her arms and comfort him.

"I'm sorry it has to be this way," Yevgeny said. He put his hand on Sebastian's shoulder. He glanced briefly at Siri. The madness in his eyes was dampened somewhat by pain. "I burn. I can't live with it anymore. I need the change."

"Leave him alone! He's just a baby."

He nodded. "I know." His voice was a strangled whisper.

Siri's hands gripped hard around the smooth wood back of the nearest chair. Fighting through Yevgeny's dark control made her dizzy. Through the swirling dizziness in her head, she could hear music playing. It was the song that had been playing in the toy store before Yevgeny showed up, but fainter now. Faint and fading. It had something to do with controlling her, didn't it? Had he used the music in some sort of spell to capture her? A spell? She was psychic and understood how to use her gift very well, but the notion of using incantations and whatnot was foreign to her. There was something unfair about using that stuff.

"You need a vampire to become a vampire, not a helpless child." She pointed at the silver curve of the blade and at Sebastian. Yevgeny didn't answer, but he didn't have to. She remembered now what he'd told her about needing a *dhamphir* when he'd worked an honest-to-god spell around her. When he'd forced *her* to help him with the use of ancient, arcane words.

Yevgeny's gaze settled on her again, a blazing blue fire. "This is a do-it-yourself way. Very secret. There's an incantation all vampires use at the birth of their companions. You don't know about that, do you? That the change isn't just a blood transfer?"

Siri shook her head. "I had no idea. They never tell us anything, do they? How did you find out this secret?" She wanted to keep him talking while she fought to clear the darkness out of her head. She'd figured out how. If she could just turn off the record—That was it, visualize it!

Sebastian was crying loudly, but Yevgeny was holding him close, comfortingly. He was still holding the ritual knife, though. "I've always been good at finding information. I was with the KGB, you know. Long ago." He stroked Sebastian's hair. "When I had sons. When I'm a vampire, I will make sons of my own. Have a household. Not be alone all the time. Nothing worse than being a companion no one wants. She said she did it for me." He laughed.

There was so much pain in the sound that Siri wanted to cover her ears. She gripped the chair tighter. It helped keep her balance, sliding it in front of her as she moved closer to Yevgeny. The real feel of the wood in her hands and the concrete floor beneath her feet helped keep a part of her consciousness grounded in the present—here in a coffeehouse in Claremont where a child was about to die. The rest of her awareness went spinning inward, searching through black clouds and shadows for the off switch to the music that wouldn't go away on its own. *Magic, humph!* She told herself sternly. *I just have to think my way out of this. If I can remember what the song is, I can turn it off.*

"This can't work," she assured Yevgeny. She hated to bring it up, but added, "Even if you drink Sebastian's blood, you'll need—"

"A mortal to kill," he interrupted her. His head came up, catching her gaze with his once more. "That's where you come in. I'm sorry, Siri. I would have used the slave, but he ran away." He sighed heavily, ruffled Sebastian's hair. "Time to die, little one."

In his dreams there was music, plus a hand on his dick. The music was what brought him as close to awake as it was possible for him to become. Or, maybe it was the hand circling and cradling his penis. He couldn't rule out the possibility, or, rather, impossibility of the hot aching pulse of an erection being what brought his focus out of the far-from-peaceful darkness.

Damn it, Val!

I know, hon, but we need to talk. I thought that if I went dreamwalking inside you, you might get a bit testy.

You think? He took a sharp breath as a surge of heat raced up from his groin, and he felt both the breath and the desire. Didn't dream it, *felt* it. His eyes were closed, he had no awareness of where he was, just of sensation, and that he wasn't alone. *This isn't real, is it? What I'm feeling? It's not possible.*

A month ago I would have agreed with you. I think it's me. I'm changing somehow. I can feel the bed beneath me. Can you?

Selim tried. *No. I've got a hard-on. How are you doing that?*

Got my hand in your shorts before I went to sleep. I don't know if you're actually feeling what you think you are, or if you're feeling what I want you to. Mostly, I was just trying to get your attention.

Don't. It's—

Forbidden. I know. Screw that. It's not doing any harm, now, is it? He found that he couldn't answer. A powerful surge of desire flared from the tip of his penis, down through the length of it, up his spine; ecstasy exploded in his head and flowed back down through blood and bone and flesh. He shuddered with the release, though not a muscle moved. Through it all, music played faintly, far away.

Now, don't you feel better?

Is it possible for you to share a bed with anyone without sex being involved?

It's good for stress. You need to relax, not take everything so seriously. My script, for example. You are far too concerned with ramifications and whatnot over it.

Whatnots? Indignation burned through him. He imagined his claws unsheathing to their full length, imagined striking the woman he was trapped in bed with. All he could manage to do was think. *Someone has to be concerned. How many will I have to kill?*

None.

You would say that.

Her laughter bubbled through him, gold, sparkling, warming as champagne. Bubbles of sound burst in his brain, refreshing and faintly mocking.

Darling, you're acting like anyone in this town actually has an attention span. You're worried about copies of the script being all over town. Forget about that. It's just another horror movie script. Nobody but us knows it tells the truth. She sighed. Deep, deep disappointment, heartache, and aching capitulation flowed from her into him, a sad, syrupy river. Her heart was bleeding; he could feel it. He thought nothing. Offered nothing. Eventually, she thought, *So much for Valentine. I'll never feast on the flesh in this town again over this, but I'll do it. For you, sweetheart.*

What is—it?

I'll walk on the production deal, withdraw the script from circulation.

Why don't I believe that?

Because you think I'm crazier than I am. Writing it freed my creativity. That will have to be enough. I will have to accept being able to write again as victory. With victory comes the end of my bloodless Hunt. I'll let telling the truth on film go for your sake, my dear.

She'd been planning on putting his life before

thousands, perhaps millions of people. He shuddered at the very notion, and not only because of the broken Laws or her violation of his mind to get her story. She was who she was. She had some right to delve inside him. She was who she was: ancient, powerful, kind, loving. Unstoppable. At least, he knew he couldn't bring himself to kill her. He wouldn't know how to start.

Your heart is in the right place, Selim told her.

She chuckled. *At least for now. You're wondering what I'm really planning, aren't you?*

Of course.

Her laughter returned, crystal clear, with dark, depressed undertones. *Rewrite it and do the thing as an indie after all. No way do I give up making movies just because of a bunch of nervous vampires. I'll do the script revisions everybody's been begging me for anyway. No real strigoi will recognize it when I'm done, I promise you that. Should have gone that route in the first place, I suppose.*

Her distaste for this solution covered him like a heavy blanket. He didn't understand and didn't think it was wise to ask. He'd learned far more about the film business than he wanted in one night's time. He didn't trust her. He was going to have to watch her very carefully, monitor every move she made. That was better than having to kill her.

No Hunts in this movie, he told her. *Not a hint of how or why we have to Hunt.*

No, dear. Of course not. But we do need to talk about Hunting.

Let me rest, Valentia. He didn't trust her. He didn't entirely believe her. It had to be more complicated than she thought, didn't it? He was too tired to think about it any more right now. And there was something else fighting for his attention. *Damn it, I just want to get some sleep!*

Not until we discuss that poor boy.

What poor boy?

The one sleeping on the couch. Am I right in assum-

*ing that you fed him last night? You did, didn't you?
You do know what that means? That you're now responsible for him.*

How would you know—

*I agree he deserves the right to take out Kama, and
he has the gift, but you can't possibly provide him with
all he needs. Not you.*

Selim would have answered, but the faraway music
swelled up from the depths of his mind, and he stopped
listening to her. It happened swiftly, like diving down
into deep, black water. He didn't fall into total darkness.
He was enveloped in seething black smoke underlit with
lightning flares of blue white and fire red. All through
the smoke drifted the music, a monotone voice sang to
him, words he couldn't understand. It was puzzling,
troubling. There was emotion in the lightning flashes.
The light and emotion formed into human shapes laced
through with flame. A third cried for its mommy and
daddy. One of the flame beings—the scarlet fire—
needed his help. He tried to make out faces in the light,
to push past the smoke to reach the crackling red flares.
He had to break through the blackness, find the concentration to dreamwalk, get to her. Siri needed—

*Valentine shook him, a spectral hand on a nonexis-
tent shoulder. Do you hear music? Wake up, boy. Talk
to me. No. Don't talk. Listen.*

He opened his eyes and stepped into a long, narrow
room full of small tables and cluttered with chairs. Fans
whirred slowly and silently in a hammered tin ceiling
high overhead, but no air moved. All the lights were on,
but the place was dark. Shades were drawn over the
windows. A Closed sign hung on the door, and it was
locked. The people in this room were isolated, caught in
a high, horrible drama. He wasn't really there, neither
was Val, though she held his hand in hers. He didn't
feel her touch, just knew it was there. He took a step
forward, focusing as hard as he could on the burning,
shadowy trio in the center of the room.

Selim forced the fiery mental image to coalesce into

its mortal form. No, not quite mortal. The man with the silver knife was tall, broad, with sun-yellow hair and a gold fuzz of beard stubble on his hollow cheeks. Mad-as-a-hatter blue eyes stared out at the child stretched out on the table in front of him. He was holding the boy down easily with one big hand. He reminded Selim of a grizzly bear. Here was a Hunter in the making, but unformed, unfinished. Power pulsed around him, shot off in uncontrolled electric arcs and waves. The not-mortal spoke, and every word rang with power, shone with it, directed his will into the others.

What is he?

Yevgeny, was Valentine's soft, fearful, pained response. *Lady of Snakes, what have I done?*

That was Yevgeny? And Siri was with him. Selim couldn't stop the jealous snarl, even though it was obvious Siri was not voluntarily in this empty place with this—Yevgeny. *Your Yevgeny?*

Mine. For the last fifty years.

A companion? Impossible.

Look what I've done to him. My poor baby.

The baby in trouble was the one on the table, still and pale as death, surrounded by an opalescent cloud of energy. Sebastian. Siri was trapped by energy nets as well, but she was fighting them, working her way out of the spell. Pride and fear for her mixed within Selim. He had to help her. Had to get to her. But he was fast asleep, somewhere in the center of Los Angeles. Yevgeny raised the knife up, the tip of the blade poised over Sebastian's heart.

"Please don't do this!" Siri shouted. The madman kept weaving his spell.

Selim listened and watched. *I know this!* He glared at Valentine.

She nodded through silent, wracking sobs.

You did this!

Another nod.

It's in the script. Just like when I—the Enforcer char-

acter stops Istvan from sacrificing Sebastian in a ceremony to gain power.

It's a real ceremony. He read the script. She gulped on tears and wiped the back of her hand over her face. *This is my fault.*

Damn right it's your fault. Stop him!

How?

He's your companion!

He can't hear me. Won't hear me.

Try.

I am!

Music swirled around Selim, the sound an irritating, plaintive, distracting noise. *What is that song!?*

Something by Dire Straits, I think. Valentine's surface thoughts were terrifyingly calm. The emotions beneath the words she sent him were anything but calm. *Mark Knopfler once did the soundtrack for a movie I worked on.* She gazed helplessly on the people they couldn't reach. *Dire straits is certainly what they're in right now.*

Dire Straits?

Siri's gaze flashed to him, even though he wasn't there. "Dire Straits! That's it!" She laughed, an evil, nasty, triumphant sound, and whirled back around.

The music stopped.

She moved nearer to Yevgeny. "You don't want to do this," she told him. "You're crying. You don't want to harm a child."

"No," he answered. He turned his head but not to look at her. He looked straight at Valentine. "I don't want to do it this way." He waved the knife around wildly. His shout was a deafening roar. "Damn you, Valentine! I don't want to do this! I can't do this! I can't go on like this!"

Yevgeny turned the knife in his hand, bringing the point of the blade toward his heart. At the same instant, Siri hit him in the back with a chair. She kept on hitting him long after he stopped moving, long after the blood from the wound in his chest had flowed into a wide pool on the cold, concrete floor. She swore and snarled and laughed, and prayed, and occasionally kicked the still body of the man who had invaded her mind and threatened the child.

Selim watched until, after a long while, Siri finally grabbed the unconscious little boy and ran with him to somewhere safe and full of sunlight.

Chapter 24

"DON'T LOOK AT me like that."

Selim continued to glare at Valentine, who was standing at the end of the bed. He'd only woken up a few moments before, with the last of the sunset, but she seemed to have been up for a while. She was dressed, her hair combed. Her eyes were red-rimmed. He wondered if she'd been grieving in her sleep, but the idea of any physical activity while sleeping was still too foreign for him to get his mind around. He sat up and swung his legs over the side of the bed.

After a few confused moments, Selim asked, "Where are my clothes?" He distinctly remembered dropping them on the floor when he stripped down to his shorts before getting into bed. They were not where he'd left them. He glanced back at Valentine. "Well?"

"In the laundry. Darling, those chinos and shirt were covered in blood, remember? I'm not letting you out of the house like that."

He stood up. Yawned helplessly, and rubbed a sweaty palm over his grimy chest. He was disgusting. "This is a ploy to buy you time, isn't it?" he asked as she tossed him towels. "You know I have to find and dispose of your darling *Yevgeny's* body.'' He sneered at the name.

Valentine pointed toward the bathroom as she wiped away tears with her other hand. ''We have more important things to discuss.'' She left the bedroom before he could ask what.

He came into the living room a few minutes later, feeling much better for the shower. He had a companion to find and comfort. He needed to talk to Don Tomas. He wasn't through with Kamaraju yet. There was still the Hunt. Valentine needed to be watched like a nighthawk as she canceled plans to make this movie of hers. The last person he wanted to see was Geoff Sterling, and the boy's problem was the last thing Selim wanted to deal with. But there Sterling was, seated on the couch, his head in his hands, with Valentine hovering over him like a worried nanny.

She waved Selim aside when she saw him. He followed her reluctantly to the corner where her desk sat. She pointed to Geoff. ''The bloodburn is eating him up. We have to help him.''

Selim cocked an eyebrow at her. ''We?''

She looked disgusted, distracted, and very, very unhappy. She sighed dramatically. ''We. You can't do this on your own.''

''Can't do what?'' Selim demanded. ''Listen, Valentine, I do not have time for Sterling's problem right now. He'll be fine for a few more days. Not fine,'' he amended as Sterling fell to the floor with a hideous groan. The boy clutched his belly and rolled into a fetal ball. Selim couldn't stop the wave of sympathy for the young vampire, but he did try to ignore it. He forced himself to face Valentine squarely. ''I have to put out some fires you started, woman. That's my first priority.''

''As soon as your clothes are dry.'' She took a step back to look him over in all his near-nakedness. ''You aren't going to save the world wearing only a pair of briefs.'' She crossed her arms. ''Even Superman wears a little bit more than that.''

He mirrored her gesture. ''Can I borrow a cape?''

"No. You can eat breakfast, and we can make some plans while you wait for your pants. Half an hour," she added before he could protest. "That's all I'm asking for. Then you can rush off as heedlessly as you like— if you still want to rush off heedlessly, that is."

Selim couldn't keep from looking back at Sterling. The bloodburn had hit the boy fast. He recalled his own stupid, angry gesture the night before. "Stupid," he muttered.

"Feeding him before he was ready?" Valentine nodded. "Yes, it was stupid. Now we have to deal with the consequences."

Once again, Selim said, "We?" And how was it she knew about the burn? The feeding?

"It's a family thing," she said and led him to the kitchen counter.

There was a heaping plate and a full mug of coffee already waiting for him there. He hadn't realized he was hungry until he'd wolfed down most of the high-protein breakfast. The thinly sliced meat was smothered in grilled onions, garlic, and mushrooms. Selim stared at the plate. He poked his breakfast with his fork. After staring at the remains on his plate for a few moments, Selim asked, "Who is this?"

"Oh, just some strig I had in the freezer. For years, actually. Why, is the flavor off?"

Selim looked from the plate to Valentine, then from Valentine to the plate, then back to Valentine. She had sounded so innocent. So very *smug*. "You're not a Hunter."

Behind them, Geoff Sterling groaned again. She looked over her shoulder, gave a sympathetic shake of her head, then turned back to Selim. "Aren't I?"

He couldn't take his gaze off the gentle little storyteller. She smiled. And changed.

Selim jumped off his chair. It fell over backward with a loud clatter. He pointed at the monster, with the fork still grasped tightly in his hand. "You're—you're—!"

"The Mother of all Hunters," she answered around

a muzzle full of hideous fangs. "Retired." She sighed, and her features settled back into human form. "Where the devil do you think you got it from?"

"But—but—" He was not used to being incoherent and didn't like it one bit.

"Where do you think Olympias got it from? Amenarib? Patrician? Auliara?" she went on naming names, mostly of people he'd never heard of, as he tried to grasp hold of his fleeing sanity with both hands. She crossed her arms and looked at him sternly. "I know you never saw me as a Hunter. How often do you show Siri that face? Certainly not when you're in bed with her."

"But—"

"How?" She attempted to look coy and modest at the same time. "It's a long story."

He sat down in the chair that hadn't been turned over. He managed to pry the fork out of his hand and put it down carefully on the counter. His heart raced. His breath came in great, sobbing gulps, like he'd run a marathon. He wasn't taking this in—not into a mind already stuffed to overflowing with too many problems. There was a part of him—a raging, territorial animal part of him—that was deeply furious, bloodthirsty in the most literal sense, at finding another Nighthawk on his territory. Another part of him was shocked and ashamed that another Hunter had been on his territory for decades without his knowing about it.

"I don't get out much," she said. "And I haven't hunted in California in years. You were having Mexican for breakfast, dear."

She was so damned good, and she knew it. So confident of her power.

"I have every right to be."

He snarled at her, but she only laughed. Selim calmed down, mostly because his curiosity won out over his instincts, his temper, and his chagrin. He leaned forward, resting his hands on the counter. He looked Valentine deep in the eyes. "If it's a long story, tell me the abridged version."

She put her hands on the other side of the counter. "It was a gift from the Goddess. I do believe in the Goddess; it's just the practice of her religion that I gave up." She took a sharp breath, as if to catch herself from going off on a digression. "Once upon a time, which is the best way to start a story," she went on. "There were great crimes committed by our kind against humanity. We were born of humankind and had no right to abuse those who did not deserve the life and the death we brought. We were powerful creatures; many forgot all morality. Those who wanted justice for our kind, and for the kind we were born from, begged the Goddess for a way to control the evil ones among us. This was long before the Strigoi Council was formed, by the way. That's another story."

Another breath.

"The Goddess sent dreams and signs to the most holy among us. The signs were interpreted to mean that one of us was to perform certain rituals and sacrifices and trials and the Goddess would grant our prayers. I got the short straw, hon."

Breath.

"All right, I volunteered. I was young and fearless and strong and righteously indignant about all the evil goings-on. I performed the rituals, and . . . changed. It was one of those experiences you never forget but never quite remember. I believe I actually drank some of the Goddess's blood, but it's all very fuzzy. Transcendent, but fuzzy."

Selim listened to all this with a certain skepticism. A certain awe. A large grain of salt. But he didn't disbelieve her. He'd seen her wearing the Hunter's Mask, and it had nearly scared him out of his skin. Nearly given him a heart attack. He smiled faintly at the thought. That was what Hunters did, after all, gave heart attacks. He felt Valentine catch the thought. She laughed with him.

"How much of a hold do you have on me right now?" he asked. "Was . . . that . . . change an illusion?" She stiffened with indignation and lifted her hands before her. Her claws came out . . . and out. "Good, God," Selim murmured.

"Goddess," she answered. She leaned across the counter to rest her hands on his shoulders, pricking the bare skin of his back with needle-sharp claw tips. "Do you want a demonstration?"

Selim shook his head.

"Good." She moved away. "Because we haven't got all night."

Another groan from Sterling punctuated her words.

Valentine padded across the room to kneel beside the suffering boy. She took his head in her lap and ran her hands through his sweat-damp hair. "You're just hungry, sweetheart," she told him softly. "Don't worry, we'll make it better soon. Won't we, Selim?" she added with a significant look his way.

Selim followed her into the living room. The blood-burn was so strong in Sterling that the air around him shimmered with heat. Selim stared at him helplessly; it was a sensation he was almost getting used to. It seemed like he'd been nothing but helpless since this whole thing started. Sterling's back arched in a spasm of pain. Seeing the boy's anguish drove the self-pity out of Selim. "Why is this happening so fast?"

Valentine shrugged. "Trauma, maybe. Maybe he has some Rom in his genetics. Who was his bloodparent?"

"I have no idea."

"Doesn't matter." Her fingers kept combing through Sterling's hair. "He has to Hunt. Tonight." She looked up at Selim. "You can't do it." Before Selim could protest, she added, "We both know why. Unless you've changed since I met you—and I don't think you have."

For a moment, he didn't understand what she meant. Then he sat down slowly, cross-legged on the floor. The thick carpet tickled his bare legs. He looked at Geoff Sterling. "Oh."

"You've never had sons," Valentine elaborated. "Have you? Never made a male Nighthawk, either? You can't, can you?"

Selim rested his hands on his knees and took a deep breath. He probably looked like he was meditating. Inside, he was panicking at images of what was necessary in the making of any type of vampire: blood and death and . . . sex. He shook his head, looking bleakly at the other male. Revulsion twisted his stomach. "I can't do that." His gaze went to Valentine. "If I could—" He shook his head as bile burned the back of his mouth. He wiped the back of his hand across his mouth. "I can't. I thought there'd be time to get him to Olympias, or one of the others. But—"

"No time," Valentine cut in. "You fed him, Selim." The words were harsh accusation.

"I know he's my responsibility!" Selim snarled back.

"Then why aren't you helping him now?"

He watched the woman cradling the young vampire, comforting his suffering with her touch. He shook his head again. "I can't." It shouldn't matter. He was too straight for his own good; he knew that. Too much so for Geoff Sterling's good, that was certain. He focused on Valentine and realized that her concern for Sterling was real, but there were also streaks of triumph and cunning coloring her emotional landscape. There was a bright, considering glint in her deep brown eyes. "What?" Selim demanded. He reached forward and snagged her by the wrist. "What is it you want from me? What are you offering?"

"Yevgeny," she answered, meeting his look levelly. "I want Yevgeny. I want his safety." She sighed. Her words rushed on. "It's time he moved on from me, whether I like it or not. I screwed up with him from the beginning. I took a happily married man from his wife and children without his permission. Took him from a culture and career he loved because of my own needs. Do you know how we met? At a party at the Disney studio. He was part of a Russian delegation doing a goodwill tour. He was the official translator, and a spy, of course. It was the middle of the Cold War, after all.

I took one look at him and jumped. It was assumed he'd defected, when a lust-crazed vampire had abducted him. He never asked for what he became.'' Her face took on a dreamy, bittersweet expression for a moment. ''He was so full of unfocused power, so beautiful and virile. I screwed him over. I thought better of it, eventually. Tried to make up for what I'd done, but my solution didn't work. But I'm trying to help him as much as I can.''

It was a touching story. Her sentiments were admirable. ''Yevgeny,'' Selim said slowly, ''is dead.''

''He's not. I would have felt him die. He's hurt, wounded, in pain . . . but he is not dead.''

Selim would have felt it as well, having been so closely entangled with Valentine during their daydreaming. ''Yevgeny,'' he repeated, words and intent as hard as titanium, ''is dead.''

''No.'' She was just as firm.

''He threatened Siri. He threatened the child. Whatever condition he's presently in, I will be putting him out of his misery soon.''

Valentine jerked her arm from Selim's grasp. ''You most certainly will not!''

''He's insane, Valentine! That makes him a threat to everyone in my territory. I won't have it.''

''He needs help,'' she replied, just as adamant as he was. ''You're going to find it for him.'' She pointed at Sterling. ''A bargain. I assume your responsibility for Geoff, you assume mine for Yevgeny.''

Selim sprang up, fury seething through him. ''No! Do you hear me, Valentia? No.''

She rose majestically to her feet, exuding force and power. ''It's the only solution, and you know it.''

Selim stood his ground despite the impulse to back away from this little goddess. ''You can't have everything your own way. You—'' If Sterling hadn't started screaming at that moment, Selim would have gone on at great length about her being spoiled, selfish, imperious, and impossible. As it was, the sound and piteous sight of the young man writhing on the floor did all Valentine's work for her. The fight went out of Selim. All he could say as his shoulders slumped in capitulation was, "Shit."

Valentine patted him on the shoulder. "I knew you had some compassion left in your heart." She turned and walked out of the room.

Sterling fought for control while she was gone and managed to meet Selim's gaze as Selim stared at him. The awareness fighting through the pain in those eyes was even more startling, and it stabbed deep into Selim's conscience. Sterling managed to mouth a silent *Thank you.* He fought hard for control and even managed to twist up onto his knees by the time Valentine returned. She tossed Selim his pants and shirt, then knelt and put an arm around Sterling's shoulders.

The clothes were warm from the dryer, scented with fabric softener. He went back into the bedroom to dress and put on his shoes. When Selim came back, Valentine had coaxed Sterling to his feet. "What are you going to do?" Selim asked her.

"Take him Hunting right now, of course," she answered. "It was your idea, remember?" He didn't, but she went on before he could point this out. "When you were Hunting Jager, you had a notion about taking out all the other strigs in town for their Hunt. That's what we're going to do, Geoff and I. Go strig hunting."

Selim wasn't even tempted to argue with her. The night was racing past, and there was so much to do. He wanted to be with Siri more than anything else. He needed her, and she needed him. He closed his eyes for a moment, forced himself to keep his priorities in order. Siri would have to wait, damn it! This devil's bargain over Yevgeny would have to come first. He opened his eyes.

"Fine," he told Valentine. "Do what you have to. I'll check back tomorrow night."

Valentine gave a firm nod, then left Sterling to walk Selim to the door. "Go." She opened it for him. "We'll both do what we have to, and that's that.'' Selim might have said something else, but she pushed him out and closed the door firmly behind him.

She collapsed weakly against the door and breathed a thankful sigh once she'd felt Selim's presence moving swiftly away. ''Elvis,'' she murmured, ''has left the building.''

She waited a while longer before she moved. Geoff needed her, but she had to gather her courage first. That had been quite a performance she'd put on for Selim. Now, for the sake of the poor, suffering boy she'd talked Selim into leaving in her keeping, she had to turn in an even stronger performance. She had to find the strength to live up to her end of the bargain.

She walked past the couch and out onto the balcony. She looked up at the stars, down at the walled garden of her Bunker Hill building, out at the skyline of the skyscrapers in the center of the city not too far away. This was her world. A few rooms and a view. A computer modem, a television, a fax machine, and a telephone fitted nicely into this small world, made it as large as she wanted. She wrapped her arms tightly over her stomach, protectively. It couldn't be about what she wanted right now. Couldn't be about her fears and phobias. Geoff needed her. Yevgeny needed her to keep her bargain. Selim, in deadly peril, needed her most of all.

Then again, she faltered, maybe the vision wouldn't come true.

Her head spun dizzily at the very thought of leaving her safe retreat. The sky tilted down, and the steel and glass buildings in the distance rose up higher and higher. She knew they were going to fall on her, flatten her, crush her. She threw her hands up to cover her face, took a frantic step backward. If she could just get inside, close the door, draw the heavy drapes across the view of the outside, then she'd be—

A hand grasped her shoulder. She backed into a solid wall of muscle. A reek of sweat filled her nostrils, and a shock of pain transferred from soul to soul at the point where Geoff touched her. Valentine gasped and spun to look into Geoff's tortured face. He was beyond words, but his thought came to her clearly, acid-tinged with agony. *How long since you've been outside?*

"Three years," she answered honestly. "Give or take a month or six."

He gave a brief, curt nod. His eyes were full of pleading. *Help me. I'll help you.*

His hunger burned into her. Hunger for revenge as much as the bloodburn that desperately needed to be released. That he was on his feet and lucid amazed her. Pleased her. Gave her hope, as well. He was a tough one. He reminded her of herself when she was young.

Why not? I'm your grandson, aren't I, Lady of Snakes?

Her eyes went wide at his presumption, at the blasphemy. Then she smiled. "So you are." She patted his cheek, though he winced from the gentle touch. "And a smart little owlet, too." At least his thoughts gave her a certain amount of courage—or at least helped return her focus. She could do this. Would. Must.

She told him, "Wait here while I get my dagger."

Chapter 25

SELIM HAD TWO choices after racing up the steps and crossing the wide, fountained plaza at the top of the hill a few blocks away from Valentine's neighborhood. He could take the steep concrete steps that led down the sharp descent of the hill on this side of the plaza, or he could take a car of the old-fashioned funicular railway known as Angel's Flight down to the street far below. He paused at the rail for a few moments, considering options, gazing down through the night at the old, beaten up backside of the city, sharply divided from the flashy new skyscrapers and prosperous housing just the height of the hill away. It was a long way down. Union Station wasn't far from where he stood, the hour wasn't that late. He could probably grab a seat on a commuter train out to Claremont.

"Or I could just go home to Siri," he murmured. "And hope she'll be there." He continued to lean against the rail and found himself wishing for a cigarette for the first time in years. They helped him think. He'd given up the smoking habit when he'd met her, at her insistence. He smiled at the memory of those arguments over health and secondary smoke. He was a henpecked Hunter, and she was right, he loved it.

He wanted to be with her, ached to, physically and psychically. Home was where she was. Selim knew that if he'd been with her, paid attention to her, given her his strength, Yevgeny would never have somehow wormed his way into her mind. He was the one who'd put her life and sanity at risk, thinking he did it for her own good. Which was the excuse Valentine gave herself for her selfishness with Yevgeny. Selim could almost forgive Yevgeny what he'd done in light of what had been done to him. What he'd started doing to Siri— because he loved her. Wanted to keep her forever in a world where the inhabitants were immortal but relationships were ephemeral. He and Siri had a lot of making up to do. He had a lot to pay for. All he could do was love her for as long as he could have her.

"Screw it," he growled and jumped over the railing.

He landed in the middle of the street below and sprang on top of a car roof to avoid being hit. The driver honked and swerved, not sure of what he'd seen but radiating an adrenaline rush of terror that reached out to perfume the night. Selim leapt off the car, got his bearings, and decided not to bother with the train. He needed a long, hard run to clear his head. He hoped something would clear his head soon, because if it didn't, he was going to go as crazy as his darling, little, fanged horror of a bloodmother.

He followed the train tracks all the way to Claremont. Streaks and traces of the mental energy and magic shot out earlier today permeated the center of the town. Selim had to stand for a while at the base of the hill beyond the train station to sort out the lines of scarring on the psychic landscape. He knew where the events at noon had taken place, but the trails that led from the site were more important right now. He drew in long breaths, searching through physically perceptible scents. There was a wealth of those in the air, as well. Finally, it was a fresh trail of emotion he recognized and chose to follow. He knew within a few blocks where the trail led and took a shortcut to head off the hunter.

Selim stepped out of the shadows on Miriam's front porch when Don Tomas reached the steps. "You shouldn't be here, Tom."

Tomas looked up, his face illuminated by the weak yellow glow of the porch light. His eyes were wide black pools; a pair of fangs protruded from beneath his upper lip. Tomas pointed a clawed finger toward the door. *"He*—whatever he is—shouldn't be in there."

Selim nodded his agreement. "I'll take care of it."

"Out of my way, Selim."

Selim moved to the top of the porch steps, blocking Tomas's way. Tomas's anger gave off a hot, deep red psychic glow, but he radiated cold determination as well. "I said I'd take care of it."

"You should have already taken care of it! You promised to protect my son, Hunter."

Guilt scratched inside Selim. "I know I did." This was no time to offer excuses, to justify his failure with a tale of being disoriented and distracted because someone more powerful had been raping his mind. An Enforcer didn't show weakness. An Enforcer of the Law didn't explain. "I am sorry," he apologized.

"Is Miriam part of this? Part of a plot to kill my child?"

"I have no idea how Miriam is involved," he admitted. "Not yet."

"Then let's ask her." Tomas snarled, and jumped toward him.

Selim caught and held him. They struggled, and Selim went over backward, landing heavily on the wide wooden porch, with Don Tomas on top of him. Selim grasped Tomas around the waist while the angry vampire swiped at Selim's eyes. Selim turned his head, and Tomas's claws scratched across his cheek. Fangs snapped at his shoulder.

"Ouch! Shit! Tom, don't make me have to hurt you!"

"Get out of my way."

"Get off my porch."

Selim hadn't heard the door open while he struggled with Don Tomas, but Miriam now stood behind them. Selim tilted his head back to look at her. "Good evening."

"Hello."

Tomas looked up from where Selim still held him in a tight grip, and he snarled a challenge. Miriam's features began to change in response, but she caught herself and remained calm and human-looking. "I understand what you're going through, Don Tomas, but don't push it." She came forward a few steps and nudged first Tomas, and then Selim, with her foot. "I won't have you fighting like schoolboys out here. It will draw attention. Bring it inside," she ordered them and stood back to hold her front door open. "I'm inviting you into my nest, Tomas," she added as Selim and the angry vampire disentangled themselves. "Answer the invitation properly, and we'll have this sorted out quickly."

The implied threat of reprisal hung in the air, and Selim had to acknowledge her rights. "She can beat the crap out of you, Tom," he reminded the *hidalgo*. "Then you'd be stuck here when Cassie and Sebastian need you at home."

Miriam could beat the crap out of him, if truth be told—and what a stupid title for a movie that was—having been a vampire for a very, very long time. She was also a sweet, civilized woman with no interest in outmoded dominance games. She wouldn't have dealt with her human stalker in a violent way if she hadn't needed to Hunt. She didn't want violence now, unless Tomas forced her into it, that is. "Let's listen to what she has to say," Selim urged. "We're on her territory." Selim carefully released his hold on Don Tomas.

Tomas rose to his feet, his gaze locked with Miriam's, but he reached down to give Selim a hand up. Selim stood by his side and waited through a short mental confrontation between the other vampires. It took a while, but Don Tomas's features gradually returned to normal, his anger toned down to a banked, manageable fire. Selim held in his sigh of relief.

"Apologies, doña," Tomas said, after silently acknowledging Miriam's superiority. "I will accept your hospitality for now."

Selim didn't ask for an apology, and none was offered. He took Don Tomas by the arm. "Let's do what the lady says, and take it inside." He had quite a few questions for Miriam himself, but out here in the open dark was no place to voice them. Once they were in Miriam's book-lined bedroom with the door closed behind them, Selim said, "Where is he, and what is he doing here?"

"Why is he alive?" Don Tomas demanded. "*He* tried to kill in your territory."

Miriam took a seat in a deep leather chair and gestured for them to sit. Selim and Tomas remained standing. Joseph and Gary hovered on either side of Miriam's chair, protective and worried. The household's other vampire was not present. Miriam looked calmly up at Selim. "Yevgeny is here because he failed in a suicide attempt. Suicide," she went on, her gaze locked hard on Don Tomas's. "Surely, you saw what happened at Andrew's place today? I know I was aware of much of what went on." Tomas nodded, his jaw tight with tension, his hands balled tightly at his sides. Miriam cut her gaze to Selim. "How is Siri?"

"Fine," he answered, though he didn't know that at all and wanted very much to find out. That was why he had to get this over with quickly. Was it suicide? He wondered. Or had Siri helped direct the silver knife toward Yevgeny's heart? He didn't question Miriam's interpretation, not with a promise to Valentine to keep.

"If it wasn't suicide," Miriam said anyway "he would not be under my protection now."

"How can you protect him?" Don Tomas demanded. "After what he tried to do to my son? Where is he? I promised to bring his heart to my wife."

"That's very touching, Tomas," Miriam said, quite

unperturbed. "But I won't allow it. The man is disturbed but not evil. Believe me, I *know*. I've been inside his head; so have Joseph and Andrew. I trust my judgment and theirs. Gary and Joseph went back to the coffee-house late this afternoon and found him," she explained before Selim could ask. "The plan was to finish him off if he was still alive." She glanced fondly at her companion and her slave. "They couldn't do it. This was cold-blooded killing, not a Hunt. So they stuffed him into the back of the car and brought him home for me or Andrew to dispose of. He was coming around, and thinking very loudly by then. What they picked up from him was very unsettling. Not the emotions of a child murderer, certainly."

"He tried to kill my son!" Tomas looked frantically at Selim. "Why doesn't she understand that?"

"Because he set out to kill a monster, not slay an innocent child." Miriam stood. Joseph and Gary moved closer to her. "Honestly, Tomas, why are you being so single-mindedly stupid about the whole affair? Look at it from his point of view!"

"I am the victim's father," Tomas pointed out. "I don't need any other point of view."

"No, I suppose not," she agreed. "Look at it this way, then. Yevgeny did not set out to kill a child. In fact, he couldn't kill a child. He set out to ritually sacrifice a monster in order to gain the immortality he'd earned after five decades of enthrallment to a vampire who denied him his rightful birth. It turned out he was an honorable person who could not harm a child, even though it meant sacrificing his chance to join the strigoi. Now that," she went on, her attention mostly on Selim. "Is the sort of person we need living in this little world of ours."

Selim gave her a grudging nod. He wasn't going to disagree with anything she said in the blond bastard's behalf. He said to Tomas. "Let it go. Sebastian's home, he's safe. No harm has been done."

Tomas shook his head unbelievingly. "No harm—"

Selim took Tomas aside. "No one's going to change your mind," he said quietly to the outraged father. "So let's make a deal, instead."

"Deal?" Tomas spat out the word, but he didn't turn away. Selim had no doubt that Tomas knew what was coming.

"You and Cassandra," he said anyway. "She shouldn't be living with you. It creates a great deal of tension and resentment, but I've allowed it for five years now. If you don't let this Yevgeny matter go, I won't allow her to live with you any longer." Selim didn't mention what everyone suspected, that Tomas and Cassandra were still, somehow, lovers as well as a parent and child living in the same nest. He couldn't help but recall the vivid dream about making love to Valentine, vampire to vampire. Remembering it, he didn't blame Tom and Cassie a bit, though it was wrong and evil and forbidden on pain of death by the Law. *Don't ask, don't tell,* he thought and went on. "You need to Hunt, my friend. Once you do, Yevgeny won't seem so important to you."

Don Tomas stood before him, wiry and intense, dark eyes blazing, deep voice rough with emotion, cold as death. He ignored Selim's mention of Cassandra. "You're saying I'm irrational because I'm hungry?"

Selim nodded, hoping Tomas would accept this. He almost held his breath while he watched Tomas battle with his anger and pride. "I will Hunt," Tomas said finally. He glared at Selim. "Tomorrow. Where you said. Arrange it." With that, he was gone, moving so swiftly that the front door slamming behind him was the only indication he'd been in the house a moment before.

Selim breathed a sigh of relief and turned his attention to Miriam. "What do you plan to do with the nut case?"

She frowned at his attitude. "Heal him, of course. He deserves our help."

Selim refrained from voicing his personal opinions on the matter. "How?"

"Take him under my wing, of course." She smiled. "Andrew's solution, really. In fact, Andrew will be the one who gives birth to Yevgeny. If that's all right with you?" she asked, for form's sake. "He's been wanting to visit some friends in Texas, anyway. We thought that after Andrew helped Yevgeny make the kill, he'd spend a year or so in Austin with his friends. That way I can concentrate on the fledgling, and no Law will have been broken."

"Bent a little, though." Selim sighed and shrugged. It seemed that every vampire in Southern California was becoming expert on bending the Law lately. "Fine. Do it, Miriam. Do you have someone in mind for the kill? Or am I supposed to help with that?"

Her smile widened. "We have a plan." She glanced fondly at Joseph. "You remember the man who was stalking me?" There was no need for him to reply to that. Miriam looked disgusted as she went on. "While we were disposing of him, he emptied a great deal of what was on his nasty little mind into ours. There is a rapist he occasionally ran with before he caught sight of me. We couldn't help but find out this person's name and what he's done. Joe managed to track down his address. We have all the information we need. We thought it would be good for the world if we took this slime off the streets. With your permission, of course, Hunter."

"Sounds like a plan." Selim looked toward the door. "I'm going to go home now, okay?"

Gary spoke up for the first time. "Siri needs you."

Followed by Joseph. "What about the other matter, Hunter?"

"Yes," Miriam added. "What about this script Joseph says mentions us by name?"

Selim did his best to project casual unconcern. He managed a nonchalant smile. "No problem," he told the worried nest members. "It's already taken care of." Valentine couldn't be trusted, he knew, but her Yevgeny couldn't be in better hands. And he'd have the weak, vulnerable, fledgling Yevgeny to use as a bargaining

piece if Valentine tried double-crossing him over the rewrite she'd promised. He looked at Joseph. "I believe
the term for what's happening with *If Truth Be Told* is
that it's lost in development hell. This is good, and I'm
going home now," he said again, and left before anyone
could say anything more.

Selim wasn't there. He hadn't been home when she arrived at his apartment as soon as she could after taking
Sebastian home. She'd almost been too tired and drained
to care. Exhaustion and reaction claimed every bit of
energy she had left as she fell into his bed, wondering
where he was. She'd slept alone through the last of the
day for hour after nightmare-riddled hour, only to wake
in the night, still alone. It was so damned unfair to always be alone that all Siri wanted to do was lie in the
big, lonely bed and scream and scream. So she lay on
her back, gazed at the blank beige ceiling, and did just
that. She drummed her fists and heels against the mattress, too. After a while, her throat hurt, and she felt like
an idiot. So she got up, took a shower, then made her
way to the living room.

She hadn't noticed the wreckage left from the night
before when she'd arrived, though she supposed she
must have picked her way through it. All she'd cared
about then was getting to the bedroom. Now she surveyed it with a mixed sense of utter distaste and gleeful
delight. She hated his pack rat ways, hated the ancient
furnishings. She was well aware that the world was falling apart around them, that her vampire was probably
out trying to save them all from death and disaster. She
also knew that he wasn't here with her where she needed
him to be. The best way to keep her mind off approaching chaos, and get even for Selim's absence, was em-
bodied by this scattered mess before her. Siri stood in
the center of the living room, rubbed her hands together,
and cackled evilly. Then she went to get a broom and
trash bags from the kitchen.

She was filling the second plastic bag when she became aware of Selim. Her mind was bruised, her gift dulled, but she could feel him, though she had to close her eyes and concentrate very hard. He was nearby. He was coming home. He was coming to *her*. She relaxed with relief and found herself sitting on the floor. It hurt too much to try to hold onto the awareness, so she let it go. Only to have the vision slam her like a nail right between the eyes.

Too exhausted to clear the razor wire, the panting strig slid down the fence. She turned to face the pair behind her, bloodied hands raised defensively. One of the pair behind her moved forward. Geoff Sterling's form flashed into and out of the glare of a passing train's lights. The train roared. Geoff dashed straight at the other vampire, dodged a kick, blocked a downward arc of claws with a forearm. Geoff snarled. Something silver flashed through the air behind him. He snatched the blade from the air. Brought it down with all his strength across the strig's face. Another strike buried the blade to the hilt in strig's throat. The screaming strig went down. A small figure raced forward, grabbed Geoff, and dragged him to his knees. Two sets of fangs and claws attacked the body on the ground. Heat soared through the attacking creatures. Huge, obsidian-bright eyes met, their bloody hands reached for each other. Then—

Siri's vision cleared at the sound of the door opening. She sprang to her feet, panting with terror and need. Selim was there, as wide-eyed as she was, as full of the hot, heady emotions of the vision. He held his arms open to her. She rushed forward on a wordless cry. Hearts pounding, blood burning, they came together in the center of the room.

There was no stopping after a chaste kiss and swift, affectionate hug this time. Not after 390 days. He'd counted those days as much as she had, suffered through each lonely hour with her.

"No more. We aren't going to be alone tonight," he promised the fierce little woman in his arms.

She bit him first, before he could even kiss her. Her teeth sank into the flesh of his throat, not sharp enough to break the tough, supple skin, but hard enough to drive all memory of the Hunting vision out of him. He'd been struck blind with another's need as he reached his own door. Once inside that door, with Siri in his arms, being with *her* was all that mattered. Her touch filled his senses, her scent surrounded him, the texture of her skin, the firm, familiar weight of her small body as he carried her into the bedroom. Her hair brushed his cheek and sent waves of fire through him. The tips of her breasts pressed burning points into his chest.

She was beneath him on the bed before she lifted her mouth from his throat. The bite mark throbbed. He shared the sensation with her. "You scared me to death," he told her between sharp, short, teasing bites on her ear, her shoulder, on her breasts through the soft cotton of her blouse. He drew blood only once, and licked it off in long, slow swipes of his tongue across her lovely, long neck. He savored her taste like a cat licking cream. She panted beneath him, dug her nails into his back. Eventually, he let her pull off his shirt. He didn't bother with any subtlety in ripping her clothes off her, though he was very careful not to mark her skin with his claws.

"Don't you ever put yourself in danger like that again," he warned, and kissed her before she could manage an indignant answer. It was the only way to shut Siri up, really, to kiss her until she was crazy. His hands moved over her, rediscovering all her soft, sensitive places, drawing moans of pleasure from them both.

She kissed back, mouth hot and eager against his. Her tongue stroked against his upper teeth, stimulated and teased at the protective sheath above his canines. He took her mouth as long as he could stand it, until there was no stopping the hard thrust of his primary fangs any longer.

He knelt back on the bed, and Siri scrambled up. She wrapped her legs around his hip and thrust herself down hard on his erection with a sharp cry of need. She settled around him, hot and tight and deep. She shifted her weight, and he cried out in response. She thrust forward and threw back her head. He cupped her small, perfect breasts with his hands, savored the feel of them, savored the throbbing pleasure of being sheathed deep inside her. Shared need and pleasure shifted through them, mingled, taking, giving, and blending. Selim lowered his head, slowly, reveling in the building need for sweet blood.

"Selim! Come on!"

"Whiner!"

"Now!"

He laughed at her demand, then nearly screamed as she retaliated with a hard stroke of her hips. He cupped her ass and held her still. "Savor the moment, woman!"

Her eyes glittered at him, full of half-angry need. There was humor there as well, understanding, trust. All the love in the world. "Screw patience!" she snarled. "Bite me."

"No, screw you!" he answered. He laughed again, happy for the first time in a very long time. And then he bit her.

Chapter 26

"WE NEED TO talk."

"We need to get out of bed." The flat of Siri's hand landed hard on his bare chest. "Ouch!" Selim turned on his side and snagged her around the waist. "Presumptuous wench."

Her eyes narrowed. "Do I look like a wench to you?"

She looked gorgeous and well-used, her naked skin covered in a half dozen already-healing bite marks. He touched one, circled the mark slowly with the tip of one finger. "I don't know; I never met one." He turned onto his back and brought her with him.

Siri settled on his chest, held his face between her hands, and looked him in the eye. "We need to talk."

The night had passed in making love, they'd slept cradled together through the day, and now it was night again. He fluffed his fingers through the feathery strands of her short hair. "Am I supposed to apologize again?"

"I'd like that, but later. You can make love to me later, too. Without teeth," she added as his sharp concern radiated to her. "We can do it without biting each other."

"It's not as much fun."

"Don't pout, Selim. You started this." She shook his head from side to side. "Just promise me it won't happen again. That we won't go for a year between nights like we just had. Promise me that you'll explain the reasons you do things—and not try to hypnotize me into not thinking about them."

He rubbed his hands up and down her spine. "You noticed me doing that?"

"Eventually. Stop making me forget that I'm going to become a vampire. Promise me."

It wasn't easy, but it wasn't as hard as the last year had been. Nothing could be as hard as that. Except losing her. He took a deep breath, and Siri shifted on top of him. He let out the breath and kissed her nose. "I promise."

She grinned. "Plus promise we can take swing dancing lessons."

Laughter exploded from him. Rather than give in and tell her he'd do anything she wanted, he filled her in on everything that had happened since she'd dropped him off in front of Valentine's apartment building. She explained to him how Sebastian came to be in Andrew's coffeehouse. He was relieved that she showed more interest in Geoff Sterling's transformation into a Nighthawk than in Yevgeny's being allowed to live. Her only comment on Yevgeny was, "Miriam will keep him out of trouble." They left it at that. They had comforted each other through a bad bout of reaction to the whole hellish situation with last night's lovemaking.

"I have go to work," he told her, reluctant to go but unable to stay.

"I know." She rolled off him, and out of the bed. He watched with great pleasure as she stretched and rolled her shoulders. Having his full attention, she went on, "That's what we have to talk about." He sat up in bed, frowning, knowing what was coming. "You remember the cops who shot the store owner? Your excuse for starting a riot?'' He nodded slowly. ''I was watching the news while you slept through the afternoon.''

That she hadn't been in bed beside him all day both surprised and delighted him. He wasn't *supposed* to be aware of the daylight world. Vampires were supposed to sleep like the dead while they wandered through their own interior world. He'd been too satiated and exhausted to even dream last day. All had been blessed darkness; even Valentine had stayed out of his head. Siri had been beside him when he woke; who cared what happened while he was unconscious?

She did, from the worried feel of her. ''What about the cops, Siri?''

''One of them was involved in another shooting. He wasn't even suspended after the first one! Imagine the reaction on the street to that. You want a riot, well you're probably going to get one without having to do anything to help.''

Selim filed away the information and ignored her bitter annoyance. And her concern that the city was about to go up in flames. Don Tomas would be happy to hear the news. He gave her a brusque nod and got out of bed. Her accusing gaze and silence as they showered, then dressed, was worse than any verbal argument. The disappointed hurt in her eyes was worst of all.

Siri accepted Selim's silence on the matter grudgingly. She wasn't going to argue, couldn't. She was too aware of how badly Tom's nest needed to Hunt. The incident with Sebastian had resulted in Tomas forbidding Cassie to even talk to Siri, in commanding that Sebastian have no contact with the outside world, and the severe punishment of the two slaves that had let Sebastian go with her and Yevgeny. They were lucky not to be dead, she supposed, and Cassie had resorted to E-mail rather than the usual phone calls. Tomas wasn't going to calm down and see reason until after he'd killed someone.

''I just want to get this over with,'' she finally acknowledged. She came into his arms after they finished dressing and moved into the living room. Pressing close to him, she said, "Just do what you have to."

Knowing that she was disappointed in him was a nagging ache in his soul. It made him want to apologize. He kissed her instead. "It'll be over soon." He stroked his fingers across her forehead. "Then we'll go dancing."

She smiled with an effort. "For years and years? How much longer can we dance together, Selim?"

She felt his reluctance to answer and was relieved when he did. "Another ten years, perhaps. If we're very, very careful."

She held him tightly, fiercely possessive. "Twenty years together. Most mortal couples don't have that long." They kissed again, long enough and passionately enough to stir mingled blood, but neither made any move to take it any farther. *Later.* They shared the thought. Then he drew his head away, and she let him go. "Go to work." She pointed toward the door. "I'll be here when you get home. Redecorating," she added just before the door closed behind him.

Siri hugged herself tightly after Selim was gone. She refused to think of Yevgeny and what too much time as a companion had done to him. She wasn't like Yevgeny. Selim wasn't like this crazy woman he'd told her about. What she did think of was her friend Cassie. Now, she was a great deal like Cassie. She saw no reason for letting thousands of years of custom and the strictly enforced Laws of the feared Strigoi Council get in the way of her having the same marital arrangement her friend Cassie managed to have with a vampire at least as conservative and traditional as her darling Selim.

"Twenty years, my ass," she said to the empty room. But she wasn't going talk to Selim about their future just yet, not when she had ten more years to get him used to the idea of living happily ever after. Literally.

Selim knew having Siri drive him on tonight's dangerous errands was stupid, even for the pleasure of her company. He didn't want to get into any more arguments over ethics, anyway. So he left her to mess with his stuff and traveled on foot. Check on Valentine and Sterling first, he decided, then join Tomas's nest. He still had Mike's and Alice's Hunts to deal with, he recalled. Things had to get back to business as usual, and it had to start tonight.

He moved swiftly, making plans, though his thoughts kept drifting back to Siri. And to Valentine, and Miriam, and even Alice. Things they'd said, and the things they'd each done in the last several days affected him more than he wanted to think about. So he ended up thinking about them anyway. Women, he scoffed. Gentle, soft, impractical, idealistic, and they made him look damned bad. That was the galling part. He laughed at the thought and ran faster, eating up the miles from Pasadena into downtown L.A.

Something struck Selim as odd about the area around the Farmer's Market when he neared it. A darker darkness to the night, an empty quality, though there were cars and people on the streets. Not enough, he thought. There was a dullness, a distance to the mortal figures. Not enough lights in the buildings. Where were the produce trucks that should be lining the docks at this time of night? Shouldn't the annoying roaring hum of their refrigerator units be filling the air? Shouldn't there be a small army of workers swarming around the trucks that weren't there? Or should they be? Selim wasn't sure what day it was, and the run-down neighborhood wasn't exactly his usual haunt. Maybe it was Sunday. Was the market closed on Sunday?

He stopped at the foot of the stairs next to the steep slant of the Angel's Flight railway track, shrugged, and looked around. He could tell that there were no cars in the parking garage on the other side of the funicular tracks. That was impossible, and there was a cold, evil feel to that impossibility. The corner streetlights were lit and so were the lights on the long, sharply angled stairs, but their light did little good against the thick darkness.

"Not good," he murmured. "Not good at all." His softly spoken words were absorbed into the enveloping night; he could almost see it happen.

Shadows. There were too many shadows. Forms waited in the shadows, and enough psychic energy swirled around the shadows to keep all but the most mind-blind mortals away. They'd been waiting for him, clouding his mind with their concentrated energy as well. Selim didn't know if they'd released their hold or if he'd fought his way through it. Either way, the trap was sprung. He glanced at the sign post that arced overhead at the base of the narrow railway tracks. Angel's Flight.

The vision had angels in it. In the vision, he was involved in a terrible fight. In the movie version, the fight was with Istvan. After confronting Kamaraju over the death of Moira Chasen, he'd assumed that was what the vision of angels meant, since she played one in her television series. That hadn't been it at all.

"Kamaraju." Selim turned around slowly as the shadows drew near in a tight, confining circle. "I should have expected this."

"You read the script, too, I see," Kamaraju said, stepping out of his shadow. The others appeared one by one after him: Lisa and his remaining fledglings. Selim sensed all of Kama's slaves nearby as well. Mike Tancredi came up beside Kamaraju. Mike's people ranged around him: three young vampires and a trio of companions.

Selim glanced sourly at Lisa, the woman who worked in an agent's office. And Kama had investments in the film industry. Of course they'd gotten their hands on the script. Selim looked to Mike. "Leave now, and I won't kill you."

"You won't kill any of us," Michael Tancredi answered. "We read the script." He laughed and gestured his fledglings closer. The young vampires moved reluctantly, but they did as he commanded. "We learned a lot from the script, Selim. We learned that even these kids can take you.''

Selim sent a glare at the young ones. Two of them stepped back. The one that held her ground trembled as she did so. ''I don't think so, Mike.''

''We've all been scared of those big teeth of yours,'' Kamaraju said. ''But they're just big teeth. We learned who you really are.''

''You weren't born in the time of the pharaohs,'' Mike added. He sounded really offended by this.

Selim shrugged. ''I never said I was. I am the Enforcer of the City, though.''

Lisa spoke up. She quoted the script as she went on:

''I wasn't born in a cage, but I grew up in one, Siri. There's a palace within the Topkapi Palace in Istanbul, within the seraglio. It was called the Cage. Where the Ottoman sultans sent their unwanted sons. I was unwanted there from sometime around 1725 until I met—her.''

''You've been bluffing all along, Hunter. You've earned your reputation by taking out only the young ones and the strigs no one cares about. Now you're going to have to face some real vampires.'' Kamaraju smiled. It was nasty, even without the fangs. ''We're going to take you home and play with you for a very long time.''

''We're going to own the Enforcer,'' Mike went on as a gang of children began slowly circling around Selim. ''Then we can do anything we want.''

Selim nodded his understanding. He didn't quite believe the stupidity of this situation, though he was well aware of the danger they presented. He kept his hands at his sides but let his claws fully extend. The young ones kept circling, with a row of companions behind them. It sickened Selim to watch Mike and Kama fall back, willing to let the ones they should be protecting face death. It was a good strategy, though. Kamaraju would probably call in his slaves as well. Selim would become exhausted having to fight them off, then the older vampires would move in. They couldn't kill him. What they would then do to him would be worse.

He focused on Mike. "You'd know this was crazy if it wasn't for the bloodfever, Mike. We don't need these dominance games. We have peace here, stability. You like the good life, Tancredi. You'd remember that if you weren't Hunt mad. Go away now and I won't have to kill all your kids."

"Go ahead and kill them," Kamaraju said. "Mike and I can make more when we have you. Can't we, Mike?"

"But that," said Alice Fraser, stepping out of her own shadow, "would be such a damn waste." Rene and Angela came to flank her. Behind them were the rest of Alice's household. She waved at Selim. "Hello, hon. Hi, Tom," she added, looking past where Selim stood.

Selim turned to see Don Tomas standing on the staircase, holding the hand of a tall, auburn-haired beauty. His four fledglings were there as well, glaring with stone-faced aggression at Kamaraju's and Tancredi's households.

"Hello, Tomas," Selim said to the *hidalgo*.

"You're late for our appointment," Tomas replied.

Selim waved at the crowd. His heart was racing with relief. He was glad somebody other than Siri had responded to his psychic cry for help. Though Siri had likely gotten on the phone and made a few calls to get everyone here. He kept his manner cool. "Got held up."

"You're interfering with my Hunt," Tomas said to Kamaraju.

Mike turned to Alice. He pointed at Selim. "He's a fraud. We have proof! Join us, and the city will be ours."

"I don't want the city," Alice answered. "I'd take a piece of you, though, hon," she added, fangs showing. She laughed, harpy and siren at once. Others joined in, but it sounded more like the howling of a maddened wolf pack than laughter.

She had the fever as well. Heat rolled over them all, the dark, ever-present *need* to stalk and terrorize and strike had reached boiling point in every vampire in town. This *was* every vampire in town. There was no way out of this fight, was there? The nests going after each other was the last thing he wanted. Slaves and companions would die, weaker vampires would end up serving the stronger until they could challenge for dominance themselves. It was all allowed under the Law, but it was no way for civilized beings to act.

Selim wasn't sure who he blamed more, Valentine, Kamaraju, or himself.

One of Alice's people moved forward. Lisa lunged at him. One of Tomas's fledglings jumped to defend Alice's man. Everything was up for grabs after that.

"Valentine," Selim decided. But Kamaraju was here. He changed and leapt.

Snarling, fighting forms swirled around him, mixing teeth and claws with martial arts training. Blood scent rose on the air. Through the loud crack of bones and meaty thud of blows, Selim singled out his target. Kamaraju saw death coming his way and turned to run.

The spray of bullets that slammed into his chest as he spun away from Selim slowed Kamaraju down considerably. The sound of gunfire brought the riot to an instant halt. More bullets flew into the silence. Kamaraju fell to his knees, blood pouring onto the concrete. Selim raced toward him, but a dark figure in black leather reached Kamaraju first. Geoff Sterling put a bullet into the older vampire's brain before he kicked him in the chest. Silence reigned as Kamaraju flopped over onto his back. Sterling tossed the gun aside. It was caught by a small woman, who swaggered forward, the AK-47 cradled with easy assurance in her hands.

Selim stepped back, transforming back to normal, and watched with the same silent fascination as the rest of the crowd. Bloodfever had died down considerably with the introduction of this new danger in their midst. Cooled, but it wasn't gone. Selim felt the atmosphere humming with the need for release, like the insides of a lightning storm.

"Now, that's how you kill an older vampire," Valentine instructed Sterling. "You just have to distract them long enough to rip out their hearts." She beamed at Selim. "Isn't that right, dear?"

He couldn't find words to answer. All he could do was watch as Sterling's claws grew out and out, to Nighthawk's length. He'd felt the boy kill several times the night before; now he saw the result before him. The boy's face changing into a muzzle that accommodated all those nasty, sharp, multiple rows of fangs. Impressive. There were gasps from among the watchers. Selim nodded his congratulations to Valentine on her work.

Kamaraju groaned, tried to lift his body off the ground. Valentine pumped a few more rounds into him. In the distance, police sirens began to sound. They weren't very far from Parker Center, after all. The sirens might have nothing to do with the gunfire. "Hurry up," Valentine instructed.

Geoff stood over Kamaraju for another moment, savoring his victory. Then he knelt and ripped open Kamaraju's clothes. A second later, he ripped open Kamaraju's chest with his fangs. He laughed when Kamaraju screamed. When Sterling stood up, he held Kamaraju's heart in his hands. Selim didn't begrudge him the kill. Revenge for Moira was Sterling's right.

He turned and tossed the meat to Selim. "You take it, man. No way I'm touching that scum."

Selim glanced disdainfully at the still-beating organ. "Yuck! What makes you think I want it?" He tossed it toward Valentine. "Somebody has to," he told her. He wiped his hands on his pants. "You do it, Mom."

It was Alice who spoke as Valentine made a face and disposed of the immortality of Kamaraju. "Is this a demonstration to show us that there are now three Enforcers in Los Angeles?"

"She's a smart girl," Valentine said after she'd gagged down the heart. She beamed around the crowd. "Does anyone have a napkin? If not," she added, "why don't you all go home?" She was still holding the AK-47, and there were more mortals than vampires in the crowd. Most of them took the hint with only brief looks of permission from their masters. Kamaraju's people had already fled.

Selim went up to Mike Tancredi. "I like Valentine's trick—Have you met Valentine, by the way?—Do I have to use it on you?" Tancredi's gaze was on the sidewalk. He shook his head. Selim put his hand on the car salesman's shoulder. He was determined not to hold a grudge. He was determined to maintain peace in his town. "Go home, Mike," he said quietly. "Get some rest. I'll take you Hunting tomorrow night."

Selim knew that Tancredi didn't trust him or quite believe him, but he went without arguing, with all his people following closely behind. Selim let out a loud sigh of relief after they were gone. He turned around and found Valentine standing over Kamaraju's corpse.

She looked his way. "Kama made the mistake most people do in this town. He began to believe his own press." She looked around her at the buildings and up at the sky far overhead. Then she looked at Geoff Sterling. "I really would like to go home now."

"I'll take you," he answered. "Soon." He looked down at the body. "I have to clean up this mess first, just like you taught me last night."

He'd become a Hunter in one night. Amazing. Maybe Valentine was the Mother of All Hunters. She was certainly Something Else. Selim didn't want to think about what. He noticed the dark Mercedes pull up across the street. He waved a hand toward the car but didn't go to Siri yet. He gestured Alice and Don Tomas over.

"I've been thinking," he told them. And he knew what he was about to suggest was for Siri. And Valentine. And Miriam. And especially for Moira Chasen. And—he sighed—because it was the right thing to do, if one was the sort who let ethics get in the way of self-interest. "There's a serial killer in your neighborhood, Alice. Why don't you take your people into Griffith Park and take him out?"

She smiled, radiated pleasure. "I had been meaning to suggest that to you."

"Right. Tomas." He turned to the other nest leader. "I think you get the job of making East Los Angeles a safer place. There's a police officer that needs killing. Why don't you and yours . . ." Selim gestured toward the group gathered around Tomas's—companion? lady? wife?—Selim did not want to try to define the relationship just now. "Why don't you prevent a riot instead of exploiting one?"

Don Tomas shruggèd. "If that's what you want, Selim. As long as we Hunt tonight."

He could see Siri standing in the street, leaning against the door of her car, arms crossed. She was listening very intently, with her heart and her soul and her vision. She was smiling. Selim couldn't help but smile back.

"Be right back, Tom."

He trotted to Siri's side. "Happy now?" he asked her.

Siri nodded. "It's a start. Someone once said that a little revolution now and then is a good thing." She frowned. "But I don't know who."

"A woman called Valentine," he told her. He kissed Siri's cheek and glanced at the small, lovely, mad, and marvelous Hunter on the other side of the street. He thought that perhaps she was called Valentine because it was impossible not to be in love with her. In an annoyed, exasperated way.

"I don't want a revolution," Selim told his companion. "I want a vacation." He checked his watch, though he didn't need it to tell him how fast the night was going by. "But right now, I think I have just enough time to save the world before bedtime."

Glossary

Bloodbond The spell that enthralls slaves and companions to their vampire masters

Bloodburn The instinct to Hunt

Bloodchild What a vampire calls a mortal they've changed

Bloodfever Another term for bloodburn

Bloodmother Vampire's female maker

Blood Parent A vampire that has changed a human into a vampire; a Nighthawk who has changed a vampire into a Hunter

Bloodsire Vampire's male maker

Coin Gold coin imprinted with an owl symbol unique to each nest; symbol of authority

Companion Someone chosen to be a vampire's lover

Curse, The Vampirism

Dhamphir Child born of a vampire father and mortal Romany mother

Dream Riding Telepathically eavesdropping on someone's thoughts and dreams

Enforcer of the City Vampire appointed by the Strigoi Council to police a territory

Enforcer of the Laws Vampire cop

Fledgling Young vampire

Fosterling Young vampire living and training under the protection of a nest leader

Gift, The Psychic ability

Goddess Some vampires believe they were created by a curse because of sins against the Goddess

Hunt Sanctioned taking of human prey, regulated by enforcers

Hunter Members of the Nighthawk line, and courtesy title of enforcers

Mindrape Forced telepathic intrusion into another's mind

Nest A group of vampires, companions, and slaves that live and Hunt together

Nest Leader Senior vampire in a nest; teacher and adoptive parent of younger vampires

Nighthawk Another term for Hunters/Enforcers

Owl Bait Term of affection

Silver Dagger Symbol of Enforcer authority

Strig A vampire that lives outside the protection of the Laws; a loner

Strigoi The vampires' name for themselves

Strigoi Council The secret society that rules vampire society

Transient Mortal psychic unable to form a permanent mental bond with a vampire